I0543464

The Girl with Chameleon Eyes

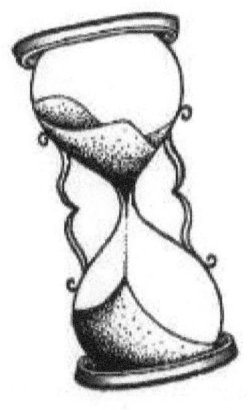

Laurel Houck

The characters and events in this book are fictitious. Any similarity to real persons, living or dead, places, or events is coincidental and not intended by the author.

If you purchase this book without a cover you should be aware that this book may have been stolen property and reported as "unsold and destroyed" to the publisher. In such case the author has not received any payment for this "stripped book."

The Girl with Chameleon Eyes
Copyright © 2019 Laurel Houck

All rights reserved.

ISBN: (ebook) 978-1-949931-01-3
(print) 978-1-949931-19-8

Inkspell Publishing
5764 Woodbine Ave.
Pinckney, MI 48169

Edited By Rie Langdon
Cover art By Najla Qamber

This book, or parts thereof, may not be reproduced in any form without permission. The copying, scanning, uploading, and distribution of this book via the internet or via any other means without the permission of the publisher is illegal and punishable by law. Please purchase only authorized electronic or print editions, and do not participate in or encourage piracy of copyrighted materials. Your support of the author's rights is appreciated.

THIS IS DEDICATED

To The One I Love

ONE

Summer

My vapor solidifies with no warning whatsoever. Abrupt. Compact. Unexpected.

I'm near a dumpster that squats behind a floodlit Sheetz gas station, the stench of hot dog grease and burnt coffee strong in my nostrils. My feet are last to materialize, so that for a moment when I look down, I'm floating about five inches above the pavement, white mist above black asphalt.

With the physical transformation comes the rest of it. Light and cool converts to heavy and hot. Yearning and searching morphs to fear and uncertainty. Naked and misty transforms to flesh-bound and clothed. I'm grateful for the garments that cover my skin, even if how that happens is a mystery to me.

The nausea and dizziness are stronger than the last time I can recall. I lean against the dumpster and slide to the ground, knees up, head in my hands. It will pass soon. I hope.

"Miss, are you okay?" A deep voice rumbles above the traffic noise. The tall, ruddy-faced cop is standing over me, wearing a black uniform and a hat with a band of navy and gold squares. "I'm Officer Sullivan. Did someone hurt you?"

"I'm fine." I scramble to my feet, glad it's dim in the shadow of the dumpster. I'm still shaky and have no clue what color has risen in my eyes. Between the lights and my startling arrival, anything is possible.

"You're sitting beside a trash can at a gas station, and it's ten o'clock at night." He shines the light in my face and stares. "What's your name?"

"I'm...not sure." That's true, at least partially. Each incarnation requires a name that matches the time and place. At present I don't know either. But I'm learning how to manage. After so many tries, I *should* know what to do.

"I need medics at 3092 Lothrop." The cop speaks into a microphone on his shoulder.

"No, really. I'm fine."

"Right. You don't know who you are. You need to be checked out. Unless you're lying." He raises the flashlight higher.

"I'm telling the truth." I keep my eyes downcast and don't add, the partial truth. I know that I used to be alive, that now I'm a ghost, and that I'm searching for something to expiate my guilt over...what? Beyond that, fuzzy at best. Another wave of dizziness comes over me, normal when I materialize so quickly. I sink back to the ground.

Things happen fast. A siren, followed by garish lights. Neck brace snapped in place. Lifted onto a backboard and gurney. Shoved in the back of an ambulance. The Emergency Room doors whoosh open.

I'm whisked down a hall, into a cubicle, and onto a narrow bed under a bright, hurting light. I have to do something, and fast. No way can I survive close medical scrutiny without endless questions. I could disappear and freak them all out, but if there's even a remote chance at resolution this time around, I have to try for it. Which means I need a surrogate.

I close my eyes, which must be a normal color or the nurse would already be shrieking, and let my mind roam the corridors. In the waiting room I find the perfect substitute. She's about my age, looks healthy enough, and is accompanying an older woman in a wheelchair. She'll be here for a while.

It only takes a second to kidnap her essence and haul it back to my body in the exam room. Fitting her larger frame inside mine is uncomfortable, but it's the only way. I feel my molecules squishing together to accommodate hers, a process somewhere between an unwanted tickle and unwelcome discomfort.

Hours later, after the cognitive questions, the blood work that rules out drugs and date rape, the neuro exam, and the CT of my head, Tim the ER Doc knows nothing except that I seem to be healthy. He leaves me alone long enough that I take Waiting Room Girl back to her magazine, none the worse for the experience. She shakes her head, looks around, and goes back to an article entitled, *Hot, Hot, Hot—Summer Dating.* My mind returns to the cubicle. It feels good to be in my body by myself again.

"Looks like you get to leave." Officer Sullivan is still hanging around, or maybe they called him back.

There's a woman in jeans and a tie-dyed T-shirt with him, medium build, shoulder-length brown hair, tentative smile. Sullivan takes off his hat and scratches his head. "The problem is where to take you. CYF is swamped, and you can't be out on the street alone. There's no way you're eighteen."

"I'm very self-sufficient. And healthy." I know where this is going. Not good.

"Except that you don't know who you are or where you're from. And we haven't found you on any missing persons' data base yet." He clears his throat. "I do have a solution. The social worker here already got the official okay from the top. This is Jill, my sister-in-law. She and my brother are licensed for emergency shelter of minors. They agreed to take you in, until we can straighten things out."

"Hi." Jill nods, makes no attempt to be fake-concerned.

"That's really nice of you, but—"

"You don't have a choice." Officer Sullivan waves his arm toward my clothing. "Get dressed, and we'll take you there. They live out in the suburbs." His gruff voice softens. "It's gonna be okay, kid."

Jill must see the confusion on my face. "This is the city of Pittsburgh, Pennsylvania. We live in Murrysville, about fifteen miles east."

Jill and Sullivan leave me alone. I would run if I could. But my new caretakers are outside the door. If I return to my default mode and float away unseen, will I doom myself to roaming forever? I just don't have enough information to know for sure. Can't take the chance.

The jean shorts, California Dreamin' T-shirt, and flip flops I picked up when I landed one time in LA slip on in seconds. My Vera Bradley tote bag—blue and brown design from the sale rack at Goodwill—goes cross-body, and I'm set.

Sullivan's personal wheels—a beat-up Ford truck—is parked outside the Emergency Room. He climbs in the drivers' seat, Jill takes the middle, and I hug the passenger door. The truck creeps along with vehicles clogging the highway. "Isn't it late for so much traffic?" We slow down even more as we enter a tunnel; the sign says Squirrel Hill. It's dingy and dirty, under some kind of construction that can only be an improvement. Nothing looks familiar.

"The game just ended. Extra innings." Sullivan glances at me. "Baseball. Pirates. They're on a roll this year, for a change."

Jill is silent, but sits as close to Sullivan as she can, giving me a tiny bit of space.

While he drones on about RBIs and unassisted triple plays, my mind is free to wander. I'm tired. From wandering too much. And wondering what the hell I'm supposed to do to end it all. If only I could remember Azul's instructions. Something about doing it until I got it right. Finding someone. Someone specific so I can be converted, and rest. But who? And why? Was my life so awful that I now have to atone for major bad crap? That's what the pervasive guilt I carry tells me. But how am I supposed to find out?

"Uh, we're here." Sullivan is standing by the passenger door, which is open.

I exit the truck and stare down an unpaved pathway.

Jill climbs out behind me and gestures to the long incline that snakes through tall pines. "Welcome." At the bottom of the hill is a cottage-like house.

Light pours out of three skylights, and a spotlight brightens the path. Everything else, sweet-smelling flowers, leafy trees, details, is swallowed by the darkness. I follow Jill and arrive at the small frame structure. The screen door is country fancy.

It bangs open, and a little boy wearing Batman pajamas bounds out. His red-brown hair sticks up in clumps, bed-head style.

"Uncle Mal." He appears ready to hug Sullivan, stops when he sees me, and settles for a manly fist bump.

"How's it going, Finn?" Sullivan gestures to me, just as a man appears on the porch—also in nightwear—and steps out beside Finn. "This is the young lady I called you about."

"You must be hungry." The man smiles but makes no attempt to touch me. "I'm Daniel. And you already met our son, Finn, who is *supposed* to be asleep."

After the good-byes to the cop, I follow Jill and Finn into the house. Daniel locks the door behind me. I like that the windows are open instead of air conditioning being on. It feels free, even though I could vaporize and drift outside at any time. Jill makes me a ham sandwich with barbecue chips and a can of Coke. I expected to do the wary dance, but they seem comfortable with me. I'm glad they ask no questions.

"Is it true you don't know anything?" Finn's eyes are shining. "Not even your name?"

This must be a cool adventure to him, something worthy of playground bragging rights: the strange girl with no name who appeared in the dark. If he only knew.

"Finn." Disapproval is heavy in Daniel's voice. "We don't interrogate our guests."

"No, it's okay." I smile at the kid and get a dimple in return. "But I guess I should come up with some name, just to make things easier." The thought *Dovie* passes through my mind, don't know why. I remember the magazine article the hospital girl was reading, that baseball is being played, and the air is warm. "It's summertime, so how about that? I'll be Summer. Until my memory comes back." Or, my mind whispers, *until I can leave.*

"Summer. I like that." Jill nods her approval. "With that pretty blond hair, you look like a summer surfer."

"Except she's not tanned. She's *really* pale." Finn holds his browned arm next to my white one. "Don't you go outside?"

"*Finn.*" Daniel shakes his head. "What part of *she can't remember* don't you get?"

Daniel ushers the kid down a hall. A toilet flushes, and I hear Finn's, "Good night, Summer," before a door opens and closes. Jill leads me up a set of spiral stairs to a loft bedroom with its own bathroom, and then leaves me alone.

There are toiletries in the bathroom, nice ones from Crabtree and Evelyn, scented with lily of the valley. I shower and pull on a pair of soft cotton shorts and a T-shirt that are hanging on a hook, the pajamas fragrant with the scent of fabric softener. There's a futon in the bedroom, open and inviting, covered with rosebud-sprigged cotton sheets. A TV sits atop a fake fireplace in the corner, but I don't turn on either one. Instead, I switch off the lights, lie down, and let moonlight from the unadorned window bathe me in silver. An unseen creek burbles me into contentment.

Until I wonder, yet again. Why am I here? And who am I, really?

LAUREL HOUCK

TWO

Summer

I have learned to control everything—all my otherness…except for my eyes. And those, well, spin the color chart and take your pick. Stormy-sky gray, sphagnum moss green, smoky topaz brown—the so-called normal colors. Throw in amethyst, carnelian, cyan, and all the rest, and it makes living as a sixteen-year-old girl a major challenge.

Most don't notice my eyes for a long time. No one pays much attention in the physical world these days. On computers, and iPhones, and tablets, everyone assumes it's some artsy-fartsy new download. In person, there's too much going on to get up close and personal. At least that's the way I keep it. I tried contact lenses in LA, but for some reason, my aberration shows through. Fortunately, the days when my wayward eyes decide orange is the color du jour are infrequent. Those days, I stay home. By sheer force of will, I can sometimes push back the more garish shades that surface when I'm seriously stressed.

Then there's the—

"Summer?" A light tapping on the bedroom door ends

as the hinges squeak, and Jill pokes her head into my space. "I've been calling you for dinner, honey."

"Hey." I close the laptop. It's not like I can submit what I just wrote for Mrs. Geary's English class anyway; the truth never works. I'll save it for when she gives us a creative writing project. "Oh, sorry. I was doing an assignment. I'll be right down."

"Pepperoni pizza, salad, and chocolate cake." Jill hesitates. "I'm sorry the police haven't been able to find out anything about you. Mal has been working on it. But it's really nice to have you with us."

"It's nice to be had." I shoot her a grin and a thumbs up before she leaves. She doesn't seem to notice that my hand wavers, translucent for no apparent reason. Maybe it's because I don't know if I'm happy or sad that the cops have no leads about me. Or maybe the air conditioner from downstairs made it happen. I thrust the wayward appendage behind my back as she leaves.

Popular fiction has everyone believing ghosts bring cold with them. Maybe some do, but my aura is heated, like an electric blanket. I don't know why, any more than I understand what I'm doing here, why I can't rest, or what's going to happen to me. I push aside the negative thoughts that consume me. One of the perks of manifesting is definitely pepperoni pizza.

I curl my tongue in my mouth, inhale, then exhale slowly as my tongue unfurls, until my hand regains flesh. A quick glance in the mirror reassures me. My white-blond ponytail is in place, my pale skin retains a skim of healthy-looking blush, and my eyes are an acceptable light brown. Along with the Abercrombie T-shirt, jean shorts, and flip flops, I look like the pictures I'm trying to imitate from *Seventeen* magazine. "Fake it 'til you make it," I murmur as I head down the stairs to the kitchen. The mantra is getting old.

"Hey, sistah." Finn greets me from his seat at the table. A telltale drip of pizza sauce dots his ten-year-old chin. He must have sneaked a slice already.

"Hey, brother from another mother." After spending three months in this house, we've grown comfortable and familiar, like real siblings. A pang hits as I realize it's all for show. If Finn—or Jill, or even Daniel saw my apparitional form, they'd end up in a psych ward. It's like I'm betraying their kindness.

"I read in the Penn-Franklin that Homecoming is scheduled for October twenty-ninth." Daniel pops a pepperoni into his mouth and talks around it. "The game should be a good one. The Panthers are playing Hampton."

"And there's a dance on the thirtieth. Sheila from my yoga class is a chaperone." Jill's eyes twinkle. "You should go, Summer. We can shop for a dress—something pretty, lace maybe, with a sparkly belt and matching pumps. And you could get your nails and makeup done at Vintage Rose, and—"

Daniel frowns. "And maybe she isn't interested in dancing."

"Or maybe she is."

Jill has this dream of me being popular and doing normal things. Instead of sitting in my safe, comfortable room trying to figure out what I'm supposed to do next.

"Summer, you don't have to go to the dance." She glares at Daniel. "I just thought that maybe if you got involved at school a little bit more, it might jog your memory. You're smart and doing beyond grade-level work, which means you must have been in school...wherever you lived before..." Her voice trails off.

"Now look what you've done." Daniel hands me a napkin. "You made her cry."

I feel the red rising through my core and know I have to get away before it lodges in my irises. "No, it's fine. I touched the pizza sauce, then my eyes, and they got irritated." I push back the chair and exit the kitchen. "I'll be right back."

After several minutes of doing the breathing exercises Azul taught me long ago, my eyes remain red. I sneak back upstairs to my room. So much for dinner, although since I don't really *have* to eat, it's no big deal. Of more concern is Jill's never-ending desire to get me involved with the activities and other kids at school. She's trying to help, but the thought of spending the evening with so many at one time and hoping not to slip back into nether-form is frightening. When I can concentrate on classes and information, it's all good. But to socialize and relax? I've tried that gig before. Enough said.

"I'm going to finish my work and turn in early." I call down the stairs. Opening the computer, I knock off a trite fantasy about The Person I Am Inside for Mrs. Geary. That finished, I relax on the futon with a marathon of *Ghost Whisperer* reruns on the TV. What a hoot. And boring. I close my eyes just to shut out the sight of a totally bogus "ghost", but the pull of sleep lures me in…

"I want my mama." My insides shake. There is no grass, no trees, no sky, no Mama. The strange creature staring at me is made of moving shades of blue, like the pond after it rains. "What are you?"

"I am Azul, the Navigator."

"I want Mama, not you." I stomp my foot, but instead of the *thud* I expect, my toes sink into a swirling mist. Where are my shoes? Where is the ground?

"Your mother is dead. You are dead."

Dead? My breath comes in short gulps. I'm only twelve years old. Strong children don't die…do they? I thought dead either meant happy-happy time or nothingness. I see Azul watching me with his deep-set eyes. *Is he the devil? Is this hell?*

"No to both questions."

He answers my thoughts. Uh oh.

"Where is my mother? If we're both dead, we can still

be together."

"She went higher. Your soul is burdened and must remain...for a time."

"How much time?"

"You will stay here with me for the next forty-eight months, until you reach the human equivalent of sixteen years. During that time, you will grow as a normal child, be educated in worldly topics, and also be guided toward a higher plane of consciousness."

I don't understand, but try to hide my thoughts from him by focusing on a spot of yellow light high up in the mist. I shiver and summon anger to push away the fear. How can my soul be 'burdened'? I'm twelve. A punch of nausea hits my gut, and with it, little fingers of guilt squeeze my heart. "What did I do?" My voice is barely a whisper. I know I did *something* wrong. Very, very wrong.

"It is not for me to say." Azul's blue lightens a bit. "You are safe...for now. Detritus is not yet interested."

"I want to go home."

"You have no home, save this one."

Beyond Azul's shoulder I see a black iron gate, partially open. Daring not to even think about it, I run through him as fast as my bare feet can take me. It's hard to gain momentum on the slippery mist, but I push my muscles as hard as I can. I'm the fastest runner at school. I can outrun William, even though he's taller than me. I *have* to find Mama.

The gate looms, inviting me to pass through, to where I don't know, but anything has to be better than this damp, silent, colorless place. I slip past the iron spikes and skid to a stop. My mother is above me in the distance, laughing, with flowers in her auburn hair and wearing a long, beautiful white dress that flows about her feet.

"*Mama.*" I run toward her, but she stays the same distance away. "*Mama.*"

"She can't hear you, doesn't even know you died." Azul settles beside me as the vision of my mother disappears. "I granted you this glimpse, so you can see she's happy. All she knows now, and for eternity, is goodness and light. Perhaps the day will come when you join her. That's up to you."

"How?"

"You will learn."

"And if I don't learn?" I want to vomit, shout, wail. But I bide my time. I'm not patient by nature, but hours of embroidery taught me more than how to do tiny stitches.

Azul merely shrugs. It says it all.

I look up as my mother appears and disappears from view. "Mama, please…"

"Summer, are you okay?" Finn's morning breath is ripe in my nostrils.

I scoot over on the futon, and he perches beside me. "I was dreaming."

"You called for your mama. Maybe you remembered something."

"Nope. Nothing that will help." The ache from the dream hasn't dissipated. When Azul visits in the night, it takes a while to recover. But at least this means my memory bank isn't completely empty. And maybe the next time, I'll learn even more. That thought brings hope. But the pull of guilt from my unknown offense explodes the hope into tiny pieces that melt away.

THREE

Kota

"Go 'way." I pull the pillow over my head, knowing it's a brief reprieve. Mom gave up. Dad will play clean-up.

"Kota. Now." Dad yanks away the pillow and pokes me in the ribs. "Come on, big guy. I'll drive you to school—if you hurry."

"Or I could drive myself." Another loser move, and it's only six o'clock in the morning.

"Or not." He throws me a clean T-shirt and finally leaves.

I hate my name—Kota Landis. I hate school—Fawn Valley High. I hate life—in general. Sixteen, getting my driving permit, starting junior year, all supposed to be milestones. They feel more like millstones around my neck. Too many expectations. Spoiled only child, yeah, right. Smothered is more like it. And lately restlessness has settled into my bones, an edginess that doesn't respond to exercise, or any other form of distraction.

Dad drops me at school and hurries off to a meeting downtown, trying to beat traffic on the parkway. I keep my head down and make it to my locker before the torture starts for another day.

"Yo, chief. Got a tomahawk in there?" Douchebag Doug smirks, but knows to stay out of my reach.

"Yeah, it's got your name on it, Dougie." I mime throwing a hatchet at him. Good thing there isn't a teacher around. Zero tolerance for violence would get me screwed, even for making the gesture. Zero tolerance for racial slurs, too, but try to prove that one.

"We're playing the Seneca Indians on Friday. Who you gonna cheer for?" Doug includes a couple of his brain-fart friends into this hilarious comment, and they laugh all the way down the hall.

"They're just jealous." Preston Burke opens the locker next to mine. "You have an identity. They're into identity fraud."

"Whatever." I shrug. Preston has enough money to say and do whatever he wants. But he's decent to me. We started pre-school together, back in the days when I always had to be the Native American at the Thanksgiving play, because some ancestor somewhere slept with a Seneca Indian and passed the genes along to me. Except for Dad's straight, black hair, I'm the only one in my family who looks the part.

"Hey, Preston." Kayla sidles between Preston and me, batting her eyelashes.

I'm forced to step aside to avoid her butt. I run into something, try to balance, and end up on the tile floor. "What the hell?"

"I'm sorry." A new girl who rarely speaks takes a step back, then with seeming reluctance holds out one pale hand to help me up.

"It's fine." I ignore the hand and get to my feet. By now a crowd has gathered, the boys leering and the girls giggling. Nothing better to do in high school.

"Are you okay?" Preston bypasses Kayla and steps around me to address the silent one.

"Me?" She glances over her shoulder and back at him.

"Sure."

I take a closer look at her, because Preston is known for his fine taste in females. I must have been in the ozone for the past month since school started, because she is *hot*, and I never really noticed it. Not your classic smokin' babe with big boobs, sultry smiles, and tight jeans. This girl is different, in the kind of way that takes more than one quick glimpse to appreciate. Trust Preston to zero in on her first, not that I care. After Marlie, I'm done with women for a while. Or maybe forever.

"Break it up, here." Coach Patterson, already in shorts with a whistle around his neck, disperses the crowd. He appraises me, Preston, Kayla, and the girl. "Everything okay here, Summer?"

"Yes, sir." The girl—Summer—nods, frowns at me for some reason, and heads down the hall. She moves gracefully, like a hockey player gliding across the ice.

"I see that look in your eyes, my man." Preston gives my shoulder a playful punch. "I saw her first. Your loss."

"Yeah, sure." I make it to class just in time and slide into my seat. Although I normally don't mind biology, I can't seem to concentrate. Instead, I doodle in my notebook while questions run through my mind. What's the deal with Summer? Where did she come from? Why did it take me an entire month to notice her? How long will Preston be interested? I know the answer to the last one, because he changes girls more often than most guys change underwear.

The morning passes like a snail, leaving me hungry and hopeful that Summer is in my A lunch period. Preston eats C lunch. The Great Spirit must be smiling on me today, because I see Summer, seated alone at the table beside the trash bin, where no one ever sits. I endure the cafeteria line, let the ladies with hair nets load up my plate with today's menu, grab a chocolate milk, and hurry to join her.

"What?" Summer looks up from the book she's holding in one hand. The other hand grips a mostly-eaten apple, white fingers turning the fruit to pulp. "Oh, it's you."

"Yep, it's me." I almost groan out loud at the lame reply, but sit my tray and my butt down across from her anyway. I notice that it's really warm in this part of the cafeteria today. "You're new this year, right?" I take a big bite of my hamburger and try to ignore the drip of ketchup that plops onto my lap.

"Right." She goes back to her book, *Heaven, the Occult, and Mysticism in Twenty-First Century America.*

"That's an…interesting thing to read. Is it for a class?"

"No."

"So you're into the occult?"

"Not really."

"Is it because Halloween is next month?"

Summer closes the book and sets it on the table, lays the apple core on her tray, and looks at me as if she's going to stare me down. Her eyes, an amazing smoky brown, suddenly begin to roil, like clouds before it storms. I can't look away. The color is consumed by what must be some shade of brown—except it looks very much like orange. Without a word, she gets up and leaves the cafeteria, head down. She takes the book. Her tray remains on the table.

I let the burger drop to my plate, ignore the milk, and sense rather than hear the usual commotion going on around me. Chills travel up and down my arms. I've known kids with hazel eyes that sometimes look green and sometimes brown. But this was more like a chameleon I once saw on vacation, a startling change to a color that doesn't normally exist in human eyes.

The day is a waste, school-wise. I ignore everyone after classes end, even Marlie, who wants to be friends again, whatever that means. I can't get the sight of Summer's eyes out of my brain. They remind me of some alien in a sci-fi flick I once streamed. But of course she's human—any other crap is part of the world of fiction, not fact.

I slide into a seat on the bus, wishing very much that I

had my license and could drive to and from school. Not in the mood for people.

"You going to the game Friday?" Kyle, a freshman, sits beside me.

"Probably."

"It's gonna be a good one. We'll scalp those damn Seneca redskins." He looks at me, swallows, and shrinks back against the seat. "Hey man, just kidding, uh, you know, talking trash kind of stuff."

"Look, just because I have a certain ethnic background doesn't mean I take offense at every little thing." Then it hits me. What he said, the way Doug always makes fun of me, looking different from everyone else I ever met—it just plain sucks. And I'm sick of it. "You know what? You should shut up unless *you* want to be scalped." I realize the bus buzz is silent, and everyone is hanging on my every word.

Kyle moves, and no one else sits with me. I've read a lot about my ancestors and their many stories. I'm the lone Native American around here and want to understand my heritage. My dad and his family laugh it off or change the subject, like even they think there's something wrong with being an Indian. Maybe it's because I'm the only family member with brown skin and red-tinged cheeks to go with the black hair. I push aside my mental rant. It's with me often enough, and there's more to consider from today.

Home at last, I make microwave mac and cheese and carry it to my room. My parents won't be back from work for a couple hours, which gives me the solitude I crave to figure out what happened at lunch. The macaroni grows cold.

I stare out the window instead of eating or doing geometry homework, and try to quantify what's going on. I'm drawn to Summer, suddenly and inexplicably. She's different from everyone else. I'm making too much of what I saw—*thought* I saw—in her eyes. It must have been the glare of the fluorescent lights, or the reflection of her clothes, or…what? I'm a very grounded kind of guy, not at all superstitious. There has to be a logical explanation. But nothing makes sense, at least not now.

I flip on the computer and type *eyes changing color* in the search box. After fifteen minutes of reading about hazel eyes, eyes that change color due to emotions—debunked on Snopes—and one particularly interesting bit of crap about extra-terrestrials, I can't find anything that talks about the roiling change from brown to orange that I witnessed in Summer. So she's unique. Who cares? Let Preston worry about it.

I open my geometry book, then shove it aside. It lands on the floor. On its way there, it takes the crusty macaroni with it. The startled-doe look in Summer's strange eyes haunts me. She has chameleon eyes. And I am *compelled* to find out why.

FOUR

Summer

It's only two miles or so from school to the Sullivans'
house. I almost think, *school to home*, but don't want to get
too attached to this place. I cut out of school after Kota
sat across the table from me at lunch. Confusion was
etched on his face, which means my irises were something
unnatural, some color he didn't associate with eyes. His
fault. I didn't want him at my table. He gives me the
creeps, not because he's got some Native American thing
going on—who am I to judge those who are different,
after all—but there's *something* about him
that's...unsettling.

The leaves are starting to change; a ruska of brilliant
red and gold lines the road. I get caught up in the moment,
loving the coolness of autumn, the scurry of squirrels as
they prepare for winter, the doe that is spooked by my
presence. Will I be here a few months, all winter, until I'm
supposed to be years older yet still stuck at sixteen?

No doubt I'll be missed in afternoon classes, but
whatever. I wonder exactly how many times I've been to
high school. Los Angeles was the last place I landed, a big,

smelly city with more homeless than famous. Nothing there interested me, not the people I met in acting class, the phony psychics along Hollywood Boulevard, or the other displaced persons searching for something.

The time before that is clear as well...at least I assume I didn't miss any place in-between. El Refugio, a rural community near the border of Mexico, became my brief home. Too small to hide me, too few people to give me any clue about what I need to find. Not a refuge, in spite of its name. Beyond El Refugio and LA, my memory bank is overdrawn. It mustn't be important to know, or surely Azul would help. But I have the sense it has been a very long journey, one with no end in sight, since I haven't a clue what I'm actually doing roaming the earth. What will end this? True love? Valiant quest? Death again? A sale at Bloomingdale's?

"*Ahh.*" A shriek greets me as I cross the sun porch and enter the great room. "What are *you* doing here?" Finn jumps up from the couch, and a bowl of popcorn empties onto the hardwood floor.

"Me? What about you?" I automatically start scooping warm popcorn kernels back into the bowl until the floor is clean.

"I asked you first."

"I asked you second. And I'm older."

"Summer, you're really cool. Like, the perfect big sister." Finn jumps up to hug me. I avoid his outstretched arms.

"Seriously? You're gonna run that con on me?" I roll my eyes.

"I knew Mom and Dad would be working late. So, I, uh..." He gulps.

"You skipped school. Not very smart. They'll put out an Amber Alert for you, get the police, give you detention until you're my age."

"I'm not stupid." Finn raises his chin. "I told the cafeteria monitor I felt sick, and she said to see the nurse and that she would tell my teacher. The nurse won't know anything about it, and the teachers will think my parents picked me up. So there." He crosses his arms. "You, too?"

"Yeah, but I'm not as smart. I just walked out." I shrug, empty the spilled kernels into the trash, and slide another bag of popcorn into the microwave. While it pops, I pick up a long piece of string lying on the counter. When the beep sounds, I carry the popcorn and string back to the couch and plop down next to Finn. "Want to play cat's cradle?"

"I never heard of that video game."

"Silly. Here, watch." I tie the sting in a loop, put my hands through and keep my thumbs out. Using my fingers, I create a web of string. "Now you pinch the X-shaped parts." It takes a while, but after a few tries, Finn is able to take the web from my fingers onto his own.

"Cool. Where'd you learn it? No one does stuff like that."

"It's not so special."

Finn puts on a DVD that belongs to Daniel and is usually off-limits. He shoves popcorn into his mouth. I sit with him while motorcycles race through town and buildings get blown up. He shouldn't watch the violence, but why skip school to do what you're supposed to do? I continue to work the string though my fingers and mentally tick off the games I'm playing: *The Manger, Cat's Eye, Diamonds.* Where did I learn to do this? I struggle to remember. The percolating of my brain is draining. I seem to recall sitting in front of a fire. There was a cat...no, a dog, warming its backside to the flames. Then...nothing.

"I'm going..." Finn won't care what I do, because he's slumped over, snoring gently. He must not have been all that interested in exploding buildings. I take out the DVD and put it away before Daniel comes home, cover Finn with the furry Pittsburgh Steelers throw that hangs on the back of the couch, and tiptoe up the spiral stairs. We can both get a nap in before Jill and Daniel get home.

Sleep claims me, more than a doze, a real, deep dive into unconsciousness. I fight it for a while, because I can lose control if I get too comfortable, but the exhaustion of the day finally wins. As I drift off, my limbs grow light and airy, my torso softens, and my head is free from the vice of gravity…

"You are tired more often this time." Azul's blue essence is a welcome bit of my poorly remembered past, because he's been with me since the beginning of this journey. I know this, though I don't know when or how my wandering came to be. I notice his usual form is less distinct, as if he's fading away.

"No…well, maybe. Tired of not knowing how to truly rest. Will you tell me now?" I'm drifting in open space, letting the nothingness of his realm soothe the rigors of a phony life on earth. What began as alien and frightening right after my death is now comforting reality to me.

"Time is not your friend." Azul darkens to navy, as if a filter has been pulled across his normal cerulean-based essence. "Detritus grows restless. He will soon awaken."

"What does that mean?" A frisson of unease causes my vapor to crinkle. "Who is he?"

"You must *think*. A past not remembered is doomed to be repeated. You were given time to learn and grow. But every clock here eventually winds down, one soul at a time. And there are stumbling blocks in your path."

I become aware of mournful moaning I've never heard before. Specters dart past, quickly, like fireflies. They seem to have no purpose, no destination, no autonomy, as if captives in a glass jar. "What are they?"

"They are your future. Aimless, unrequited, tortured."

"*No*. Please. Tell me what to do." The moaning grows more fierce as the specters beat against the gate. It's open but they can't seem to get out. Panic nibbles at my brain, pushing aside all rational thought. I reach for the answer.

It slides away.

"You have outpaced your allotment. In fact, I stretched this final phase because you have tried so hard." Azul's essence quivers. "But your body is now aging in real time. I can give no further extensions. When you reach seventeen human years, you will belong to Detritus." He gestures to the specters. "As do they."

"But I want to make things right. Show me. Please." I think, *who is Detritus*? But if I can work things out, I never need to know.

"You hold the key. Unlock the door of your mind. Step inside. Reconcile your soul before it's too late."

"Finn. Summer. Now." Daniel's voice jars me awake.

I'm floating above the futon, my vapor slightly yellow and musty smelling, instead of its usual pure white and honey sweet. Questions ricochet in my brain: how much time is there before my seventeenth birthday? Will I then be lost for eternity? Did I have a human nightmare caused by stress, or a ghostly visitation? And yet I know the answer. Azul speaks clearly to me, but only in visions. I have no more dreams left.

"I said, *now*." Daniel is angry. In three months, he's never raised his voice to either Finn or me. We really screwed up.

I focus on one body part at a time until flesh appears, and I settle onto the sheets in human form. Once again, my left hand wavers for an added minute before solidifying. A quick glance confirms my fear that my eyes are a strange shade of red-purple, but as I take deep breaths and try to think human thoughts, they finally fade to an acceptable violet.

"It's about time." Daniel stands in the kitchen, Jill beside him. Finn is sitting on one of the caned chairs, his head hanging. "I had an interesting call today. Two calls, actually."

I stand behind Finn, my hands on the back of his chair, touching his shaking shoulders with my thumbs. He's a good kid, not used to breaking the rules. For some reason, my breathing is faster than usual. I realize—with surprise—that I feel guilty for letting Daniel and Jill down by skipping school and making Finn think it was cool for him to do it, too.

"I'm sorry." I blurt this out; uncharacteristic for me. Is that a memory resurfacing? Is part of my eternal offense an inability to take personal responsibility?

"For what?" Daniel waits.

"My eyes were bothering me at lunchtime. So I came home to take a nap. I should have gone to the nurse or called you."

"And you?" Daniel addresses Finn.

"Me, too. I'm sorry." Finn's shoulders shake, and he sniffles.

Jill wrings her hands. "Did you two plan this together?"

"*No.*" Finn and I say it at the same time, which, in other circumstances, might be funny.

Daniel and Jill let out big breaths.

Suddenly, I get it. "I'm an unknown girl with an unknown past. You were worried I might have done something to Finn. Or at the least been a bad influence." My words come out flat. I see the truth in Daniel's eyes. And with that my wayward left hand becomes translucent. I slip it into the pocket of my jeans. I blink away tears, before they cause a radical change to my irises.

"It's not that we don't trust you, Summer." Jill, the peacemaker. "But Finn never did anything like this before, and when we found out you weren't in school, either..." Her voice trails off, leaving words hanging in the air. Words like: devious, bad influence, mistake.

"Summer didn't make me do anything." Finn jumps up, glaring at his parents. "It was my own plan. She just had the same idea."

"On the same day." Daniel is deadpan. He confers in

whispers with Jill before turning back to Finn and me.

"Summer, we expect you to be a good role model for our son." Jill is grave, but the frown lines between her eyes are gone. "And to take advantage of the good education being provided while you live here. And Finn, there better never be a repeat of this behavior."

"Breaking the rules may be fun, but there are consequences for bad behavior." Daniel shakes his finger at Finn. "No video games or computer for a week—unless it's for supervised school work. And you'll have to miss the hockey game on Saturday."

"For the next week, our dishwasher is taking a vacation. You two can clean up after dinner and wash the dishes the old fashioned way." Jill appraises me. "I'll make arrangements for you to help out at the nursing home down the road on Saturday afternoon. They usually have an activity and are always looking for volunteers. Call it community service."

"I'm sorry." I repeat it, because this needs to end before they notice my hand.

"Me, too." Finn runs to his mother and gives her a hug.

Jill wipes the tears from his cheeks and looks at me over the top of his head with a tiny smile. "If we didn't care about you both so much, it wouldn't matter."

A great blob of pain rises in my chest. I realize that I am now part of this family. I love them. They love me. Yet I'm still a ghost, still held hostage to something I once did, still clueless about how to be released from earth—and no longer sure I want to leave. It's not like I have much of a choice. The ache in my heart intensifies. But instead of evaporating into vapor, as I did in LA and El Refugio when things got uncomfortable, all but my hand remains solid.

Not thinking, I reach to pat Finn's arm and quickly shove my translucent hand behind me. But I hear the quick intake of the kid's breath as he steps away from me. He saw.

LAUREL HOUCK

FIVE

Kota

The sneeze explodes, spraying snot all over the lab table before I can grab a tissue from my pocket. "Sorry." I wipe up the gooey mess with a paper towel.

"Allergies, Mr. Landis? A cross to bear in Pennsylvania in October." Mr. Curtioff the jag-off glares at me. "You have now compromised your experiment. Start over." He waves his hand at the petri dish and walks away.

"I can't believe you. Worst lab partner, *ever*." Marlie rolls her eyes and rubs hand sanitizer on her hands and forearms. "You are *so* gross and disgusting. I just want to be done with this before I get bubonic plague or something and have to miss the homecoming dance."

"What happened to 'I want to be friends?' You're the same as always." I go up front, get a new petri dish, and return. Not interested in her, anyway. For a while it went okay, someone to hang with, but when she got clingier than plastic wrap and meaner than a rattlesnake, there were no more dates. The only things I miss are her lips—the girl can kiss, I'll give her that.

"You messed up everything." Marlie throws her hands

in the air. "The experiment *and* us. I'm just being honest."

"We're supposed to grow bacteria in this experiment. My germs might be more interesting than the cultures the school provides." I ignore the 'and us' part of her comment.

"What*ever.*" Marlie nudges me with her curvy hip. "Want to stop at Eat 'n Park after school?"

"No." I ignore the familiar echo of her discontent with me. What a crock that we ended up as lab partners. I wonder if she made it happen to get what she wanted— another chance to torture me. Once upon a time, it seemed like a great idea to date the delectable Marlie Morrissey. Lately I don't feel like dating—or even hanging out—with anyone.

Class ends after a beyond-boring lecture on microbes, delivered in a monotone by Curtioff. He could put a meth addict to sleep, no joke. I take advantage of Marlie's distraction at being complimented on her new hairstyle (is it different?) by a gaggle of girls and escape to the bathroom. If I hide out in a stall for a few, the halls will be almost empty. I'll still make it to study hall on time.

Don't know what's wrong with me. I take a crap, study the four-letter words scratched into the side of the metal stall, and mentally examine myself. Not sick—no vomiting or anything classic—but kind of *heavy.* As in sick of everything. I've always been a loner, curse of the only child, but never like this. Am I depressed? Why? *It's not like I want to hurt myself...*now where did that thought come from?

"Dude, you in there?" Preston's rumble precedes the vibration from his hand smacking the door. "Stinks, man."

"It's a bathroom. This is the way they smell—unless your shit doesn't stink, which, I assure you, it does." I pull myself together, flush, open the door, and wash my hands. Preston is busy at the urinal. "Want me to wait for you?"

"Go ahead." He finishes and looks in the mirror. "Gotta comb my hair. I won't get in trouble." And he won't. Somehow, he gets away with almost everything.

"Yeah, later."

The halls are, as hoped, almost empty, save for a few losers like me sliding into classrooms. I see her before she sees me. Summer. Staring at the courtyard through the tall glass windows. She has her left hand in the pocket of her jeans, her right splayed against the glass. Sideways, she's so skinny she could be a boy; not much up top and few curves. But there's *something* ultra-feminine about her long, almost white-blond hair, her pale, pouty lips…but what about her eyes? I want to see them again, see if they really are some bizarre shade of orange. It's a test of my powers of observation. My sneakers carry me closer, not even squeaking on the polished tile floor.

"I know you're there." Her voice is mellow, neutral. She takes a deep breath and holds it, then slowly pulls her hand out of her pocket. "What do you want?"

"Nothing. I mean, I just thought…" *I thought what? I'm not usually tongue-tied like this.* "Uh, are you lost?" Her eyes aren't orange. They're deep, deep brown, a startling contrast to her fair skin.

"Yes. That's exactly what I am, lost." She turns and frowns at me. "But you're not the one who's going to find me."

"No, I meant lost as in couldn't find your class."

"Summer, hey." Preston walks up behind us. I didn't even hear him coming. "I've been looking for you all day." He gives her the patented Prestonian grin, guaranteed to melt girls' hearts—and cause nausea in guys. "Homecoming dance is in two weeks. It's usually cool, for a high school thing. Not country club, but fun."

"Oh, okay." Summer edges away from the glass, but Preston and I stand between her and her escape down the hall. The only other option is the stairs that would take her to freshman floor and make her really, really late. She turns and heads for the exit sign above the stairway door. Better late than us, I guess. Before Preston can say anything else, she's gone.

"So much for your magic powers over women." I laugh. "She's not interested in you."

"Like you're her type." There's an unfamiliar undertone of nasty in Preston's remark.

"What does that mean?" A surge of mad rises in my chest.

"I'm rich. And good-looking." Again with the crap attitude.

"And I'm poor and ugly?"

"What are you gentlemen doing out here? The buzzer rang five minutes ago." Principal Romero steps between Preston and me.

"Mrs. R., sorry." Preston rolls out his ass-kissing persona. "Kota and I were discussing pre-revolutionary America and the role of the Native American to the British military establishment."

I keep quiet, amazed by his ability to ooze B.S. If I speak, I'll get detention, and he'll end up having lunch with Romero in the teacher's lounge.

"I'm always pleased when students engage in debates based on their studies." Romero nods. "But you boys have to get to class. Go on, before I change my mind and give you a tardy slip." She walks with us until Preston enters his classroom, then points me to mine, as if I'm too much trouble for one more second of her precious time.

A bored teacher barely glances up as I enter. It's study hall, so who cares? I pull out my phone and ear buds. Music fills in the blanks in my head while I churn out my homework. Eighth period study hall, one of mankind's greatest inventions.

I scan the handout from history class and almost groan out loud. Great, just great. We have a chance to study a local historical site, Hannastown. Seriously? Mrs. Mayhew will be all into it. Hopefully it won't mean a field trip. I think my parents went there once for an antique show, which I skipped. I read on: *Westmoreland County seat from*

1773-1782, first English court west of the Allegheny Mountains, colonial center of justice and order, blah, blah, blah.

I pause to yawn and find a new song before picking up the paper again. *Burned down on July 13, 1782. Residents saved from...*I stop to close my eyes, then open them and start again. *Residents saved from a Seneca raid by fleeing to the fort.* So now we're going to study the way some ancestor of mine destroyed an entire town. My stomach turns over. Doug and his peeps will be merciless. It was a very long time ago. It shouldn't even matter. But I know it will. Maybe, since field trips usually don't happen until spring, we'll be on another unit, Fort Pitt or something, by then. The burn in my stomach subsides just in time for the bell to ring.

"Hey, wait up." Preston jogs up beside me.

I ignore him.

"Dude, 'sup?" He punches my arm.

"Not interested in hearing more about your good looks or my loser status." I get to my locker, pull out my stuff, and slam it shut.

"No clue what you're talking about." Preston's forehead is wrinkled, and one eyebrow goes up.

"Summer, Homecoming, your pissy insults—any of this sound familiar?" I stare at him, but he doesn't seem to get it.

"Summer, yeah, sure. I was going to ask her to Homecoming, but she left for class." He shrugs.

"What if *I* ask her to the dance?" Normally I would never move in on Preston's date, except that I'm still annoyed...and really want to go out with Summer.

"Hey, whatever. We've been friends forever. No girl can spoil that." Preston sounds normal again. "But I'm not backing down on this one. We can both go for it, and she can choose one of us. No hard feelings when it's me, okay?"

"Sure." I have to laugh. He has every reason to believe he'll win. On top of his obvious advantages, Summer has made it clear she wants nothing to do with me. But for some reason, I know I'll still try.

SIX

Kota

Dad chuckles as the kid in the commercial googles: *How to Ask a Girl Out on a Date.* "I remember those days." He winks at Mom.

I barely glance at the TV as I cut through the family room from the kitchen, nachos and cheese in hand.

"By the time you got to me, you knew exactly what to do." Mom is blushing.

"What about you, Kota?" Dad mutes the sound on the television.

"What about me?" I edge for the door, escape to my room within two steps.

"Honey…" Mom looks at Dad, then back to me. "Since you and Marlie broke up, you've been moping around the house. We're worried about you."

"It's like riding a bike, son. Once you do it, you never forget how. Girls come and go in high school, we know that, but—"

"But you seem so, oh I don't know…" Mom interrupts then lets her voice trail off. "…depressed?"

"We know you wouldn't do drugs…" Dad's turn to

throw out words sure to annoy me.

"So you think I'm a drug addict who's ready to blow out his brains?" I stare at them. A tiny nudge of guilt works into my brain—they're concerned because they love me. But still, it sucks that they've seen my mood taking a dive. I wish I could blame Marlie, because then I'd know the reason. Instead, the lethargy and heaviness—I avoid the d-word—hit me without any cause that I can imagine.

"There's no stigma to depression." Mom sucks it up to provide a rational argument. "Maybe, if you talked to a professional counselor, you could figure things out together."

"Or try dating someone else." Dad is a guy to the core.

"Look, I get it. Don't worry. I'm not depressed, I don't do drugs, and good riddance to Marlie. It's junior year. I'm just working hard to keep up my GPA." I head for my room.

"Your grades have always been good." Mom's not letting go.

I feel like a rubber band breaks apart in my chest. "Just freaking leave me alone." I escape to my room, the sound of Mom's heavy sigh and Dad's ominous growl in my ears.

Finally by myself, I set down the nachos on my desk, no longer in the mood. Maybe there *is* something wrong with me—never turned down corn chips before. On a whim, I open my laptop and google *How to Ask a Girl Out on a Date*. After scrolling through wikihow's *Five Steps* (with pictures), SonicSeduction's *Surefire Methods* (ANY GUY CAN DO IT), and eHarmony's *Advice* (it need not be nerve-wracking), I'm disgusted. I've asked girls out since eighth grade. Why is Summer, the one girl I can't get out of my mind, so different?

Maybe it's because this is the first time I've been up against Preston in the dating wars. So I need to up my game. Think outside the box. Get radical. "Okay." I mutter as I surf the web. "Girls like…what? Romance, fairy tales, diamonds. Can't afford gems, happily-ever-after has to be very individual, and romance…that I might be able to pull off."

Normally I would consult Preston before making an unfamiliar move, but right now he's the enemy. My mind churns throughout the evening, while Mom and Dad watch me like hawks, as if I'm gonna off myself in their presence. I sleep poorly, just make the bus in the morning, and get to the school office before going to my locker.

"Yes?" The bored office lady barely glances at me as she sucks down her morning Starbucks.

"I want to get two tickets for the homecoming dance." I pull some rumpled bills from my jacket pocket and smooth them out on the counter.

"They'll be on sale starting tomorrow at lunchtime." She examines her nails.

"But you have them here now, right?" I pull out the best smile in my arsenal and lean over the counter. "If I wait, a very special girl might go with someone else. You understand."

She finally looks at me, shrugs, and opens a drawer. "Fifty dollars. And don't tell anyone you got these early, or I'll be in trouble."

"Thanks. No worries." I tuck the tickets in my back pocket. The rest of the plan will have to wait until later. By tomorrow morning, Summer will be my homecoming date. As long as I ask her first, in the right way, she won't say no.

The day seems to last forever. A pop quiz in math, a fistfight at lunch between two girls, and a freshman who vomits in the hall blocking the way to the bus—all conspire to make it a bad day. But I'm so caught up in my plan that my only concern is getting out of school.

"Wanna shoot some hoops?" Preston sidesteps the puking kid to catch me as I leave the building. "I'll pick you up in the 'Stang since you don't have your license yet. You can have dinner at my place."

"Not today. Stuff to do." Is he being nice, or rubbing it

in that he can drive, has a vintage candy-apple red Mustang, and a full-size indoor basketball court? Or am I being paranoid?

"Something's up. I know you." Preston grins. "What could it be? Maybe a certain mysterious girl we both want to date? Don't even bother. I'm getting dance tickets tomorrow as soon as they go on sale. Marlie's still sniffing around. Ask her, and save yourself some grief."

"Good advice." I wave and climb up the bus steps. His puzzled frown follows me, but he leaves as soon as I take a seat. Once he's headed for the student parking lot, I get off the bus. It's a nice day. I'll walk. And take care of business along the way.

A bell rings as I open the door to Colegrande's floral shop. The strong scent of flowers makes my nose wrinkle. It reminds me of Gran's funeral, not a good thing. No one is around, so I browse the small place. There are too many blossoms—white petals with yellow centers, big orange blooms, and bouquets of fake silk in fall colors. This was a stupid idea. I'll just hold out the tickets and ask Summer to go with me. It doesn't have to be nerve-wracking, according to eHarmony.com.

"May I help you?" An elderly woman with a lifetime collection of wrinkles on her face appears from a back room, wiping her chapped hands on a yellow towel.

I back toward the door. "No, thanks. Sorry."

"It's pretty confusing in here. First time?" She nods, not making fun but seeming to understand.

"Yeah. I had this idea, but it's not going to work."

"Let me guess." She closes her eyes briefly, then opens them. "Flowers for a girl. Not a girl*friend*, someone new you want to impress. But you don't want to look like a geek."

"How'd you know?"

"I've been doing this for quite a while, and we're right down the road from the high school." She moves around the room, gesturing to flowers along the way. "These are daisies, a simple country look that says, *You're nice, and I'd like to know you better.* Then we have mums, fall flowers that make a traditional statement like, *I'm a regular young man but I know the season.* And then we have the roses." She opens a glass case, reaches inside, and pulls out a tall container filled with fragrant blooms in red, yellow, pink, and white. "These very special ones say, *I've got class, and so do you.* Simple, yet elegant. And you can do one rose with a tiny sprig of baby's breath and not break the bank."

"They have thorns." The last thing I need is to draw blood from Summer.

"I'll take care of that, wrap it in tissue, and add the baby's breath and some ribbon free of charge. Just pick a color. What do you think?" She passes the container under my nose, and the sweet scent makes up my mind.

"Okay. Great." I study the four colors and can't decide. Sweat dampens my pits. Too many choices. "The girl's skin is pale, like she never met the sun. Should I match that or go for color?"

"Hmmm. Of course it's up to you. But most girls like pink."

"I'll take a yellow one. She's not 'most girls'."

"Good choice." The clerk picks a bud that's still tightly closed. "Yellow roses stand for friendship, joy, and happiness."

The end result is a long-stemmed yellow rose, surrounded by a cloud of tiny white blossoms and dark green tissue, tied with curls of shiny silver ribbon. The clerk puts a plastic holder in with it. Instead of using it to hold a card, as she suggests, I'll put in the homecoming tickets. If this doesn't get Summer to go out with me, nothing will. I have it on good authority—wikihow—that flowers always work. I just hope I can get home before someone sees me.

I make it to the end of the road and turn onto my street, practicing in my mind how to make things work. Summer, this is for you. Will you go to Homecoming with me? Lame. So, Summer, how about it? Moronic. Summer, I really want to take you to—

The blast of a car horn makes me jump. The flowers quiver in my hand.

"Yo, Kota, my man. What have we here?" Preston pulls his Mustang to the curb, blocking my way, and gets out.

I shove the flowers behind my back, even though I know it's too late. "What are you doing on this side of town?"

"I thought you might change your mind and hang with me. But you didn't get off your bus. Then I saw you strolling down the street with *flowers*." Preston grins. "And they're for...let me guess. Your mother?" He throws back his head and laughs.

"Exactly. I was an a-hole last night and thought she'd like them. Also hoping it will keep her from grounding me." I shrug. "No big deal. Gotta get home. See you tomorrow."

"Uh huh." Preston stares at me. "Like I believe that crock. But whatever. Later, dude."

I hide the rose in the back of the refrigerator behind seafood cocktail sauce and other stuff we rarely use. Why endure a bunch of comments from my parents about the whole thing? I'll tell them when it's time, especially if I need a new shirt or tie. Can't help but feel good, though, knowing Mom will be excited to take endless pics, and Dad will think Summer is pretty.

I have trouble sleeping, but it's okay. I just can't wait to ask Summer to the dance.

SEVEN

Summer

"Finn, got a minute?" I give him my warmest smile and yank on the dishtowel he's holding. Since the day we skipped school, he has avoided me. Because, I suspect, the momentary translucence of my hand freaked him out. We've been doing dishes together as part of our punishment, side by side at the sink, but our normal comfortable banter has been absent. Usually Daniel and Jill are around, but tonight they finally left us alone and went to Home Depot.

"Uh, I have homework." He lets the towel drop. A sheen of sweat appears on his upper lip. Even at ten, he shaves—needless and bladeless—every morning; there isn't a single downy hair to catch the moisture.

"Sure. Need any help?" I pick up the towel and snap it at him.

Finn jerks away. "No. I'm good."

"We need to talk." I make two glasses of chocolate milk and sit them on the breakfast bar. From the drawer I pull out the red plastic straw he likes, shaped like a snake.

"I have homework," Finn repeats. He remains

standing.

I perch on a stool, eyes on the milk. "You saw my hand." I don't know quite what to say or do.

Finn closes his eyes briefly, sighs, and chooses the stool farthest away from me. "Your hand disappeared." His whisper is that of a frightened little boy. "Am I going crazy? I don't want to be weird and get locked up at a mental hospital because I saw a reality show about that and the kids in there can be really really mean and—" The litany of words stops abruptly.

"That's what you've been worrying about? You think you're hallucinating?" His silence is assent. Now what? He's suffering, but what will the truth do to him? Before my brain can think it through, my mouth opens. "I'm a ghost. That hand thing happens sometimes. It's totally inconvenient."

"So you *do* know who you are. Except you're not alive, you're dead." Finn scoots his stool closer to me, until he can touch my hand as it rests next to the glass of cold milk. "You feel normal, just kinda hot. Are you telling me the truth? You're not a vampire or a werewolf, are you?"

"Oh, for goodness' sake." I feel my eyes roll. "First of all, vampires and werewolves aren't real. And second, I tell you I'm a ghost, and that's all you have to say?"

"Oh, yeah, right. I should be scared." Finn's dimple shows. "I'm not going to the loony bin, and you're not a creature of the night. That's all I care about. It's cool that you're a ghost. I mean, I wish you weren't dead, but it seems like you have an okay life, so maybe it doesn't matter?" His brown eyes study me, roving over my head, torso, legs, and feet. He touches my hair, spends a few minutes examining my left hand, which looks normal at present, and sniffs me like he's a dog. "You smell like that flower crap Mom buys, not like a moldering corpse. And my hand doesn't pass through you. But if you say you're a ghost, I believe you."

"'Moldering corpse'? Where did you get that one?" It's

easier to talk vocabulary than about my tenuous hold on humanity.

"Duh, spelling. We get words that go with the time of year. You know, right now it's all about fall and Halloween and stuff." Finn's turn for an eye roll. "My teacher thinks it's cool and keeps us 'engaged in learning'." He goes very quiet for several seconds, then, "What happened? What's it like? Will you be a ghost forever? How long have you been dead? Are you here to haunt this old house? Does everyone become a ghost when they die?"

"Slow down." I take a drink and wait until he slurps his milk through the straw. The chocolate rises through the maze of red plastic, a maze that's as convoluted as my situation.

"Okay. Now I'm slow." Finn burps. "But I have so many questions." He bounces on the stool. "I never met a ghost before."

"Fair enough." I decide to condense what I know and fill in what I suspect. "I died a long, long time ago. Don't remember when or how. I did something…very wrong. But I don't know what. There's a task I have to do to atone for my mistake. Again, don't know what's expected. Oh, and if I don't get it right by the time I'm seventeen, I won't ever be able to rest. I'll have to roam as a specter forever."

"You think you're sixteen, right? When's your birthday?" Finn's eyes are owl-wide. He doesn't even ask me about specters.

"I don't know."

"You don't know much."

"True, that." I think about what he said. "Let me think. I remember the last two times I appeared. Both were earlier this year, once in mid-April and once in June. I was sixteen each time." I don't add that it seems likely I've been sixteen for longer than the earth-years equivalent. If I'm wrong about that pesky detail, it will give him false hope.

"It could be today." Finn's eyes well with tears. "I don't want you to be a spectator."

His emotion touches a cord in me that I don't recognize. A great tsunami of emotion rolls through my body, a yearning to hug this child, kiss his sweaty head, protect him from harm. As tears fill my eyes, I sense a color change coming, but I don't run away. For the first time I can recall, a live person cares about me, isn't judging me, wants to be with me. Instead of giving him the hug that yearns to break free, I automatically correct his vocabulary. "Specter, not spectator. Like a restless shadow."

"Whatever. Wait. Your eyes." Finn stares.

"What color are they this time?" I blink my lashes. "Totally radical red? Amazing yucky yellow? Funky outrageous orange?"

"Rad red." Finn giggles. "But I'd like to see the other ones, too."

"Stick around. Not a problem." *At least not for you.*

"We have work to do." Finn is all business. "You must have a birth certificate somewhere, we can look online. Or research the places you were before you came here. And I have books about ghosts. Maybe there's help in one of those. Wait there." He runs out of the kitchen. His footsteps clatter down the hall toward his room, there's the momentary whoosh of the throw rug skating across the hardwood, and the bang of his door hitting the wall.

As I have no name, social security number, or police record, Finn is going to be disappointed. And the drivel in books is fantasy. But it will keep him busy and make him feel like he's helping. The problem of my birthdate won't be easy, unless Azul helps. *He* must know. He seems to know everything even though he doesn't share. But I sense he wants me to succeed, so maybe everything will work out. Big maybe.

"I've got it." Finn returns, only one book in hand. He holds up the slim, paperback volume, a smug smile on his lips.

"*Hypnosis for Idiots.*" I read the title and stifle a laugh. "You're going to hypnotize me?"

"Yep. I got this at a flea market. The lady said it really works. She used it to hypnotize her cat, and got the cat to stop peeing behind her chair. I spent two dollars of my own money on it, so it's not junk." Finn's cheeks are pink, and his eyes are shining. "I practiced on a squirrel once, and it stood really still for a whole minute."

"Look, this is a cool book and all, but maybe it works best on animals. I'll just keep trying to remember. But thanks. Great idea." I fill my voice with as much enthusiasm as possible and try to ignore the hurt that makes Finn's face droop.

"But, you don't want to end up," his arms flail about, "out there somewhere forever, do you? Isn't it worth at least trying? Have you ever been hypnotized before?"

He is so earnest and interested in my future, that for the second time in one evening my heart explodes with what must be love. "You're right. I'm just nervous. And no, never tried it."

"Leave it to me. I read the whole book and even watched a reality show about past lives, so I know how to take care of you." Finn looks me up and down. "Go put on comfortable clothes. Then meet me in the dungeon."

"Sure. Right back." I go upstairs, use the bathroom, and put on a pair of old gray sweats Jill gave me. They're loose, but the drawstring keeps the pants from sliding off my hips. I descend the spiral steps to the great room, then the second set of stairs to the basement. Daniel has a man-room they call 'the dungeon', filled with milk crates holding old books, the hot water tank, some gardening supplies, and a threadbare brown recliner.

"Okay. Great. Now sit in the chair, and get comfortable." Finn has donned a red cape from the Halloween costume bag and looks more like Little Red Riding Hood than a hypnotist.

I sit, pull the lever to recline the chair, and lean back. The fuzzy fabric is soft under my hands, and the cushions support my body. "Now what?"

Finn holds up one finger, flips through his book, and nods. "Do you understand what we are planning to do today?"

"Yes. You're going to hypnotize me so I can remember my past." I keep my tone serious. Why not humor the kid? "I trust you."

"You will remember everything that happens. I can't make you do anything you don't want to do." Finn is reading from his book, seeming to skip a paragraph or two, but hitting the highlights. He sits the book on an upturned milk crate. "Ready? Close your eyes."

I nod my assent and close my eyes.

"Think about a happy place in your mind, like the meadow behind our house. The leaves are red and falling off the trees when the wind blows. There are deer, and turkeys, and groundhogs." Finn's voice is a monotone, as he describes every possible detail of the meadow in autumn.

I can picture what's he's talking about. The way the wind blows the long grass, and the deer appear at twilight to nibble on chrysanthemums in Jill's garden, and dusk scatters the shadows early.

"Let your body be comfortable, your neck, and shoulders, and everything. Take long, slow breaths. You are sooo relaxed. As you listen to me, you feel heavier and heavier, more and more peaceful as you focus on my voice. You're sinking into the chair. It feels good. You want to go deeper. It feels *really* good. Now you are the most comfortable you've ever been." Finn's words run together.

I'm encircled in a warm, snug cocoon. But instead of feeling 'heavy', I am floating down a lazy river that sparkles in the sunshine. Finn's voice is the buzz of a honeybee in the background.

"What is your name?" The buzz is close to my ear.

"Summer."

"You have another name, too. What is it?"

I breathe in the scent of something sweet. "Dovie. Critchlow."

"How old are you, Dovie?"

"I am twelve."

"When is your birthday?"

Mama walks toward me through the meadow, a cake balanced on a plate. There are buds on the apple trees, but no apples. The other foliage is pale green and new, and the air is sun-warmed cool.

"My birthday is in the spring."

"What month were you born?"

I see a robin. She has a nest in the oak tree that is piled high—strange—with eighteen pale blue eggs. "April. Eighteenth."

"What year is it?"

This time the buzz of words is annoying, puzzling, frightening—a cacophony of confusion and screaming. A great heat rises in my body. I hear myself moan out loud. It is cut short as oxygen-deprived air catches in my throat. I hold my breath until my lungs burn. I try to stay very still, even though I yearn to thrash about.

"Summer, I'm going to count backward to one. When I get to one, you'll be awake and feel great. Five, four, three, two, one."

I open my eyes as "one" reverberates. Finn is standing beside me, his eyes wide, tears glistening on his cheeks. "Summer? It's okay. Whatever it is, it's okay. You're safe."

The floating feeling remains. My body has partially vaporized, and I'm actually several inches above the surface of the chair. As my flesh returns, I shiver. My clothes are drenched in sweat.

"Summer?" Finn wrings his hands, reaches out to touch me, then retracts his hand.

"I'm fine." With effort, I release the chair lever and sit

upright. The import of what just happened hits me. I manage a smile for Finn. "My name is Dovie Critchlow. I died when I was twelve years old."

EIGHT

Summer

Dovie Critchlow. Dovie Critchlow. I had been mentally exhausted after Finn hypnotized me. Instead of researching my background, I came upstairs and tried to nap. But the name—*my real name*—reverberates in my brain, making sleep impossible. *Dovie?* It must be short for something else, but what? I get out of bed, power up the tablet, and begin to search.

"Dovie is of English origin, symbolizing a dove of peace. Nickname for Margaret." I mumble my way through several websites, most of which say the same thing. After typing "Dovie Critchlow" in quotes, Google gives me next to nothing. There are a total of five people from the current US Census with that name, but I'm fairly sure my life began before present-day records. I give Ancestry.com a try, but they want a credit card number.

Part of me wonders why I cling to the idea of having been dead for a long time. I just know I have an old soul, in the same way I know my essence isn't really at home no matter how well I've learned to adapt to current culture. I try going through older records, but come up with nada, except for a grinding headache.

I force myself to lie down and to let my mind go blank. "Azul, speak to me." Nothing happens, except that eventually I must pass out. The alarm jars me awake into a gray, overcast day that matches my mood. I know who I am, but what good is it doing me? Thanks to the snooze button, I'm late getting up. I grab jeans off the rocking chair, pull a cinnamon-brown shirt from the drawer, and sling my hair into a ponytail. It doesn't matter how I look. I'll either figure things out or get to my eternal rest soon, or I'll—nope, not going there.

"Good morning, *Summer*." Finn grins as I descend the stairs.

Last night we agreed that I would remain Summer. Too confusing to explain anything else to Jill and Daniel. I push aside the niggling thought that Dovie might be nothing more than the memory of someone I met before. "Hey, Finn."

"This is a big day." Jill smiles over the rim of her coffee mug. "The dishwasher can start working again tonight and Finn, you can use your video games again." She shrugs. "You're almost done, Summer, after you help at the nursing home tomorrow morning."

"Sure." It's kind of funny that I could be older than any of the nursing home residents, but of course I don't share that thought with Jill. "Later." I pull on a fleeced hoodie and walk up the hill. The air is crisp, only the most tenacious leaves still clinging to almost-bare branches. Too soon the bus arrives, belching fumes that taint the scent of autumn.

"Saved." A red-haired girl puts her hand across the empty seat beside her, one of the few places left to sit. Near the back of the bus I slide in next to Marlie, a girl from my history class. The bus starts moving, hitting a pothole in the road.

"Curse of big boobs." Marlie giggles as her chest bounces with the motion of the bus. She adjusts her shirt, which gives me more than a peek at her ample cleavage. "Not that the *guys* seem to mind." She glances across me to the pimply kid on the other side of the aisle. "Enjoying the show, loser? *Honestly*," she settles back in the seat, and her smug gaze sweeps across my flat chest, "it's *exhausting* being me."

"I'll bet." She speaks as if every other word is in italics. That alone must be tiring. I fight off a sneeze, her perfume heavy and cloying in my nostrils. Maybe even the bus exhaust is better.

"Did you get your homecoming dress yet?" Marlie claps one hand over her mouth. "Oh, sorry. You're *new*, and have mental *issues*, and so…" Again she looks me up and down. "No probs. Lots of girls don't get asked. Since you don't even know who you are, *no guy* will want to get involved. You could be a *serial killer* or something." She makes sure there is room between us on the narrow seat.

A twinge of pain shoots through me at her words. Is that what I am? A serial killer? Surely if that were the case, I'd have gone straight to hell when I died. And as for the dance, I don't want to go anyway, but her attitude pisses me off. Mental issues, my skinny butt. "The tickets go on sale today. Are you sure someone will ask *you*?"

Spots of red appear on her already peach-blushed cheeks. "*I* date Kota Landis."

"Really?" Can't imagine a glowering hulk like Kota with a princess like Marlie.

"Well…it's complicated."

I shrug, preferring to think about dry toast rather than the life and times of Miserable Marlie and her Bouncing Boobs.

"We were, you know, like *this*." Marlie crosses her fingers, as if she and Kota used to be one pretzel. "We *both* decided to explore other options, but *somehow*," she winks, "we ended up as lab partners, and he's *totally* into me again. Once he asks me to the dance and sees me in my dress— strapless and fits like a glove—he'll be mine for good." She shrugs. "*If* I decide to take him back, that is."

If I were a betting girl, I'd win the "will Marlie take Kota back?" bet in a heartbeat. The bus pulls into the school, and I get ready to stand. If I'm quick enough, Marlie won't try to walk with me.

"Summer, I'm *so* glad we had this little chat." Marlie's long, purple-polished claws dig into my arm and skewer me into place. "Kids can be *so* cruel to those who are…*different*, like you. But you can *always* call me. And Summer," she looks around the crowded bus and lowers her voice, "keep what I said about Kota to yourself. I just *hate* gossip, don't you?"

"Yes, I do." I yank my arm away. "Have fun at the dance."

"At the dance—and *afterwards*." Marlie stands, wiggles her hips, and mimes a kiss with her full crimson lips.

I push my way off the bus and hear Marlie as she catches up with her BFF. "I sat with that *horrid* crazy girl on the bus. You know, the one who lost her mind? OMG, I am *so* over being a friend to *every* loser in school."

I'm not liking this place and if not for Finn might take off before the first bell. But there is Finn. And there's the deadline for my restoration. It's October now. I glance at the date on my phone: October twenty-first. Six months until April. "Azul, you have to help me out here," I mutter through clenched teeth.

"Talking to yourself?" Preston is leaning against my locker. He's smiling, but not in a way that seems like he's laughing at me. "You can talk to me anytime."

"Thinking out loud is more like it." I wait for him to move. He doesn't. "I have to get in my locker."

"Right." Preston's head dips, as if he's shy. Which he isn't on a normal basis. He's the guy every girl thinks is hot, the one for whom they doodle *Mrs. Preston Burke* on their notebooks in study hall. "I, um, wanted to give you this." He holds out a long-stemmed yellow rose surrounded by a cloud of tiny white flowers, green tissue, and curled silver ribbons.

"What is it?" I keep my hands at my sides. It's too weird. Flowers for me? Before first period? From someone I barely know? At school?

"Look at the card." Preston thrusts the bundle into my hand.

The paper crinkles when it touches my hand, and the tendrils of ribbon tickle. I put the bloom to my nose and inhale the sweet aroma. There's a plastic stick, forked at the end, holding a white envelope. I lift the flap, look inside, and pull out two cardboard rectangles. "Tickets?"

"Will you go to Homecoming with me?" Preston is serious. He stares at me while I struggle for an answer. His eyes narrow.

I suspect what's happening. "My eyes are hazel. They change color."

"Your eyes are...yellow...like the rose." Preston doesn't move, but there are a million questions moving across his face.

"Right. Like the rose. My eyes reflect things around me. It's a genetic thing." I wave my hand to dismiss his query, wondering how I came up with this new excuse, but glad I did.

"So your eyes are as mysterious as the rest of you." The famous Preston grin is back. "What do you say? You in a dress, me in a suit, music, dancing—no strings, just a good time. With a beautiful girl."

I am not used to this. "Why me?"

"Why not?" Preston laughs, then sobers. "I want to go out with you. You're not like the other girls around here. You're unique, interesting. I want to get to know you better. It's just one dance, Summer. If you hate it, I'll take you home."

He thinks it's just one dance. His interest in me is startling, uncomfortable—yet not unwelcome, I realize with amazement. Since I can't ever remember being the object of a cute guy's interest, it occurs to me that maybe it's more than one dance. Maybe Preston has something to do with my restoration. Maybe a relationship, with the right person, is the way out of the nightmare I've been living. Maybe he is exactly what—whom—I've been searching for.

"If you don't want to go, you can say it." Preston sighs and looks at the polished tile floor.

"I'm just surprised. Tickets don't even go on sale until lunch time."

"I have connections." One eyebrow goes up, and a smile lifts the right corner of Preston's lips. "So…"

"Yes. I would like to go to Homecoming with you." I feel the shift in my eyes, not sure if they've headed red with excitement or lavender with promise.

"What's this?" Kota looms behind Preston, his face more threatening than the thick gray clouds outside. He pushes past his friend, knocking him aside, and stares at the rose in my left hand and the tickets in my right.

"Summer just agreed to go to Homecoming with me." Preston straightens his shirt and moves beside me. His arm goes around my waist.

I start to pull away, but he feels warm and smells amazing. I address Kota. "That's right."

"I can't believe this." Kota is up in Preston's face. "You lying, miserable sack of shit. We've been friends for all these years—and now this. How could you?"

"If you wanted to ask her, you should have done it sooner. Not my problem you're always late, my man. You snooze, you lose." Preston doesn't move an inch.

"Look, I don't know what this is all about, but it's just one dance." I echo the words Preston used moments ago. And I step away from both of them. Kota's brown cheeks have a flush of color, his eyes squint in a deep frown, and a pulse beats at his neck. Preston is tight, balanced on the balls of his feet, as if ready to run.

"That's the way you want to play this?" Kota's eyes close briefly, he takes a deep breath, and his face relaxes.

"Don't do this, man. You know it's wrong. This was all my idea—she belongs with me."

"Excuse me? I belong to myself." My heart pounds as I notice a crowd gathering around us. Attention—one of the things I dread. "Preston was sweet enough to get flowers, the tickets—and I'm going with him. It's really none of your business." I turn my back on both of them, elbow my way through the ring of students, and head for class. A loud *bang* stops me. I look back.

"How could you do this, huh? Answer me." Kota smacks the metal locker again and gets nose-to-nose with Preston, his hands clenched into fists. "Afraid I'll spoil that baby face?"

I can't hear Preston's response and don't have a clear view of his actions as the bodies in front of me press forward toward the altercation. What I do hear is Kota's growl, right before his fist connects with Preston's jaw.

The flower in my now-translucent hand shaking, I make my way to the bathroom. Shouting, teachers' voices, the cheers and jeers of the crowd, all filter into the stall where I sit and will my flesh not to disintegrate. It's clear Kota has anger problems and must be jealous. Since I've never given him any indication I'm interested in him—because I'm not, he freaks me out—it makes no sense.

I leave the stall, watch in the mirror while my eyes roil until they settle into a shade of brown, and then go out to the hall, which is empty. The flower and tickets go into my dented locker. I won't let Kota ruin this for me. Preston is gorgeous, rich, and interested in me. Maybe, just maybe, this is the beginning of eternal peace.

NINE

Kota

"Because he stole the flowers and tickets *I* bought, and asked Summer to the dance with *my* stuff and *my* plan." I glare at Mrs. Romero and try to shrug off my father's hand. It tightens and clamps down on my shoulder, pushing me into a chair.

"I bought those things." Preston leans back in a chair, an ice bag on his jaw. "He's losing it. We both talked about asking Summer to the dance. He's just jealous that I came up with a winning idea, and it worked." He glances at me. "Get over yourself."

"This is unbelievable. I walked to Colegrande's yesterday, bought the flowers, put them in our refrigerator, and stowed them in my locker this morning." And planned, after combing my hair, to catch Summer and ask her to Homecoming before classes started. Until Preston, former friend and current scumbag, came along.

"So you said." Mrs. Romero taps a pencil on her desk. The annoying noise irritates me even more. "I called the flower shop. They don't remember you."

"Why would they remember one customer? But I had

the flower at home in the refrigerator all night." I hold my breath. Surely one of my parents noticed it behind the crusty condiments.

There is silence from Mom and Dad. At a pointed stare from Romero, Mom shakes her head and Dad mutters, "Didn't see it."

"And you're also saying Mr. Burke stole these things from your *locked* locker?" Disbelief drips with every word from the principal's lips.

"He knows my combination."

"No, I don't." Preston, lying again. We always trade combos in case one of us forgets something. "I'm lucky to remember my own."

"I am not getting into a he-said-he-said situation." Mrs. Romero stands behind her chair, as if the whole thing is over.

It's not. She walks around the desk and hands me a packet of printed pages.

"What's this?" I look at the top paper. The Fawn Valley Code of Conduct stares back.

"Assuming you can read, you will note that these are the official school rules." Mrs. Romero frowns. "You received a Student Handbook in September and signed the form stating you had read and understood its contents."

Like anyone reads the handbook they give us every year. I wait for Preston to get his own personal copy of the rules. He doesn't. "What about him?" I jerk my head Preston's way.

"Regardless of whether or not Mr. Burke's actions were above-board—which you in no way have proven them *not* to be—you are the one who indulged in violent behavior. Which carries serious consequences." Romero, chief inquisitor, handing down my sentence. "You will note on page one that the school board gives me the authority to discipline. On page six, there is an outline of disciplinary measures."

I flip to page six. One to five day suspension, with

make-up work on Saturday from eight to twelve. "You've got to be kidding."

"Because this is your first violation, and your parents have assured me they will follow up at home, I am suspending you for one day. You will be off tomorrow, Friday, and arrive promptly on Saturday to make up your work. You will also pay for repairs to the dented locker door. I am being very lenient. Do not make me regret it." A small child could get lost in the frown lines between Romero's eyes.

"Preston punched me in the stomach. First. As I already told you. And he gets nothing?" I rub the sore spot on my gut where Preston's fist landed before I could get off a punch.

"I never touched him." Preston widens his eyes, as if he's done nothing, when he started it, hit me, and lied about everything.

"Kota, please." Mom's face is a mixture of sadness and anger.

"I spoke with several witnesses to your actions. There is no proof to what you *allege* he did." Romero ushers everyone to the door of her office. "Mr. Landis, I am very, very disappointed in your behavior. Right now, you think everything is about a pretty face, but by next month you won't even care about this particular young lady or the dance. I'll be watching you. Make sure you curb these tendencies toward violence, or your one-day suspension will end up in expulsion."

"Get your things. I'll wait while Mom pulls the car around." Dad escorts me out of the office.

It hurts that Preston has turned on me. It hurts worse that my parents don't believe me.

"I have to use the men's room." Dad frowns. "Don't talk to anyone, especially Preston. This can be over by Monday, at least at school. I'll meet you at the front entrance." He walks away, leaving me digging in my locker for my coat and a few books.

"Tough luck." Preston is at my side, his smile triumphant, no bruising or swelling on his jaw. "I told you I would win. I always do. If you remember that, we'll get along fine, like always."

"It's just you and me." I gesture to the empty hall. "Why did you do it?"

Preston glances over his shoulder before answering. "I intended to take Summer to the dance. When I saw you with those flowers yesterday, I guessed what you planned. So I waited until you stowed things this morning and took it from there. You know people always believe what I say. Sorry about the jab. I thought it would keep you from punching me." He rubs his jaw. "You know how to hit."

"So you're telling me you don't mind throwing away twelve years of friendship over a dance and a girl?" I can't believe what I'm hearing, even as part of my mind registers the fact that I would do almost anything to be with Summer. Which is totally weird.

He shrugs. "Looks that way, my man. Although there's something even more important." An expression— something evil and alien to Preston's usual demeanor— crosses his face. "I will always beat you. At everything. At the end of days, Summer *will* be mine."

"What are you talking about, 'end of days?' That doesn't even make sense. You've always been competitive, but not like this." I see Preston standing in front of me. I smell his expensive Polo for Men cologne. I hear his familiar voice. It's Preston...but not, like he's giving the worst parts of himself free rein.

"I've always won. You should be used to being my lackey by now." He laughs and leaves me standing alone.

I slam my locker door, wishing it was Preston getting slammed. A sound makes me swing around.

Summer, the only other person in the hall now that Preston left, is watching me. "You need anger management classes—or therapy." She doesn't cringe, raise her voice, or call for a teacher. But her eyes betray her emotions as they fill with a deep red. She blinks several times, takes a deep breath, and shoves her left hand into the pocket of her jeans.

"What is it about me? We've barely talked. And no matter what you think, I did plan the whole dance thing that Preston stole. All I ever wanted was to get to know you." More words than I'm used to uttering, especially to a girl. But she looks vulnerable, her thin form ready to run from me, her strange eyes—don't know what to make of them. "Is it because I'm Native American?"

"I don't care what you are." Summer gets a book out of her locker. "You just creep me out."

"Oh, right. *I* creep *you* out." I hear the snarl in my voice, can't help it. "You don't know who you are or where you came from. For some reason, apparently, even the authorities can't find your real family. Your eyes do that voodoo thing—and don't give me that crap about genetics. Everyone in school should be afraid of you, and yet I've been suspended for the sin of trying to ask you out."

"Boo hoo, life isn't fair." Summer's turn to slam the locker. Instead of walking away, she moves in close to me. Her breath is spearmint, her scent earthy and fresh, her eyes faded to umber. "I'm a freak, I get it, don't need your analysis to make it clear. So you're suspended. Big deal. A couple days off school at your cozy house with the family who loves you. Try living with total strangers, not knowing if you've ever seen the ocean, fitting in with a bunch of hormonal adolescents." She turns on her heel, then back again. "Even if you did buy the flower and the tickets, I wouldn't have gone to the dance with you." This time she walks away without a backward glance.

I should be meeting my parents at the door, but can't make my feet move. I just insulted the girl I can't get out of my head. For whatever reason, I turn her off. Instead of finding out how to change that, I've made it worse. Much worse. As in fatal. Other girls have been flirting with me for years, and I couldn't have cared less. Why now, with Summer, am I saying and doing all the wrong things?

The bell rings, classrooms empty, and the hall fills with the buzz of many voices. I get lots of stares, a few high fives, and Doug's "You're on the war path, dude," along with a few other choice ethnic slurs. I head for the front door.

"I heard what happened." Marlie, last person I want to see, steps in front of me. "That girl is psycho. I know how kind you are, and that you were only asking her to the dance to be nice. So be glad she's going with Preston. She's his problem now." Marlie links her arm to mine.

"I have to go. My parents are out in the car."

"I'll miss you in school tomorrow." Marlie summons a tear and takes a deep breath. "Kota, let's go to Homecoming together. We had so much fun when we dated before. I'll even buy the tickets. Okay?" Her soft body bumps up against mine as she whispers in my ear, "You won't be sorry, baby, if you know what I mean."

From the end of the hall my dad appears, dodging students, his face in a scowl.

"Gotta go."

"Please? You and me?" Marlie licks my ear before pulling away. "I won't let you say no."

"Yeah, fine. Whatever." I join my father and make it to the car, slouching in the back seat. No one speaks as we drive down the road to our house and pull in the garage.

"Go to your room." Mom breaks the silence. "Your father and I will decide what punishment is appropriate here at home. I'll call you when dinner is ready, and we'll talk then."

I consider ignoring her. After all, I'm taller and stronger; she can't make me. Habit wins out, and I get out of the car, close the door with more force than needed, snatch up Blondie, and go to my room as ordered. My dog wriggles in my arms and licks my face—her warm tongue grazing the place where Marlie just drooled. "You're my good girl, right, pup? You aren't afraid of me, and you don't try to run my life." It occurs to me that I should stick with dogs and leave girls alone. On that thought, I flick on Twitter and tweet: That moment when you realize life totally sucks.

LAUREL HOUCK

TEN

Summer

"Summer! Welcome to Peaceful Retreat Personal Care Center." The large woman in bright orange scrubs printed with smiling pumpkins greets me at the office. "I'm Mrs. Shields. Thanks so much for volunteering to help with our Harvest Party."

"Oh, sure." I don't mention that it's a punishment for skipping school. "What should I do?" The air is permeated with the undercurrent of incontinence, poorly disguised by industrial-strength air freshener. A thin, repetitive wail comes from somewhere down the hallway. A harried nurse mutters as she pushes a heavy cart laden with medicines. Lovely way to spend a Saturday. Kota might have it better in study detention. Not that I care what he's doing.

"You can help me set up in the activity room. We'll be playing Harvest Bingo, holding a drawing, and eating goodies from Dietary." Mrs. Shields coos like an oversized pigeon. She leads me down the carpeted hall to a large room with tables and chairs. There are windows on three sides, fake fall leaves in bunches on the tables, and plastic pumpkins atop cardboard hay bales. "Put a Bingo card and a little cup of tokens at each place. I'll call out the letters, and you can move about to help the residents play the game. All righty?"

"Okay." The kitchen must be behind the far wall. I smell what has to be lunch, and it's not pleasant. The mixed scent of body functions and fried something— liver?—makes me gag. I wonder if there will be pureed spinach to make things worse. Hopefully, I'll be on my way by lunchtime.

I pass out cards, help arrange cookies on a big aluminum tray, and fill paper cups with Harvest Punch— otherwise known as sugar-free orange Kool-Aid. Residents wander in, a few using canes, some with walkers, and many in wheelchairs being pushed by staff members. There is little conversation or interest shown in the party that's about to begin. Heads droop, and a few people doze off, drool sliding down their chins.

"B-four." Mrs. Shields, using a squealing microphone, belts out the first number.

"What? You gotta speak up." An elderly woman wearing a black sweatshirt with a scarecrow printed on the front holds one hand to her ear, a token gripped between palsied fingers.

"B-four." I point to the correct place on her card.

"I can read, girlie." She plunks the token on the space.

"N-ten." Mrs. Shields giggles. "That rhymes."

"Now what's she saying?" An old man with red suspenders and a scraggly white beard spills his cup of tokens.

"I'll get them for you." I scoop up the plastic chips and sit them beside him. "I like the beard. You look like Santa Claus."

"Aren't you too old to believe that nonsense?" He glares at me. "Be quiet, or I'll miss the next number. There's a prize for the winner." But he winks and says, "Maybe the prize is having a cute young thing like you for my sorry old eyes to see."

Some of the people are gracious, some crotchety, but all a sad reminder of the toll life takes. Maybe dying when I was twelve wasn't so bad after all. I skipped this end-of-life crap. Of course, they aren't roaming the earth trying to find some peace. Mr. Red Suspenders loses to Mrs. Scarecrow—who wins a small plastic jack-o'-lantern filled with sugar-free candy—at which point it's time for cookies and punch. Somehow, even though I don't want to be here, I like the feeling of helping these folks.

"Code Blue, East Wing." The loudspeaker squawks to life. Staff members come to attention and race out the door. I'm left alone in the room with twenty residents.

"This party ain't no good." A rotund man in navy sweats looks around. "You here to do a show for us, young lady?" He's staring at me.

"I'm just a helper." I have to admit he's right. The party sucks. Even the cookies are tasteless. These poor people deserve better. A crazy thought comes to me. "But I can do some magic tricks."

"What's she saying?" Mrs. Scarecrow leans forward.

I move to the front of the room, realizing I've become the center of attention. But unlike at school, it doesn't bother me here. "I can make my hand disappear. Watch closely." I hold out my left hand, think about how much Kota freaks me out, and after wavering for a second, my hand vaporizes.

A moment of stunned silence is split by clapping. "More, more." The alert residents strain to see what I'll do next. Even the sleepy droolers open their eyes.

For a few minutes, I play around with disappearing body parts. But since some staff member must soon realize they've left a volunteer alone, I don't have much time. I close my eyes and let my spirit soar. A rush of wind whistles through my head as my flesh morphs into vapor. I hover in the air, close enough for everyone to see me, and pass out more cookies. That done, I return to the front and materialize once more into human form.

"Now that's what I call a magic trick." Mr. Red Suspenders whoops, even those formerly slumped in their wheelchairs sit up straighter, and there are smiles all around.

"Oh my." Mrs. Shields enters the room, jaw dropping open. "I'm so sorry to have left you...but it seems you have quite a talent with senior citizens."

"This girlie knows her stuff." Mrs. Scarecrow hobbles forward, leaning on her walker. She pats my hand and stares at me before toddling out of the room.

I realize that the strange *something* moving through me is happiness. For once, my ghostly presence hasn't been questioned, and it helped brighten the day. Way cool. Too bad I'm not accepted by anyone my own age.

"Come by anytime." Mrs. Shields shakes my hand and gives me a piece of paper with Volunteer of the Day computer-printed on the top.

"Thanks." I take the paper and walk to the front door of the facility.

"Just a minute, girlie." Mrs. Scarecrow blocks my path. She pokes my hand. "Those other fools believed you were doing magic. But I think you're some kind of supernatural creature. I see them—ghosts or whatnot—sometimes, in my room at night. Don't know if it's angels or demons coming for me. Can you tell me?"

I open my mouth to say something easy and shut her up. Until I notice her faded blue eyes are intent on my answer. I had no time to ponder the hereafter before I died—no twelve-year-old does—but his woman must think of little else. "I'm nothing special. But I'm sure what you see are angels, waiting to take you to paradise."

"Angels." She closes her eyes and the wrinkles between her brows soften. "Angels." She walks away, a small smile on her lips.

The fresh, crisp air outside in the parking lot is a nice contrast to the nursing-home smells. My stomach rumbles. Since it's noon and I skipped breakfast, I decide to grab a bowl of soup at Panera, then check out Goodwill for a bargain dress for Homecoming. Food is more a luxury than a necessity—but eating makes me feel alive.

Since it's Saturday, the line at Panera is long. I finally order, get my bowl of chicken noodle soup and an apple, and find a seat in the corner next to the window. I like it here. It's noisy, people either focus on their computers, a book, or friends, and no one gives me a second look. I sip the soup and let my mind wander. It goes from the inconsequential—what kind of dress is right for the dance?—to the usual—how do I figure out my eternal destination?

"Hey, watch it."

A familiar growl interrupts my thoughts. I look up.

Everything happens in a slow-motion instant. Kota, balancing a tray in one hand and his phone in the other, jerks aside as a little kid sideswipes him in a dash to the bathroom. The tray and phone fly into the air, along with a green bowl and crusty baguette of bread. Hot broth, slimy noodles, and a few stray carrots splash in my direction. My shoulder and hair absorb the mess. The phone lands, face down, in a puddle on the table, next to the bread.

"Here sir, let me help you." A Panera worker hurries over, gives me napkins, and helps Kota clean up the mess. Before either Kota or I can speak, she returns with a fresh bowl of soup and bread, which she sets on the table. "Have a good day."

"I'm, uh, sorry about that." Kota doesn't make eye contact with me. He blots his phone with a wad of napkins, tries to make it work, and shoves it into his pocket. "Dead. Of course." With a sigh, he sinks into the chair directly across from me.

"This isn't your table." Even as I say it, it sounds petty and mean. Why do I avoid this guy? He's hot, obviously interested in me, and seems nice enough. My gut usually isn't wrong, but this particular incarnation has been different than the others, so maybe I should give him a chance. "It's okay."

"You have a carrot in your hair." Kota reaches across the table and plucks a bit of orange from my damp, blond hair. He discards the veggie onto a napkin and reaches back—his hands are small for a guy— to tuck a loose strand behind my ear.

At his touch, a shiver starts in my shoulders and passes through my body. I don't know whether to lean in to his hand or slap it, such is the mixture of hot and cold that wars within me. I smell a sudden, acrid scent of fear from my armpits, even as a tidal wave of desire wells up.

Against my will, I look full at Kota. The coarse black hair framing his face shows rusty tones as the sunlight hits it. His nose is slightly wide, his chin square. He blinks long, thick lashes that every girl must envy. I notice his eyes are somewhere between hazel and dark brown, the iris surrounded by a narrow, clearly marked ring. There is both menace and magic in those eyes. I try to drink in the magic and ignore the rest.

"Summer." Kota's hand is stopped in mid-air, between my ear and the table.

The breath catches in my throat. It's almost like I know him. But my brain refuses to process any information, the notion a tantalizing tickle that goes no further.

A ringing noise breaks the moment. Kota frowns, reaches into his pocket, and pulls out his cell phone. "It's working after all." But he silences it and puts it away.

"I have to go." Seeing him frown pulled the menace to the front of my brain, chasing the magic. I've endured by trusting my instincts for way too long. And every time I'm around Kota, those instincts are screaming. Being lonely isn't a reason to ignore my survival, especially when time is no longer on my side.

"But…" Kota shrugs. "Sure. Sorry about the soup and all. Maybe we can get something less messy to eat another time. Like tomorrow?"

"Thanks. Don't think so. Marlie wouldn't like that." I

see him ready to interrupt me. "And neither would Preston."

"Oh. Right." Kota's eyes narrow. "Maybe you two deserve each other."

"Maybe we do." My chin lifts. "Like you and Marlie."

We both stand and glare, as if ready to engage in hand-to-hand combat. My heart pounds as a burst of adrenaline shoots through my veins. Fight-or-flight kicks in; I opt to leave. If it weren't so crowded, I really would fly—as far and as fast from Kota Landis as possible. He has some kind of power over me. And I know it's not good.

Before I can get out of my corner seat, he picks up his tray, slams the dishes into the bin, and strides out of Panera. People are now looking at me. I can almost read their minds—lovers' quarrel—and that thought propels me out of the restaurant. Quarrel? Yes. Lovers? Never.

ELEVEN

Summer

Goodwill is crowded with teens looking for cheap fun and the poor looking for cheap necessities. I don't know which category to put myself in. I choose "poor me" and wallow in it, even though Jill would be happy to buy me a homecoming dress. She and Daniel have done enough already. Let them spend their money on Finn. One way or another, I'll soon be gone.

The store is divided into tops, pants, dresses, shoes, household goods, and furniture. To avoid all thoughts of Kota and our recent encounter at Panera, I focus on what I'm here to accomplish. I flip through the dress rack, finding an array of plain cotton sundresses, old lady cast-offs, and the occasional glitzy club mini. A separate section filled with colorful, shiny fabric catches my attention. The Goodwill team has put all special-occasion wear on a single rack.

"Aren't these lovely?" An older woman pulls out a matronly mother-of-the-bride type thing, beige with long, transparent sleeves and a big fake purple fabric flower on the belt.

"Very nice." I edge closer and look through dresses of various colors, fabrics, and styles. None appeal to me. Preston wouldn't like any of them—not that I care what he thinks—or maybe I do. The thought that he might be my eternal love has been occurring to me more and more as the dance gets closer. I'll let Jill take me shopping.

I pick some jeans from the other side of the store and head for the dressing room. On the return rack in the back, I see it. Another girl also spots it from across the store, but I get there first. She gives me the finger as I scoop the hanger off the bar. In the dressing room I take off my jacket and shirt and let my jeans puddle around my ankles as I slip on the dress.

The fabric is shimmery white, not glaring but a muted ivory. It is a shade darker than my pale skin. The top is high and straight across, with cut-in shoulders and a fitted bodice liberally sprinkled with tiny beads the same color. Much of the back is bare. The dress is soft and hugs my slender frame, flaring from my knees to my ankles. When I turn from side to side, there is a subtle swish as the fabric twirls. I slip off my jeans and socks and stand on bare tiptoes.

"Thank you, Preston, I would love to dance." I move about the small dressing room, my eyes—which are a peaceful light green—watching in the mirror. The price tag says $19.99, and I know there isn't another dress anywhere I could love this much. It's classy, highlights my slim build, and doesn't need big boobs to hold it up.

A quick stop at the shoe rack scores me a $3.99 pair of silver pumps, a little higher than I like, but I can't pass them up. I put the jeans back on the rack. My purchases are enough to dispel the lingering sense of unease that any interaction with Kota Landis caused me. I pay, clutch my bag, and head for the door.

"You *bought* something here?" Marlie deposits a plastic garbage bag in the donation bin by the front door. "Eww. This is all stuff from dead people." She tries to peek in my bag, but I keep the top closed.

"Whatever." I step around her.

"It's not even hygienic. Or safe." Marlie follows me to the parking lot. "Of course, for those who are less fortunate, I guess it keeps them from being naked." She giggles.

"You just donated a bag of clothes, and you're not dead. Yet." I let the implication hang in the air and try to look menacing.

"Are you threatening me?" Marlie takes a step back.

"Why would I do that? Just pointing out that not everything in Goodwill is from a dead person. And that all of us die eventually." It's very funny that a dead person—me—will be wearing what Marlie finds offensive. If she only knew. I'm tempted to vaporize right here in the parking lot beside her new BMW, but she's not worth it. I have a dance to attend, an event that might begin a relationship that will lead to my eternal resolution.

"Oh. You're making a joke." Marlie barks out her nasal laugh, even though she hasn't a clue what just happened between us. And she thinks she's so smart. "Maybe you and Preston should double with me and Kota to Homecoming. We'd have so much fun, and it would give you time to admire my gorgeous new dress."

"Preston and I have things planned already, but thanks. I'm sure I'll see you there so I can 'admire' you." I say this knowing that if there's any way to avoid Marlie and Kota, I'll find it. Before she can answer, I wave and run to the beat-up Honda Civic Daniel lets me drive.

"How did it go at the nursing home?" Jill pounces as I enter the house.

"Good. I liked it." I also don't want to share too much, so I hold up my bag. "I got a homecoming dress."

"At Goodwill?" The skepticism on Jill's face fades as I pull out the gown.

"Oh, Summer, it's perfect for you. And you got shoes, too?" Jill smiles. "I'll take care of the jewelry. It's going to be a wonderful evening for you. The dance will be here before you know it."

In spite of my initial reluctance, I find myself getting into the excitement at school as the date approaches. Kota ignores me, Marlie is caught up with her giggling friends, and Preston is attentive without smothering me.

He stops on his way past my locker. "Tomorrow is the big day. Sorry we missed last night's bonfire, and that I have to help out my dad for a few hours. Otherwise, I would've taken you to the football game tonight. Are you all ready for the dance?"

"Do I look ready?" I gesture to my jeans, baggy sweater, and cross-body purse. As his smile dims I add, "Just kidding. I'm glad you're taking me. And I don't care about the game."

"Great." Preston nods, and his hand brushes the hair away from my face. "We'll pick you up at six o'clock so we can get pictures at the park."

"I'll be ready." It isn't until I'm home that I realize he said "we" for the pick-up. Maybe his parents will come along to see us all dressed up. I know Jill already has the camera sitting on the table.

I sleep in Saturday morning, take a long shower, and go to Vintage Rose Day Spa with Jill. Heather, the owner of the place, transforms my nails into glittering spheres. She applies makeup, against my better judgment. I prefer to look natural.

"Oh." Jill's hand flies to her mouth as Heather swings the chair around.

"That bad?" I take the hand mirror Heather gives me. "Is this really me?" I look exactly like myself, but better. Subtle highlights of rose skim my cheeks, and my eyes have a touch of silver on the lids. "I don't know what you did, but it's great."

As soon as we get home I hurry to the loft to finish getting ready, ignoring Jill's entreaty to eat something. The dress slips over my head, and I zip the side zipper. I crimp my long hair and let it hang down my back. The silver shoes slip on, and I make a grand entrance down the spiral stairs.

"Woo hoo." Finn whistles. "You look *hot*."

"Finn. None of that." But Daniel smiles. "You do clean up well."

"Try these." Jill hangs a white gold chain around my neck, with one diamond in the center. She hands me matching earrings.

"I can't wear these." I try to give the jewelry back. "They're too expensive."

"Nonsense." Jill shakes her head. "You spent next to nothing on the dress and shoes. At least wear some decent accessories. And take this shawl in case it gets cool later."

"Someone's here." Finn runs to the window. "A red car's coming down the hill."

"It's Preston." Butterflies flutter in my stomach. Playing dress-up is one thing. Actually going to a dance, quite another altogether. I glance in the mirror, but my eyes remain a steady gray rather than some wild shade. It's a comforting sign. Maybe Preston really is my path to reconciliation. And maybe it begins tonight.

"Summer." Preston walks into the room. He's wearing a black suit, black shirt, and silver tie. "These are for you." He hands me a small bunch of wildflowers, tied with silver ribbon.

"They're perfect." I take the flowers and bury my nose in their sweetness. An image of a meadow filled with wildflowers flits through my brain. I don't even try to determine where it came from.

"Let's get some pictures." Jill picks up the camera. She snaps, adjusts, snaps some more.

"I'll have the others come in, too, if that's okay." Preston goes to the door and waves toward the car.

"Others?" The fragile peace in my gut is shattered as Marlie and Kota approach the house. "I thought we were going alone." But it's too late now, so I stop.

"It's more fun this way." Preston takes my arm.

"Isn't this exciting?" Marlie, clad in a skin-tight, hot pink dress, almost loses her boobs right in front of Finn, who can't take his eyes off her. "It's so much more fun to double. We can spend the *entire evening* together."

Marlie looks me up and down and I catch her eye roll to Kota. Her dress is short. Very short. Is a long gown the wrong length for this particular event, or is it just Marlie showing off more skin? A trickle of sweat inches down my back. I thought I didn't care what anyone thought about me. Maybe I thought wrong. But it's too late now.

Jill takes more pictures. It's much harder to smile with Marlie simpering and Kota glaring. But Preston smells great, looks amazing, and his eyes signal his approval of me. Why should I care about anything but having fun? I'm sixteen, at least for tonight, and a rich, hot guy wants to be out with me. I won't let anyone spoil it.

Preston does most of the talking as he drives us to the high school. We troop down the hall to the decorated gym. There's a crowd of dressed-up girls who appear comfortable and their dates who are squirming in suits and ties. The dance committee did a good job transforming the site of basketball games and gym classes into a fall fairyland.

"Marlie, oh my gosh. Love the dress, girlfriend." Kayla, one of the gaggle of girls Marlie hangs with, swoops in as we move through the crowd. She stares at me. "Seriously?"

"I know, right?" Marlie lowers her voice, which is still loud enough to hear. "Can you believe she wore a *long* dress to Homecoming?"

A quick check of the room confirms my sudden fear. Every other girl in the place is in a short dress. "Let's find a seat." I touch Preston's arm, but he's talking to someone behind us and doesn't move.

"I love your *gown*." Kayla comes closer, inspects my dress front and back, and peers at the beads. "It looks really *familiar*."

I shrug. This is going to be a no-win conversation.

Kayla nods and raises her voice above the music, even though she pretends to be talking to Marlie. "That's the dress I wore to prom last year. There's a bead missing right at the neckline. I donated it to Goodwill."

"I saw her there, with a bag." Marlie rolls her eyes. "How low-class can you get? She probably remembers who she is, but doesn't want anyone to know which trailer park she came from." She and Kayla share their information about me. I can almost imagine the gossip traveling around the room. Girl with no memory wears inappropriate dress from a thrift store.

I instinctively lower my eyes, sensing the roiling change coming over them. A quick glance at my left hand confirms my worst fears, as the flesh wavers. I cover it with the shawl Jill made me bring.

"You bought that at Goodwill?" Kota, ignoring his date and her friend, addresses me for the first time all evening.

"So what?" My chin comes up, and I sneer at him. "I don't care what you think."

"Hey, lay off her, man." Preston's arm slips around my waist. "She's the most beautiful girl here. Jealous?"

"Of you?" Kota's hands clench into fists.

"Now boys, there's enough of *me* to go around." Marlie shows her ass to Preston and puts her arms around Kota's neck. "Let's dance, baby. She's not one of us. Let Preston figure out what to do with her." She drags Kota away.

But the damage has been done. Other girls I don't even know point and snicker as they get close to me. I even overhear a chaperone whispering about "that poor, poor girl who has no one to take care of her."

I try to endure for Preston's sake, keeping the shawl draped over my left hand the entire time. We dance, drink awful punch, and he tries to make conversation. Until Marlie glides past and calls me "Queen of Goodwill."

"They're ridiculous." Preston breathes in my ear. "Let's

get out of here."

"You're sure?" The promise of leaving sends a surge of hope that settles my hand. I pull the shawl around my shoulders.

"I'm sure." Preston hurries me out of the gym and into his car. He drives in silence for a long time—at least thirty minutes—until we reach the city. After crossing a bridge, he hangs a right and winds up a two-lane roadway until we reach the edge of a deserted hill. The city of Pittsburgh is spread out below, three rivers, twinkling lights, and impressive buildings. He turns off the car and reaches into the back seat. "Mt. Washington. We can be alone here. Come on."

We walk over the edge, me holding on to him as my high heels sink into the grass. He finds a spot beside a tall tree and spreads out a soft blanket. "Let's talk."

And we do talk, for a while, until there's not much to say. The evening was a disaster, and we both know it's my fault—even though he's too much of a gentleman to mention it. He must see the tears before I feel them, because he pulls out a snowy white handkerchief and blots my face.

"I'll take care of you, Summer." Preston's breath is sweet, he's wearing a woodsy cologne, and his arms are warm and strong.

I give in to the nuzzling of my neck that turns to insistent kisses. As we lie back on the blanket in the cool night, his hot weight heavy over me, I wonder. Is this the way to reconcile my eternal soul? Is Preston the love that will make things right? Is this the night?

But there are no fireworks in my heart. Instead, I silently plead with Azul to tell me what to do. Because I don't have time to screw up again.

TWELVE

Kota

"What the hell is wrong with you?" The growl in my voice makes Marlie jump.

"Me? You're the one who stared at that pathetic *loser* all evening." Marlie bends slightly, giving me a good look at her boobs.

The mounds of jiggling flesh don't turn me on this time. *Did* I stare at Summer all evening—or at least until Preston hauled her away? I mean, I noticed her, like every other guy at the dance. She looked like a queen in a throng of jesters. A pulse beats in my neck. "You called her 'Queen of Goodwill.' She doesn't have a rich daddy to buy her a dress. What's it matter to you?"

"You're *defending* her? She hates you. We rode the bus together the other day and she told me she can't *stand* you." Marlie's eyes narrow. "She's psycho—she might even try to hurt you."

"Right. Can't wait to see all five feet two of her take me on and win." But it's disturbing to think someone—especially Summer—feels that way about me. Just because she came to Homecoming with Preston doesn't mean I'm totally out of the picture. Or maybe it does, if Marlie's right. Of course, Marlie has been known to stretch the truth.

"Baby, I just don't want anything to happen to you. We're so good together. And we could be even better." She leans into me, her body soft against my chest, and whispers in my ear. "Let's go somewhere private. Right now."

"The dance isn't over." What *is* my problem? A hot chick is throwing herself at me. Me, a virgin, probably the only guy in school who never got any. "Yeah, okay."

Marlie hits the bathroom. I check my wallet for the condom that's been in there since Preston gave it to me in seventh grade. No glove, no love. I'm not about to become a teen dad—or make a lifelong commitment to Marlie. But if I'm not in love with her, it's wrong to do it. Of course she came on to me, I'm just going along for the ride. My morals collapse.

I smell Marlie before I see her, the scent of some fruity cologne stronger than when she left the gym. "So, I've been thinking—"

"Me, too." She giggles and runs a lingering hand across my butt. "Can you guess what *I'm* thinking about?"

I've got nothing. We weave our way through the crowded dance floor, aka gym. Guys throw me knowing glances, girls whisper behind their hands.

"Have fun, you two." Kayla looks me up and down, licks her lips, and smirks. "Don't do anything I wouldn't do."

From what I've heard around school, that pretty much means we can do anything. And why not? I'm almost seventeen. If it isn't Marlie, it will be someone else. Like Summer. Her skin. Is it warm like the soft white sand on the beach? Her hair. Would my hands slide through that waterfall cascade of soft blond? Her eyes. Why are they a kaleidoscope of color? Thoughts of Summer do to my body what Marlie's rounded figure failed to accomplish.

"Ooo—we aren't even at the car yet." Marlie practically purrs, her sideways glance approving. In the parking lot she pulls a metal flask from her purse and takes a drink. "Irish whiskey to help you enjoy my Irish ass."

Against everything I know is right, I swig some whiskey, and we get in the car. I take the long way downtown, through city neighborhoods instead of the Parkway. Anything to delay the inevitable. Did Preston take Summer to the place we're headed? He and I found it years ago when we snuck away from a Boy Scout urban hike. In the midst of the busy city, it's a secluded oasis. Chances are he's forgotten about it by now, or he took her to the Ace Hotel. He can afford niceties like sheets and room service. I grit my teeth.

"Why are you parking here?" Marlie's whine gets my attention. "There are too many apartment buildings and restaurants. No privacy."

"It's just a place to stash the car." Also, it further delays arriving at the Hot Spot, as Preston and I dubbed the make-out place. "Let's just be quiet and enjoy the walk."

Marlie kisses her finger and places it on my lips. "And get in the mood."

I stroll along the sidewalk that rims Mt. Washington, resisting Marlie's attempts to hurry me. Below, the city spreads out, hugged by three rivers. PNC Park, the Pirates' baseball stadium, is dark. At Heinz Field, the lights blaze and muted crowd sounds make their way through the night. Steelers versus the Raiders tonight. I'd rather watch football than punt with Marlie.

I point. "Steelers. Hope they can keep the ball tonight. Turnovers cost them two games already."

"Speaking of football…why didn't we go to the homecoming game together last night? Or the bonfire on Thursday? It's a tradition. Except you never answered my texts about it. *Everyone* was there with their date, except for us." Marlie's pouty face belongs on a two-year-old. "*Almost* everyone, that is."

"'Almost' is not everyone. The Bucks suck this year, so why bother?"

"Preston didn't take Summer, either." Marlie rolls her eyes. "He was smart enough to ditch her for the game, why not the dance, too? He hooked up with some chick from Seneca. I saw them behind the bleachers. But who cares?" Her arm links with mine in a vise grip. "I've got the *real* Seneca right here with me. Gonna use your tomahawk on me, baby?"

The Indian references kill any speck of desire I'd tried to summon for her. "What is it with you? I don't go around making lame jokes about your 'Irish ass.'"

"I love it when you get all hot and bothered." She ignores the view. "Are we there yet?"

I'm about to call her an infant and tell her that yes, we're there, when I hear voices. "Shh." I put one hand to my lips.

"Don't tell me to shut—"

Something in my look stops her mid-sentence, and she goes quiet for once. I get close enough to whisper in her ear, almost gagging on her perfume. "Wait here. It's secluded down there. Could be a drug deal going down. Don't want you hurt."

Eyes wide, Marlie nods and pulls a lipstick-sized cylinder of Mace out of her purse. She practically hugs a streetlight.

I edge down a grade through damp grass, fragrant pines, and almost-bare deciduous trees. My feet slide through the fallen leaves, making me wince at the crunch. I doubt there's a drug deal. It's more likely Preston and Summer. No need for a scene with Marlie, if they've spoiled her chance to get laid tonight. My peripheral brain recoils at the crudeness of that thought. But "making love" is a label I'm saving for someone special. Summer? Not likely.

"You and me, babe. Sheer perfection." Sure enough, Preston's usual line. How many girls have believed that and given in to him? "You want me, don't you? Say it, Summer. Say it."

"I want…" Summer's speech is thin and wavers, her pitch higher than usual. "I'm not sure what I want—or need. And…I never did this before. I don't think—"

"Let me do the thinking." Preston's voice is rough around the edges. Weird. Usually he sounds like an announcer on a YouTube video. "It's been tough for you, waking up in a strange town, getting crap at school, Kota putting the moves on you even though you hate his guts. Everyone needs a safe place for a retreat. Let *me* be your safe place."

"I never said I hate Kota." Summer hesitates. "I just feel like he's…dangerous or something. To me."

So she doesn't hate me. As far as I know, she also doesn't lie, so Marlie's version of what they talked about on the bus is probably B.S. But she thinks I'm dangerous? What the hell?

"You do make me feel safe." Less tremolo in her voice. More like decision-made.

For several minutes—maybe seconds—the sounds of kissing reach my ears. I'm beyond confused. Who am I to tell Summer what guy to sleep with? I should ditch Marlie and forget about Summer. Spring is coming, baseball season. If I concentrate on perfecting my first base catch, I can forget about *all* girls. But a worm of anxiety gnaws at my gut. There's something wrong. Very wrong. I don't know what it is, but Summer's in the middle of it. And Preston isn't helping.

I creep closer, fighting off the thought of being a peeping perv who only wants to stand in the shadows. And then I see them. Red plaid blanket—Preston keeps it in his back seat, no matter what the season. Summer is almost hidden under Preston. He slips one hand loose and eases her dress away from her shoulder, kissing her neck, and lower.

In one quick move he flips her over, so she's now on

top of him. That's when it happens. Sudden moonlight bathes the scene in silver, like her dress, which is on top of Preston. But it's almost like, I don't know, her soul escapes the clothing and floats above it all.

Preston doesn't seem to notice. His eyes are closed and his hands are roaming. Until he yanks her skirt up around her waist.

"No. Preston, no." Summer returns to earth, rolls off him, adjusts her clothing, jumps to her feet.

Suddenly it all looks normal. Just a guy and girl making out, and the girl changes her mind. Except that even at this distance I see her eyes, shining in the dark like a wild animal's.

I rub my face with both hands. Shouldn't have had the booze, the moonlight was almost blinding, my brain froze at what I was seeing and screwed with my perceptions.

Preston stands and cinches his belt. "You need me."

Summer takes a step back. "What does that mean?"

"I'm the one for you." Then, softer, "I just want to take care of you. No pressure. I'm here when you're ready. Maybe you'll dream about me tonight."

Summer picks up her shawl, brushes off some bits of leaf, and pulls it snug around her body. She flips her hair to the side and stares. At me.

I shake my head, no. And make my way up the hill to Marlie.

"What took you so long? Should we call the cops?" Marlie takes a step toward the edge of the hill.

"They have guns. We gotta get out of here. Fast." I grab her hand and yank her back toward the car. "And you can't tell anyone about this or the druggies might find out and track us down. Then we'd have to be in witness protection and never see anyone we know ever again." I lay it on thick, hoping she'll bite and keep her mouth shut. If Preston finds out I watched him with Summer, there will be hell to pay. And even though I considered him my best friend as of a few weeks ago, he isn't now.

Marlie talks the whole way home, blabbering about drugs, weapons, and 'our secret'.

I let her ramble. It gives me time to think. What did happen back on that plaid blanket? Summer has those strange eyes, okay, got it. But did she…I struggle to come up with a word…levitate, like something from a magic freak show? No. No way. I was right about the whiskey, the lighting, my wild thoughts. Preston would have noticed something that bizarre and opened his eyes.

I push away the image from the Hot Spot and vow to forget about it. Summer didn't sleep with Preston. I didn't touch Marlie. It's as good a way as any to end this stupid night.

THIRTEEN

Summer

"So, what happened?" Finn bounces on the soles of his bare feet. "Come on, you can share with me. I know you—remember? Tell Mom *whatever*, but I want the real deal. Or I'll hypnotize you again and get the information." He waves both hands in the air and wiggles his fingers, like some voodoo prince.

"It was a dance. We danced." I don't look at him. Not gonna share my almost-loss of virginity under the harvest moon last night. I picked the leaves off the back of my dress when I got home, before anyone—especially Jill or Daniel—could see and ask embarrassing questions. Part of me wishes I had gone all the way. I long to belong. The unsettling thought that Preston might be my way to reconciliation, and that I refused my only chance, has my stomach roiling. But why would sex equal redemption? It can't. Right?

"That's it?" A grin blooms on Finn's round face. "Did he kiss you?" He closes his eyes and makes kissy noises, lips against his own arm. He comes up for air. "Summer has a boyfriend, Summer has a boyfriend."

"Do not." I chase him through the house, his sing-song chant never-ending.

"How was it?" Jill, who I blew off last night with yawns, is even more eager for details than Finn. She holds out a steaming cup of coffee and pushes a plate of cinnamon rolls across the breakfast bar to me. I inhale the spicy scent. "Umm—smells great."

"How'd it go?" Daniel weighs in and waits with the rest of the family.

I chew a bite of a roll, swallow, and take a sip of coffee. "Really nice. The gym looked pretty, and the music was good."

"That's it?" Jill's eyebrows go up. "I want details, girlfriend."

Suddenly, the whole fiasco crashes in on me. "I was the only one in a long dress. They figured out it was from a thrift store. We left early." My words—particularly the last ones—hang in the air.

"Left and went where?" Daniel sets his cup on the counter with a clink.

"Just drove around. Downtown. Mt. Washington to see the city lights. Got lattes at the all-night Starbucks and talked." I keep my voice even. We did most of that. I'm old enough to do whatever, but they don't understand that part.

"Your dress was wrong?" Jill, girly-girl, saves the day.

"Turns out it was a prom dress that belonged to one of Marlie's friends. But Preston thought I looked great. He's very…nice." I give Jill the smile I know she wants.

"Then who cares about anything else? There were mean girls when I was in school, and there always will be. The important thing is to ignore their jealousy and just have fun, honey." Jill gives me a hug.

I want to lean in to that hug and spill everything about my life and death. She smells like baby powder, her concern feels very much like love, and a soft kiss on my cheek almost pushes me over the edge. A voice in my head tells me it's okay. But Finn gives me a look, as if he can read my thoughts. The moment passes.

"Who's trick-or-treating tonight?" Jill pulls away first with a wink to me.

"*Me.*" Finn, curiosity about my evening disappearing in the anticipation of Halloween night, claps his hands. "I want Summer to go, too."

"I'm too old to go door to door for candy." But his excitement is contagious. "I can take him, though."

"And dress up. You have to dress up. Right, Mom? Mom always wears a costume to take me out. Come on, it's fun. We have extra stuff in the attic." Finn runs up the stairs.

"I guess it's not cool to go out with the little kids, but if you don't mind, it would be great." Jill cleans up the dishes. "Daniel has to help his mother with a few things, and someone has to stay here to hand out candy."

"No problem. It'll be great." I think about All Hallow's Eve on the church calendar. And wonder why I know anything about the history of Halloween. Must have been a long-forgotten class. Amazing, the crap they teach in school that we never need again.

Finn spends hours putting together a costume, having decided the one he bought at Walmart is lame. "Ahoy, maties." Pirate Finn brandishes his arm like a sword. "Nah, I'm not a pirate guy." He goes back to the attic and follows up with, "Giddyup," but the cowboy hat perched on his curls is too small. Finally a spooky, "Ooooooo," precedes his appearance with an old, white sheet over his head. "I'm a ghost. Get it?" He promptly runs into the desk.

"Even ghosts need to see where they're going. If this is your final decision, I'll help you cut eye holes if your mom lets you use this." With Jill's permission, I cut two holes for eyes and agree to pin the sheet in place at the shoulders so it doesn't come off when he's gathering candy.

"What about you?" Finn grins and raises both eyebrows. "We can both be ghosts."

"Or not." I opt for the red, hooded cape from the Halloween bag—the one Finn wore when he hypnotized me—that I can wear over jeans and a sweatshirt. "Little Red Riding Hood, ready to rock and roll."

Finn watches the hands of the clock creep toward six. The fire whistle blares to announce the start of trick-or-treating.

We hit a few houses along the road. Finn stops at a dark yard. "This cuts through to the Royalty Ridge plan. They give out *full-size* candy bars."

"Does Jill allow you to go there?" With skipping school not too far past, don't want to get either of us in trouble. Although a big Hershey bar sounds amazing. Chocolate, the lonely girl's substitute for love.

"Not alone, but I'm with you. C'mon." He races into the dark.

No choice but to follow the little troublemaker. The grass is wet, and soon the hems of my jeans are damp and cold. The wind picks up. I pull the red hood over my hair, no longer caring how dorky it looks. No one knows who I am anyway, and those who do hate me. Except for Preston.

"Finn?" He seems to have disappeared into the night. I zig zag through some trees and make it to a street lined with McMansions. Each large house blazes with lights and is decorated in a theme. There's a tropical paradise with fake palm trees and ocean sounds. Next is a pirate motif with a gangplank and plastic cannons. And the requisite haunted house with cobwebs and spooky music. Kids scurry door to door with orange plastic pumpkins, pillowcases, and shopping bags bulging. I see princesses, a life-sized bacon strip, and a hippie. But no Finn.

In an instant my left hand disappears, without even wavering. I know what's coming by the rush of adrenaline through my system and the burn in my eyes. I duck behind an ornamental pine with spreading branches. The red cloak slides off my shoulders and I drop my candy bag as I feel my form take on the nebulous shape I've experienced so many times since my death: white, hazy, roughly human, if diaphanous vapor can be said to look like part of humanity. My misty hair floats back from the hint of a face that is me—and not—all at the same time.

"*Finn.*" His name issues from my mouth in a trail of letters, punctuated by a moan that causes a big kid dressed up like a rock star to drop his candy bag and run.

"*Summer.*"

I catch the sound vibrations, more than hear my name, my senses now on preternatural power. Rather than cause too much attention to my form, I silently glide toward Finn's call. A couple kids do double-takes, but must think they've seen a shooting star. They continue on their candy safari. Surveying the scene, I take in slate rooftops, foliage, asphalt ribbon of street, glare of lights on every porch and entryway. But no Finn.

I move lower, no longer caring who sees me. There was fear in Finn's voice. I *must* find him. My essence begins to vibrate. I finally spot him at the side of a big house decked out like the wild west, partially obscured from the street by professional landscaping. Finn, no longer in costume, is surrounded by three larger boys. In my peripheral vision I spot another bully on his way across the lawn. They're big enough—maybe eighth grade football players—that if I solidify they can take me. So be it.

"What the f—" Punk Rocker stumbles back as I swoop toward him. Sadly, he regains his balance.

Harry Potter screams and swats at me with a wand, which passes right through me.

The wand disturbs my essence, bringing about a rapid change. I thump to the ground, land hip-first, tumble down a small grade, and jump to my feet. Thankfully, I'm fully clothed as usual. "Back *off.*"

The action at the top of the hill pauses briefly. Superman doesn't release Finn's arms, which are being held behind his back. Harry Potter grabs the candy bag before I can get to them.

"Let go of him." I run up the hill, grab Superman, and try to wrench him away from Finn.

A fourth costumed figure races across the grass toward me, some knife-like thing held aloft. My concern for Finn morphs to an all-out adrenaline rush. *Weapon. Run.* Everything in me longs to flee, but I can't leave this little boy.

"Stay back." I'm panting and sweating in the effort to get Finn out of Superman's grip. How can I possibly take on the others who are circling me—and a guy with a knife? They apparently sense that they can overcome a little boy and a skinny girl.

Finn is in my tunnel vision. A sudden whiff of something woodsy and familiar expands my visual field. I focus on the new arrival. who dives into the brawl. He is dressed as an Indian, complete with buckskin, a headdress, and feathers. In his hand is a tomahawk. My eyes focus on his face. "Kota?"

The others use my obvious confusion to their advantage. Superman releases Finn, jams an elbow to his stomach, and takes off. Harry Potter holds on to Finn's candy and runs. Punk Rocker follows him.

"Finn, are you okay?" I sink to the grass beside him. His face is dirty, his shirt torn where the pinned sheet has been ripped off, and he holds his stomach.

"I'm—" Finn rolls over and pukes in the grass.

I wipe his mouth and help him to his feet, keeping my arm around his shoulders. My heart pounds and a rod of heat rises inside me. I turn to Kota. "Dressing up like your bloodthirsty ancestors so you have an excuse to rob little kids of candy? And carrying a blade? You're *pathetic.*" Spit flies from my mouth.

"I can explain." Kota steps closer in the dim moonlight, tomahawk still in his hand.

My brain suddenly registers that the tomahawk is only a prop. Yet my fear remains. I scan Kota's body. "You aren't worth my time. We're leaving. Stay away from my brother or you'll be very, very sorry. Don't make the mistake of thinking that when you look at me, what you see is what you get." I back away, Finn warm and firm against me.

"Summer, wait." Kota reaches out.

Let him chase down other kids. I came for Finn and can't worry about the rest.

"Am I in trouble?" Finn shivers. "Dad will never let me go out again."

"Don't worry about it. We aren't going to tell your parents. Jill will still be handing out candy. We'll go in through the back door and take care of everything before she even knows we're there. You can have my candy." I retrieve his sheet, my red cloak, and my candy, and guide him back toward the house.

It isn't until I make sure he's safe and warm, a peanut butter cup in his hand, that it hits me. I start to shake. Kota made good on the threatening vibes he put out to me, even if all he was trying to do was steal candy. And I called Finn my brother. The two thoughts don't go together. Yet somehow they do.

FOURTEEN

Kota

"Thank you, Kota. We won the Association prize this year. Having a *real* redskin made our display so authentic. It's a good thing the judges came *before* you left your post. I'm glad your mother recommended you for the job." Mrs. Montrose hands me an orange envelope. "Happy Halloween. There's a nice tip inside, too."

"Thanks." I stuff my pay—wow, fifty-*two* bucks—into my pocket, hand Mrs. Montrose the costume she rented, and get the hell out of Royalty Ridge. Mom talked me into taking the stinking gig, citing my need for money...

"Not happening. Not now, not ever, no way." I turn away from my mother, unable to hold in a snort of disgust.

"I do believe you have a cash flow problem. And no job." Mom pushes her iPad under my nose. "Just read the ad."

My inclination is to hocker up some snot onto the shiny screen, but it's not worth it. I scroll through the want-ad and read out loud in a monotone:

"Seeking a young man, aged fifteen to nineteen, to dress up as an

Indian and enhance our Halloween display. Help us to win the Royalty Ridge Association prize for Most Authentic Decorations!! Enjoy the holiday at our humble home (wink, wink), costume provided, all the candy you can eat, Italy Master cappuccino provided to ward off the chill. Fifty dollars plus tip, six o'clock to eight o'clock. Respond via email…yada yada."

"That's twenty-five dollars an hour. And a tip from people who live up there could add twenty to the total, easily, bringing your pay to seventy dollars for two hours of work. Not even work, really." Mom is in accountant mode. "Think how much fun it will be to see all the little kids in costume. Maybe even some cute teenage girls will come by."

"No."

"I don't get it." Out comes the 'I'm going to make you feel guilty' grimace. "Your dad and I provide everything for you. We believe school is more important than work. Junior year is demanding, that I understand. But we're not rich, and you picking up some spending money would help us a lot. And it's your heritage. Aren't you proud to have Native American blood?"

"No. I already get crap about how I look. Dressing up in some cheesy costume as a Native American—excuse me, 'Indian',—would only make things worse. And what if Preston drives past and sees me? He lives up there."

"Embrace who you are." Mom grabs my arm and hugs it. "I'll reply for you."

I give up. Mom, one. Kota, zip.

Replaying the entire process of getting the miserable job keeps me from thinking too much on the way home. I trudge down the darkening street as people shut off lights. Trick-or-treat is over, time once again to isolate into their phony castles. Summer's face pushes into my mind, past the wall of thoughts I try to erect. How can she think I would try to hurt that kid—or any kid?

"Yo, bro." The purr of a fine-tuned engine underlies Preston's familiar voice. His tone is friendly, normal, not his recent condescending B.S.

I stop and wait for him to pull beside me, then lean on the open window frame. "Hey."

"What're you doing up here?" Preston adjusts a perfectly pressed black cape.

"Nothing. What's with the cape? Vampire? Zorro?"

"Vampire, of course. Hitting a party over at Shanai's house. I'm late, but she won't mind. By now it'll be just the two of us and her beagle. Her parents are out of town." Preston grins. "I vant to suck her—and not just her blooood."

I wonder about Summer. But he's being like the old Preston, and I don't want to mess things up. None of my business. And if he's already moving on, maybe I have a chance. Probably not, after tonight.

"Heard the Montrose house was all decked out." Preston's grin morphs to ugly. "Also noticed in my travels a certain bare-chested heathen stationed at the front door."

"Some of us have to work." I shrug and step back from the car. "I was perfect for the job."

"Yeah, truly. Might want to wipe off that war paint before someone else sees how stupid you look. Later." He punches the accelerator and lays rubber over his laughter.

I make it home by repeating old Marine Corps chants my grandfather taught me on a hike through Shenandoah Park. Anything to occupy my brain. Bypassing the family room, where Darth Vader does some heavy breathing— Dad, gotta love his addiction to *Star Wars*—I grab shorts and a T-shirt and lock myself in the bathroom. A quick piss and into the warm shower. I lather up, rinse, and let the water cascade over my back and shoulders.

The evening plays in my mind, a movie I don't want to watch but can't look away from…

"Mommy, is he real?" A princess in yards of pink pokes my abdomen.

"Hey, where's your teepee?" A hippie grabs a handful of chocolate bars from the bowl.

"Yo, gonna scalp me, Chief What-a-Pack-of-Crap?" Superman high fives Harry Potter and a punk rocker as he elbows a ghost away from the candy.

"Not cool." The ghost's little-boy voice is muffled under his sheet. He squirms between the three older boys. "Can I please take two? My, um, sister didn't catch up with me yet."

"Boo hoo. Gonna call nine-waa-waa for the waa-mbulance?" Harry Potter gets a back slap from Superman.

"You got your treats, now beat it." I brandish the fake tomahawk—which looks very real, shiny blade and all—and notice the ghost taking off, sheet flapping. Didn't mean to scare the little dude.

A few other kids come for candy, and I lose track of the obnoxious triplets.

"Leave me alone." From somewhere out of sight by the side of the house, I hear a kid's quavering voice, attempting to sound brave but failing.

"You gonna make me?" Not Halloween fun. This is bullying.

I leave my post at the front door and race toward the raised voices and squeals, still gripping the plastic tomahawk. "Hey. What's going on?"

"Summer, watch out." The ghost, sans costume, which is in a heap on the ground, struggles against Superman and shrinks from me. It's Finn, the kid from Summer's house. With Summer right behind him.

She throws me a look of pure hatred. "Dressing up like your bloodthirsty ancestors so you have an excuse to scare little kids and take their candy? You're pathetic." Spit flies from her mouth, the droplets silver. Her hair is steaming, as if mist is coming from her head. In the ambient light, her eyes are tiger-bright, their color impossible to gauge.

Before I can explain, she drags Finn away through the yard. And I'm left feeling guilty for something I didn't even do. Damn that tomahawk. Like I would bring a real weapon to freaking Halloween.

"Kota, you okay in there?" Mom knocks on the door.

"Fine. Be out soon."

"I want to hear about your job." After a pause, during which I say nothing, her footsteps fade.

I stay under the scalding water, my fingers wrinkling and condensation heavy on the tile. As much as I hate the crap I get about being different, there is a spark of pride inside that my ancestors were Native American. That spark is dimming, because for some reason it seems that Summer holds my ethnicity against me. Is she prejudiced? I discount that thought. It seems to be *me,* not my genetics. Not sure which is worse. I've never talked to my dad about any of it, because his own Indian blood is hidden beneath an ordinary exterior.

"*Hey, hey watenay. Hey, hey, watenay. Kay-oh-kay-nah. Kay-oh-kay-nah.*" A woman's voice, intoning strange words to a simple, rhythmic melody, echoes in the bathroom.

"Mom?" I poke my head around the shower curtain. Nothing. No answer from the hall.

"*Kay-oh-kay-nah. Kay-oh-kay-nah.*"

Every molecule in my body begins to vibrate, as if I'm shriveling. I close my eyes and sway to the hypnotic music that moves in a loop through my head, music I've never heard before. Sensations bombard me. I can only manage to identify them with simple words: soft, warm, safe.

"*Kay-oh-kay-nah. Kay-oh…*"

The sounds dwindle to nothing. In their absence, a yawning hole of pain opens up inside me. Falling, falling through time and space, as if borne on a torturous cloud. My senses are smacked and pummeled: breathless, sour, empty.

I open my eyes expecting to see the showerhead spewing water. Instead, I am surrounded by emptiness, a body in a vacuum. "No' yeg." After a moment, louder, I cry out again, "No' yeg? Mother?"

"Kota? Open this door right now."

I blink and see that I'm sitting on the floor of the shower, surrounded by steam. With difficulty I haul myself to my feet, swaying as if I've just competed in a major weightlifting competition. A raging thirst makes me open my mouth and swallow hot shower water.

A rattling of the doorknob precedes the opening of the bathroom door. "Kota, honey, are you okay?" The shower curtain parts slightly and Mom peeks in, her eyes fixed on my face. "It sounded like you fell."

"I'm fine, just need some privacy here."

"If you're sure everything is okay." Mom hesitates, hands me a towel, and leaves.

I turn off the water, dry, dress, and escape to my room. My ruddy cheeks are flaming from prolonged exposure to the heat. My loose black hair hangs wet to my shoulders. My slightly slanted eyes are smoldering. I've never looked more like a Seneca than at this moment. And never been more confused. So I boot up the computer and type in Native American dreams.

"American Indians respect the sacred guidance given in dreams. They contain information about one's destiny and what direction to take." I mumble as I scan articles on visions. If that's even what I had. The odd words that started it all are slipping from my mind. I write them phonetically in the search box and sit back. "Native American lullaby...sleep little one, go to sleep."

"Kota?" Dad knocks and enters without waiting for an invitation.

I close the computer. "Hey."

"Mom's worried about you." He looks at me, waits a beat, and perches on the edge of my bed. "Anything you want to talk about?"

"No, not really." I do and I don't. So I contradict myself. "This whole Native American thing. I don't want to diss your ancestors—my ancestors—but everyone seems to think I'm a caricature or something. It sucks.

Why couldn't I look like you, a regular guy with black hair, instead of like freaking Hiawatha?"

"Genetics." Dad shrugs. "You're a unique, handsome guy, Kota. When high school is over you'll laugh about the losers who gave you grief."

I hear his platitudes but something occurs to me. "About the gene thing. Why did karma single me out? There's no one in our family who looks as Indian as me. Sure, Aunt Linda has the whole high cheekbones thing, but it makes her look like a model, not a freak." I deliver the 'not a freak' portion of my rant in a loud voice with my arms waving in Dad's face.

"'Freak?'" Dad stands. I'm taller, but he's my father, and I back down. "Let's count the ways you're a freak: tall, muscular, healthy, smart, athletic—and loved. Need I continue? Get off the poor-Kota train. Look at that girl the Sullivans took in, the one who can't remember anything. Try to imagine how that must feel."

"Summer is *not* a freak." Heat rises in my chest.

Dad stares at me. And smiles. "Oh, so it's like that, is it?"

"It's not 'like' anything. She can't stand me."

"Is that why you suddenly think *you're* a freak?" Dad puts his hand on my shoulder. "That's rhetorical. I'm not getting into your love life. As for your heritage, that's something you just have to figure out, because you are who you are. That won't change. Your mom and I love you—in case you haven't noticed." He doesn't wait for a response from me.

I head for the basement and lift weights for an hour, until in need of another shower. Why did I hear some goofy lullaby? And what's the deal with the whole disappearing bathroom? Did I fall and hit my head before all that started? If not, what happened?

The exercise gets rid of the immediate crappy shit in my gut. But at the end of it all, I'm a sweaty Native American who is losing his mind—and also falling for a girl who hates him.

FIFTEEN

Summer

"You called me your brother." Finn is serious, focused on my face with all the intensity he usually reserves for Xbox.

"That was almost a month ago." Since Halloween, Finn and I have talked about what happened several times. Including the fact that he thinks Kota raised his fake tomahawk as a threat and came to help the bullies. But he's never mentioned my slip of tongue before.

"Did you mean it?" Finn's gaze is unwavering. "Your eyes are turning gray."

I suspect he's right. Gray, the transition color. The one that says he isn't my brother, yet he is. "We aren't related, you know that."

"What if we are? What if I'm adopted and you're my real sister but you forgot about me and fate brought us back together?" His words and his breath run out at the same time.

"Finn. You're right that I don't remember much. But if you really were my brother, I would know." I put my right hand over my heart. "In here. That's something I could never, *ever* forget." I grab his smaller hand in mine. "But just because we aren't blood relatives doesn't mean all that much. You're my brother in every other way. Including in my heart."

He ponders this long enough to pour a glass of orange juice, drink it, and set the glass in the sink. "Okay. And you're the sister of *my* heart."

The sting in my eyes is one of joy. I love this kid, beyond all rational thought.

"Boots, hats, gloves." Jill opens the door, letting in a blast of cold air. "I would take you guys to school, but I'm late for work.

"So you get a warmed up car, and we get a school bus?" Finn's smile is smarmy. "I love you, Mommy."

"Ha, ha, good try. I love you too, but no ride today, kiddo." Jill brushes her lips across his cheek—raising a protest—and blows me a kiss. "Have a great day, you two."

I make sure Finn is bundled and drop him next door at his friend Josh's to wait until it's time for his bus. The hike to my stop is a short one through frozen slush. Even though the weather isn't a huge concern to me, the air is bitter enough to tempt my essence to dissolve and float to a warmer place. It might have been smart to put on snow boots after all. The knock-off Uggs I'm wearing will be a soggy mess by the time I get to school.

It's a relief to board the yellow bus, even though it's chilly and is filled with conflicting scents of over-perfumed girls and testosterone jocks. I ignore them all and plop in an empty seat in the back. Marlie laughs as I pass her, likely mocking me. Who cares about any of these morons?

"Can I sit with you?" Marlie has left her seat and is standing in the aisle beside mine.

"Whatever."

She sits, balancing her Louis Vuitton bag on her lap. Her fingers play with a strip of leather embellishment on the purse, making the zipper pull *click, click, click*. "I need your advice."

I look over my shoulder reflexively and turn back. "*My* advice?"

"You and Preston are a couple. I thought Kota and I were back together. But he's been ignoring me since Homecoming, and I don't know why. I need you to ask Preston what's going on. They're besties." Marlie twines two fingers together. "Since, like, forever."

I take my time answering her. Am I dating Preston? Sort of, kind of. Although I'm not feeling it yet, I'm afraid to let go. He has to be the one who will somehow give me release from this earth. It just takes time to fall in love. I hope. Of course I can't share these things with anyone, especially Marlie, Gossip Girl of Fawn Valley High School.

"The thing with Preston, it's not serious." I shrug. "So it's not like he'll actually listen to me, or anything. Just talk to Kota yourself."

Sudden tears well in Marlie's eyes. Soon her mascara runs in dark rivulets down her cheeks, a sad clown effect. "I've been a bitch to you. Why should you help me? It's just that being mean to you made me more popular, so I went with it. But now, I don't know, nothing's going right."

I don't want to share secrets with anyone, especially this girl. But the tug of belonging is strong. And what if my reconciliation isn't about falling in love? What if it's about helping someone, being a true friend, not just some guy's girlfriend? Is Marlie a challenge to meet and overcome? Should I take the chance and turn her away? I can almost hear the clock ticking in my brain, every second taking me closer to my birth date—and the end.

"This isn't the best place to talk." Furtive glances are aimed our way from others in the front of the bus. "Want to get together after school?" I hope she says no. It's easier to keep her in the People I Hate box than to adjust my thinking.

"That would be great." Marlie sniffs, dabs her face with

a tissue, and gives me a tremulous smile. "You can ride the bus home with me. We have a great cappuccino machine."

"Okay." I'm not certain that helping Marlie will help me, but Preston is no sure thing, either. I can't let any opportunity pass me by.

We pull up to the school, saving me from further conversation. Marlie joins her friends, making me wonder why she doesn't bare her heart to them instead of me. I need Azul's guidance, but he's been silent for too long. And, truth be told, not all that helpful with his stupid riddles—"*Oof.*" I run into a wall of warm.

"Watch it…oh. It's you." Kota takes a step back.

"Sorry." I hear the way that one word is clipped off. We've avoided each other for a month, no eye contact, no words exchanged, no apologies or arguments.

"This is crazy." He runs one hand through his longish, dark hair. "I'm not sure what you think happened on Halloween, but all I wanted to do was get those bullies away from the ghost dude—Finn. You can believe me or not. I don't give a shit."

I raise my eyes to his, sensing as I do the shift in color. Experience tells me they are likely a Monet watercolor that is settling to pale, clinical white as I ponder his words. I fight against the likelihood that it's the truth. My thoughts war between wanting to prove he's the jerk I sense he is, and wanting him to be decent. He had a *toy* tomahawk, after all. And why would he want to hurt Finn? As hard as it is to admit, he seems like an okay guy, not given to hurting kids at school—except for that one run-in with Preston.

"Fine. If that's the way it is." His don't-mess-with-me growl is back.

"No, wait." I make a choice. "Maybe I overreacted. If I did, well, I'm sorry."

"That's no apology. 'Maybe.' 'If.' Not very convincing."

"Are you always this annoying?"

"Pretty much. But I'm not the creep you seem to think

I am." He holds my gaze. "I like the simple brown eyes. Much warmer than white. You *are* strange, you know." His half-smile takes the sting from his words.

"So what's up with you and Marlie?"

"First you hate me, and now you're jealous?"

"*No.*" I grit my teeth. "It's just that she likes you...and I wondered if you like her."

"What is this, seventh grade?" Kota shakes his head. "How about you and Preston?"

"'What is this, seventh grade?'" I bite my lip. This is beginning to be fun.

"There's my girl." Preston comes up behind me and crosses his arms around my chest. His nose nuzzles my neck before he pulls away. "'Sup, Kota?"

"Guess we answered that seventh-grade question." Kota's face, almost playful two seconds ago, is carefully neutral. He nods at Preston. "Later."

"What's he talking about?" Preston frowns at Kota's back.

"Nothing." I don't argue that I'm 'his girl', even though it's questionable. Since Homecoming—one month ago—we've been to one movie, Blue Diamond—way too violent—had one chocolate milkshake at Dairy Queen—sadly with whipped cream and a cherry—and had one make-out session in his car—lips, tongues, and a sore back. Hardly what I call a relationship. But he's been my only social life, and as far as I know, I've been his.

The bell is a welcome interruption. He goes left, I head right for history class. Kota is already there, seated in the back, as usual. The only seat left is in front of him. Great, just great. I slide in and smooth down my hair.

"Good morning, ladies and gentlemen." Mrs. Mayhew, who wants us to be steeped in American history from the time we enter her class, writes on the board: Hannastown. "I have some exciting news." She ignores the collective groan. "Originally, I planned a field trip for spring, as the site is closed in the winter months. But I've been able to arrange a special tour for the first and fourth period classes when we return after Thanksgiving break."

A boy in the front row, wearing a blaze orange shirt, raises his hand. "I go hunting the whole week after Thanksgiving. I already got permission. If I miss the H-town gig, will it mess with my grade?"

"We are scheduled for the following week, Tuesday, December ninth. Go forth and bring home the venison, Master Rocereto." She writes the date on the board. "Hannastown is having a holiday open house. We will attend in the afternoon, before the general public. There will be a tour of the site, weather permitting, a docent will give us the history, and you will have time for questions and answers. Any volunteers to dress in period clothing?"

Another groan, louder this time, moves through the room.

"Very well. But please, no ripped jeans, no droopy pants, no inappropriate tops. And warm coats. The only heat will be from a fireplace, and they may not have it burning when we arrive. Now, get out your homework."

I tune out, not interested. I'm here because some cosmic force dropped me off. The rest of the class has to worry about college. All I have to worry about is my eternal destiny. Which doesn't include a dinky, local historical site. Preston is in fourth period history, so I guess we can hang out. And maybe Marlie, also in fourth, and Kota. I'll tell her about it after school. A lame double date.

The day drags. How many times have I been to high school? Why am I here now? The answer to my problem must be somewhere—someone—nearby. Preston? Marlie? They seem to be the only candidates for my soul-saving endeavor.

"Ready?" Marlie meets me at the double doors leading to the busses. We climb aboard, sit together without conversation, and get off in front of her house. "Come on in. It's freezing out here." She pulls a key out of her purse, opens a huge door, and ushers me inside a house that could hold two of Jill's and Daniel's house. "Thanks for coming over. My other friends are horrible gossips. I can't tell them *anything* important. Consuela will make us something to eat and bring it to my room. I don't want her listening to us."

Marlie pushes an intercom button on the wall, orders two cappuccinos with extra foam, chocolate cake pops— with raspberry drizzle—and a basket of homemade potato chips. If nothing else, I'll have a great snack. Worth the walk in the cold. Or maybe Consuela drives a limo to take Marlie's friends home.

We ascend the curving staircase, pass several closed doors in a hallway, and cross the thick carpet into Marlie's room. Everything matches, from the king-size bed, to the massive dressers, to the modern swirls of pink and purple on the bedspread and draperies. Silence drags on as I wait for Marlie to speak first. She's the one who invited me here.

"*Chica*." A polite tap on the door precedes a Hispanic woman who must be Consuela, a tray balanced on one hand. She nods to me, sets out cups, plates, and food on a small bistro set in the adjoining sitting room, and leaves us alone.

The coffee is hot, the cakes fresh, and the chips still warm. I munch and wait for whatever teen angst Marlie wants to spill. She is uncharacteristically quiet. The only sound is the crunch of chips.

"Did Mayhew tell you we all have to go on a field trip to Hannastown?" At her nod, I continue. "I thought it might give you a chance to hang with Kota." Maybe this will end the sharing time, my kindness will redeem me, and I can leave this world with the sweet taste of chocolate cake on my lips. Not a kiss, but whatever works.

"Good idea." Marlie pushes back her chair and folds her hands on her stomach. "Here's the thing. I'm going to have Kota's baby."

LAUREL HOUCK

SIXTEEN

Summer

Marlie's words hang in the air.

Kota's *baby*? Seriously? No *way*. I can't decide if it's the sugar rush from cake pops and cappuccino or something worse—it can't be jealousy—but my stomach heaves and a pang shoots through me. I blink away a mental image of Kota and Marlie plastered together. And keep my eyes averted from Marlie to avoid unanswerable questions about the likely kaleidoscope of colors in my irises. "You're pregnant?"

"Not yet." Marlie pats her stomach. "But I've decided it's the only way to make Kota love me. And never leave."

My gut settles. "Are you mental? That's the lamest thing I've ever heard. Only stupid, total losers do that crap." I pause in my rant to glance at Marlie. Her face is frozen in a grimace, her cheeks pink as if they've been slapped. "Oh. I didn't mean that *you're* stupid. Just that, well, usually roping in a guy by getting pregnant doesn't end up in a lasting relationship. You're way too smart and beautiful to resort to a trick like that."

"You think I'm smart and beautiful?"

"Of course. And popular, and rich, and the perfect girl for the right guy who comes along. You can't force love. And hardly anyone gets married just because there's a baby." Not sure how I ended up counseling someone who has been so mean to me. Maybe I should just leave. Or maybe, if I'm a good enough friend, I'll be whisked off to eternal rest on my way home.

"But Kota is so…straight up." Marlie, known more for her facility with cruel words than insight, struggles. "He would want to be part of his child's life, and if I'm the mother, that means we'd be together all the time, even if we don't get married. I know he likes me. And he's a great kisser."

"So you're basing the rest of your life on a high school kid who thinks you're okay, takes responsibilities seriously, and knows how to kiss? It seems to me that you're settling for a lousy second-class existence." I try to think about what I'm looking for, besides avoiding the whole roaming-specter thing. "Don't you want someone who can't live without you? Who chooses you over everyone else? And makes a baby with you *because* of that love?"

"But I'm losing him. Even when we're together, he has something else on his mind. I thought at first it was you." Marlie laughs. "Of course that's ridiculous. He's just not dating anymore." She goes very quiet. "Maybe he's gay. That has to be it. Otherwise, why wouldn't he want me?"

One look at her face and I don't respond, even though I'm fairly certain Kota is anything but gay. If it makes her feel better, why not? "I don't know what he is. None of my business. But I'm sure that you're the most wanted girl at school. Just imagine how many more hot guys there'll be in college."

"I know, right?" The old Marlie is back. "What was I thinking? Pregnancy makes you fat, after all."

"You're good?"

"Of course." Marlie lifts a hand to high five me. "I don't know why I even talked to you about it. It's not like you have a clue about love, or dating, or being popular. I mean, really. You don't even know who you are or where you came from." She glances at her watch. "So sorry, but I have cheer practice in an hour. Have to do my makeup. I have a reputation to uphold. Can you find your way out?"

I leave Marlie's room, retrace my steps, and exit through the front door. The wind is blowing harder than before, with flecks of sleet pinging against the copper roof that covers the front porch. Darkness is descending, thanks to the time of year and massive cloud cover. Not the best conditions for a walk, but Consuela isn't around to drive me, Jill and Daniel won't be home yet, and I've got no one to call. Except Preston. But what if he won't come, and I sound like an idiot? I don't want to see him. At least not right now. Best possible thing, Azul will notice I helped Marlie, and my wandering will be done. That thought should fill me with joy. Should. I'm settling in way too much, no idea how to stop it.

By flipping my hood up and keeping my head down, I avoid the sharp bite of freezing rain against my face. There's a shortcut to my house—Jill's house, have to stop thinking I'm here to stay—but it goes through a neighbor's property. Mike the Moron. He had a screaming fit one day with Daniel, afraid someone might step on his property when Finn was playing with his friends. What a jerk.

In this weather it's worth taking a chance through Mike's. No one is out. The curtains are all closed. I head for the gap in the trees inside Mike's property line. Still no sign of anyone. Good. Pulling my hood tight around my face, I move into the stand of pines and pass his house on the left, skirting the No Trespassing sign.

"You. No trespassing." Mike's raspy voice is accompanied by a loud click.

I stop and turn, facing Mike, who has a rifle in his hands. "I'm staying with the Sullivans. The house in the valley. Over there." I point, even knowing he's quite aware of who lives there. "Sorry. Leaving." I edge backward to the hill that descends to safety.

"I know who you are. That crazy girl who lost her mind." Mike caresses the stock of his rifle. "Man has a right to protect his property from a lunatic who attacks him. Self-defense, none would blame me or miss you. Should also shoot that obnoxious kid who's always trespassing in my woods."

I want to be afraid. Instead I'm pissed. "You might be able to scare Finn and yell louder than Daniel, but I don't give a crap what you do to me. Want to shoot me? Go ahead. It won't matter, because I'm already dead, you moron." With that I close my eyes, suck in a gulp of frigid air, and let my essence dissolve until I'm one with the driving sleet and sudden snow.

"Wha…" Mike drops the rifle, his mouth hangs open, and he trembles.

I give him the whole ghost treatment, throwing in a few throaty moans for good measure. Instead of being pummeled by the weather, I glide on the slick surface of the frozen pellets, swooping around Mike, letting tendrils of my misty hair drag across his face. He blinks. In that moment I use all my strength to stare at him and summon an other-worldly glow into my eyes.

A wet stain blossoms on the front of his jeans. He runs, screaming, into his house and slams the door.

I pick up the rifle, unload the shells, and drop the weapon and brass down an old well, glad to retain some human abilities even in spirit form. Time to get my body back. I concentrate on flesh. Nothing happens. I try again. And again. And again. The heart visibly beating in my chest is a pale pink pulsation going way too fast. In the past, I've blacked out and ended up halfway across the country, maybe across centuries for all I know. I've adjusted to my fickle eyes. But I've always had control of my essence when I'm conscious. Until now.

"What can I do?" The words come out like the phony moan I pulled on Mike. I can't go home in this form. Is this what happens before I'm shunted to another place by unseen forces? Am I entering eternity, saved by my kindness to Marlie? Or. What if my vision under hypnosis was wrong, and today is my seventeenth birthday? Am I going to be a specter forever?

"Your time is not yet ended."

"*Azul.* What's happening to me?" He is perched on the stone edge of the old well. His blue form is even less distinct than last time, his glow a shimmering torch as darkness descends. Then it hits me. I'm not asleep. The real world is very much around me. And Azul is in it.

"You are troubled." He nods.

"I can't materialize." A rhythmic sound echoes in the woods. I look for its source before realizing it's my heartbeat, obscene in its racing cadence. "I completed my task. With Marlie. And you're here to take me to rest."

Azul is silent.

"Am I being sent away? I don't want to leave here. This is where I'm going to find reconciliation for my soul. I know it. There's a boy, Preston, and we're in love. Not exactly love, but it will be, eventually, and that will save me."

Azul's eyes are downcast.

"Is it...my birthday?" An ache moves through my essence, a pain so exquisite that I know it's me, drifting away into hell.

"Dovie, you *must* remember. I am breaking every law of the hereafter to come to you on earth. You are so close, yet so far. When spring brings new birth to the earth, it will be the end for you. Think. Open the eyes of your heart. The hourglass is almost empty. The Deceiver is at the gate."

"No, wait. I don't need more trouble, no Deceiver, please. I *am* called Dovie. Dovie Critchlow, right? You see, I'm starting to remember. Don't make me go yet." I never beg. Or never did, until now. "You've already stretched time for me. Please, please, just a little longer. Another year. If I don't figure out what I did wrong and atone by next Thanksgiving, I'll go willingly. And I'll never tell anyone what you've done for me."

"My intervention is at an end. Your destiny is reaching its conclusion. With you—or without you." Azul fades, until all I have is his voice in my head. "Embrace the fear. Overpower it. Watch for signs and wonders in misty places. And search with all your heart for the one—and only one—thing that will bring you home."

A gust of wind blows through me, and I crash to the ground, flesh once more, except for my rebellious left hand. I retrace my steps, pulling on gloves that are in the pocket of my jacket. Their warmth gives my fingers and hand the structure they need until I'm whole. Yet even clothed in flesh, I'm only a shell, covering wisps of a soul in torment. Torment of my own making, for something so terrible that my mind refuses to remember it.

I make my way to the house. My home. My family. Finn is looking out the window. He waves and runs to open the door for me. My brother.

"Hey, Summer, what ya doing out in the woods?" Finn brushes shards of ice from my coat sleeves.

I wrap trembling arms around him, ignoring his squirming protest long enough that he stills. The overwhelming need to protect him infuses me with strength, and I hug tighter. Is he in danger? What's happening? Is Mike going to hurt him? Or is the only real danger from me, a ghost with a dreadful secret?

SEVENTEEN

Kota

"Why don't you carve this year, son?" Dad holds out the big knife he always uses on the turkey. "I'll be thankful to pass this job to the younger generation."

I stare at the gleaming edge of the knife. Dad sharpens it once a year, right before Thanksgiving. "That's okay. You always do it."

"Kota, it would be a nice, new tradition for us." Mom glances around the table at the assembled family, the usual suspects: Gram, Pap, Aunt Linda, and Mason.

"Oh, go on." Gram claps her wrinkled hands.

"I remember when your dad took over for me." Pap shoots a fond smile to Dad.

"You do the turkey," my little cousin Mason pipes up, his four year old face solemn. "At pre-school we had real Thanksgiving, with marshmallows and Kool-Aid and Jell-O. And we dressed up. I was a Pilgrim but I wanted to be an Indian so I could cut the Jell-O. You an Indian, so you s'pposed to cut the turkey." He stares at me. "You need feathers in you hair."

"Oh yeah? What else should I do and wear since I'm an

'Indian'?"

"Kota, he's four." Aunt Linda shrugs. "He doesn't understand politically correct yet."

"Oh, so if it has to do with Native Americans, it has to be PC? What about you?" I gesture around the table at my rellies from Dad's side of the family. "Thanks to Pap, we all have a Native American background. So some other Indian, please carve the damn turkey so we can eat."

Into the shocked silence I shove back my chair and go out on the deck. It's cold, but better than the stuffiness inside. The low murmur of Mom's soothing tones comes through the fogged glass. I said a bad word in front of Mason and ruined a holiday meal. I feel...how do I feel? As sharp as the blade of the turkey knife, what I feel slices through me. Then, nothing. Mild dissatisfaction maybe, with family shit. But that's almost like a practiced response. Suddenly it's like my insides are stuffed with clouds: empty, floating, chilly. The restlessness of recent months—years?—surrounds me like cotton balls. I stare at the snow-covered back yard, my mind a blank.

"How's my favorite teenager?" Pap is beside me. I didn't hear him slide open the door or walk across the deck.

"Fine." I see my breath and Pap's as we speak. "Sorry about in there."

"You missed a fine meal."

"It's over? How long have I been out here?"

"An hour, give or take." Pap puts a wool blanket over my shoulders. It's not until the warmth reaches me that I realize how cold I am. "Your mom wanted to come out for you, but your dad...well, he said to leave you alone. Gran fixed you a plate. And we didn't have pumpkin pie yet. It looks mighty good."

"Yeah, great. Be right in."

"Don't try to bullshit a bullshitter." This is a Pap I don't recognize. "What's really going on? Seems like you're mad at the world more often than not. It's not just being a teenager, is it?"

"Did kids mess with you? About the Native American thing?" It hits me that Dad never talks much about it, and neither does anyone else. A sensation as fleeting as melting snow trickles through my soul. There's something wrong. I've known it for a long time. But chose to ignore it. "What's the deal?" I turn to face him. "The real deal."

Pap glances through the glass door, a huge sigh ending in a hacking cough. "Think we could do this in a warmer place? Maybe after a piece of pie and a hot cup of coffee?"

"Sure." I follow him inside.

No one says anything about my performance. Mom sets a plate on the table, piled high with turkey, stuffing, mashed potatoes, green beans, and cranberries. A buttered roll, soaked with gravy, perches on the edge of the plate. I sit and eat while the table is cleared, the pie cut, and the coffee poured. Normal holiday chatter resumes. It's the usual: Mason yapping about the Pilgrims, Dad and Pap hearty, Mom and Aunt Linda already planning for Christmas.

"What do you want for Christmas, Kota? I want Xbox, and an iPad, and Play-Doh." Mason ditches the Pilgrims theme for the anticipation of Christmas loot. "And a puppy. A baby puppy with long ears. One that doesn't poop."

Mason sprays the tablecloth with whipped cream from a can, we eat the pie, and second cups of coffee are poured. Mom and Aunt Linda go into the kitchen to package leftovers, and Mason flops in front of the flat screen to watch a movie.

"Kota has questions about our family heritage." Pap throws this across the table to Dad along with a pointed look and a frown.

Dad spills coffee and doesn't seem to notice. He sets his cup in the pool of dark brown liquid in his saucer. "Pap had an ancestor who was Native American. You already heard about that. We don't know much more about the

125

family tree. Someday, we should go on Ancestry.com and see what we can find." His jovial voice is forced. He picks up his cup and drips coffee down the front of his sweater. And again, doesn't react.

"Ancestry-dot-freaking-com, seriously?" I shove my cup across the table. "It used to be that nothing bothered me about my background, not even the jokes. Then it got to be too much. And now?" I shrug. Even I can't keep up with the way my mood is shifting and changing minute to minute. Maybe I'm bipolar.

"Kota—" Pap starts.

Dad holds up one hand to silence Pap. "No. Not now, like this. We'll talk after everyone leaves. His mother needs to be here." He lays one hand over mine. "Hold your questions. I promise we *will* answer them."

"Tonight." I pull my hand away from his.

Dad nods and gets up from the table, his posture stooped like Pap's. Pap claps him on the back and goes to join Mason in the living room. Soon the soundtrack of an animated movie changes to football plays and the cheering of a crowd. I watch and listen to the familiar sights and sounds of every Thanksgiving. Football, clattering of dishes, opening and closing of the refrigerator door. The scent of roasted turkey lingers in the air, punctuated by cinnamon from the pies.

But this year after the cleanup is finished, Pap invites Mason to spend the night with him and Gram. Which breaks up the party early—not by chance, I'm sure.

"Love you." Gram gives me her usual hug—trying to put her short arms above my shoulders, which hasn't worked since I was ten.

"Kota." Pap holds on tight and whispers in my ear, "We all love you. That's the bottom line."

My insides begin to shake and the snow-chill from the deck re-invades my body. The bustle of coats, empty dishes, leftovers in Tupperware, and cold air yield a sudden quiet when everyone is gone.

Mom glances at the TV, where the Steeler defense is attempting to keep the Eagles from scoring again. "Maybe I'll turn on a Hallmark Channel movie instead." She frowns into the silence. "Neither of my guys is going to object to missing the end of the game?" She looks at Dad, then at me. "What's going on?"

"We have to talk." Dad's words are simple. He shuts off the TV.

Mom pales and wrings her hands. "Now?" Her voice is a whisper.

I plop in the big armchair, shoving the ottoman out of my way. Mom and Dad sit on the sofa, not touching. Dad crosses his leg; his foot jiggles up and down. Mom is perched on the very edge of the upholstery, fingering the fringe on a throw pillow.

"Kota, we love you—" Mom and Dad say it in unison.

Mom looks at me then back to Dad. "Go ahead. I'm the one who kept putting this off."

"There's something we should have told you long ago, son." Dad's preamble is unnecessary.

"I'm adopted." The absolute certainty of my statement is mirrored in the eyes of the two people who are not, strictly speaking, my parents.

"You already knew?" Silent tears course down Mom's cheeks, her makeup streaking.

"I do now."

"That's a relief." Dad's foot stops bouncing. "Want to watch the rest of the game? The Steelers were behind, but they always make a comeback in the fourth quarter." He picks up the remote.

"Screw the Steelers." The f-word wouldn't have shocked him more. "After sixteen years—and only because I sensed something was wrong—you finally confess that I'm not your real kid. And you think that's all? Once you tell me a few quick facts, like who the hell am I, who are my real parents, how did the whole thing go down, then maybe you can watch your precious game."

127

I'm panting like a dog on a hot summer day.

Summer. The thought of her breaks into my rant, unexpected, sudden. Will this new information make a difference to her? After all, she's in a foster home, and I'm also with two people who aren't related to me. But why should I care about that right now? My feelings for a girl shouldn't mean as much as whatever Dad is about to tell me. Yet they do.

"You are more important to your mother and me than anyone or anything in the world." Dad tosses the remote. It lands on the coffee table, the back pops off, and the batteries roll onto the floor. He ignores them. "You've lived here since you were a newborn, just a few hours old. We adopted you as soon as possible. So we've been a family for your entire life. And we love you."

"Right. A family who loves and lies. Great combo."

"There never seemed to be the perfect time to talk about this." Mom's voice holds an uncharacteristic whine "We never think about you as adopted. You belong to us. As much as if you came from my womb." She holds her stomach with both hands splayed.

"Not talking about your 'womb.'" I avoid gagging. "I want to know about my birth parents. Isn't that what they're called? You know, my *real* heritage. Then maybe I can at least find them, let them know I'm okay, figure out more about my background." The ache is displaced by growing excitement. Sure, it would have been nice to know all this years ago, but now I can do something about it. My fingers itch to hit the computer keys and Search.

"Your parents were likely both Native Americans." Dad stops, takes off his glasses, and massages the bridge of his nose.

"Were? Likely?"

"We don't know much about them." Mom looks to Dad, who stares at the blank TV. "We couldn't have children and were on a list to adopt. For two years we waited. Nothing. Then one night we got a call from a social worker we'd grown to know very well. The nuns at the Carmelite Monastery in Latrobe found a newborn baby on their property. Would we want to foster him until his family came forward? Of course we said yes, and she brought you here. To us."

"And they never found my *real* family?" I try to ignore Mom's wince at the word real.

"They found your mother." Dad picks up the story as he pats Mom's hand. "On the same property, behind some bushes, the police discovered the body of a young Seneca woman. She'd recently given birth in that spot."

"The body...as in dead body." My voice is dead.

"Yes. The, um, autopsy showed she died from complications of childbirth. She had no ID and the investigation reached a dead end."

I know he didn't mean the pun, but it jars me. "They never, ever figured out her identity?"

"Things were different back then." Dad stops mid-shrug. "She had no criminal record, her fingerprints weren't on file anywhere, no missing person fit her description. We don't know anything about your birth father, but again, no one came forward, even though the local and national news carried the story." He shakes his head. "Human interest."

"How did they know she was Seneca?"

"From her physical features." Mom gets up and smooths back my hair. "From what we know, you look like her. And *your* features are classic Seneca, which is why we think both parents were probably from the same tribe. But nothing can ever be certain. Which is why it seemed to make sense not to even tell you."

"So you all lied about some random Native American ancestor on Dad's side? Just to explain," I circle my hand around my face, "this?"

"No, we never lied." Dad stands and comes to me. He drops to his knees with a groan, his face directly in front of mine. "Pap did have a Native American ancestor way back.

Maybe not Seneca—no one really knows for sure what tribe."

"So basically, my mother abandoned me, you adopted me, and now it's business as usual."

"It's a lot to deal with, I know. But as your mother—don't give your father or me that look. We *are* your parents. You *are* our beloved son. As a mom, I believe your birth mother did the best she could. It was all meant to be. Beyond that, yes, we move on with our lives."

Having an unsolvable puzzle sucks more than anything that ever happened to me. The facts are clear—dead Seneca mystery mother, loving adoptive parents, happy ending. My initial reaction—hit the internet and find my roots—has drained away. Why bother? But the thread that ties me to my blood doesn't unravel. It strengthens into a skein of steel cable. I have to accept that I'll never know the man and woman who gave me life. But the turmoil in my soul is just beginning.

EIGHTEEN

Kota

"We have to talk." I approach Summer at the end of the school day. "Please."

"What, did you miss me over Thanksgiving break?" Summer flips her hair behind her shoulder. Her expression is neutral.

"No. I mean yes." I take a breath. "I found out some things. About my family."

Summer's eyes shift, this time a subtle morph from brown to black, fathomless like the bottom of a well. "I don't have to know your history. It must be fascinating for you, but since I have no clue about my real family, frankly, not interested. Thanks for sharing."

"I'm adopted." I blurt it out. She has to understand how alike we are.

Her eyes lighten, just a bit. "Oh." One word, the crack of a broken heart. "You should share this with your friends. Preston. Marlie…whomever."

"I'm sharing it with you."

"Because…"

"Because." I shrug.

"Hey, you two look all snuggly-wuggly." Marlie sidles up and places a possessive hand on my arm. She stands on tiptoe and pecks my cheek, her tongue grazing my skin with moist heat.

"Hardly." Summer shrugs. "I need help with math—my worst subject. Mrs. Romero suggested Kota could give me some pointers."

"Yeah, so how about meeting at the library? Around 3:30?" I really don't want to spill my guts at the public library, but also can't stomach Marlie's jealous crap. We're not even a couple.

"Great. Thanks." Summer nods. "See you on the bus, Marlie." She walks away.

I stare at Marlie. "You and Summer are friends?"

"She's *so* into Preston and wants my help to make sure he stays interested. I do what I can for the poor girl. You tutor her in math, I tutor her in love." Marlie laughs. "Later. Gotta make the bus."

I wonder how 'into' Preston Summer really is. I don't see them together all that much. Preston is all over the place, but Summer is a loner. Like me. As if we're meant to be together. I walk down the hall, indulging in a moment of pure fantasy: Summer's slim, naked body running through a field—no, pressed up against me, that's more like it. Her eyes a deep, passionate purple, scent of warm cinnamon and apples, lips opening to mine…

"You in la-la land, my man?" Preston grins. "Let me guess, Magnificent Marlie and her Bodacious Boobs, right? I can tell by the lust in your eyes."

"Something like that." I'm careful. These days I'm never sure if I'll get Preston, my old friend, or Preston, my new enemy.

"I hear you. On Halloween? Shanai? Oh, man, is she hot." Preston adjusts his jeans.

"Marlie thinks you and Summer are together."

"She's a good kid, but straight up and down, if you get my drift." Preston's lewd smile fades into a weird grimace as his eyes glaze over. "Summer is mine. Don't get any ideas. It's not a level playing field. Go after her, and you'll regret it."

"What is wrong with you?" Heat travels to my cheeks. "You're screwing Shanai, but no one can have Summer? That's crazy."

"I didn't say 'no one' could have Summer. *You* can't have her. We good?" Preston's breath is foul, to match his mood.

"You need a shrink."

"Oh, really? And the sad little adopted Indian doesn't need help?"

One of our vocab words, *malicious*, springs into my mind as I search Preston's face for some sign he's joking—or truly insane. "Who told you about that?"

"I have my sources." Preston shrugs. "Nice talking to you, my man." He gets his car keys out of his pocket, throws and catches them, and whistles as he walks away.

I didn't tell Preston—or anyone else—about my family. Summer would be the first to hear about it. So how does he know? Maybe he bugged my house. I almost laugh out loud. Conspiracy theory, alive and well in my brain. Probably my mother told some other mother, who eventually told Mrs. Burke, who told Preston. Gossip central.

I make it home from school in time to grab a snack, brush my teeth, spray on some Axe cologne I find in the back of the bathroom closet. Math book in my pack as a prop, I ride my bike to the library, thankful for the wintery sun that has melted most of the snow. The cold slaps my face. Yeah, I like Summer, and yeah, I would normally never mess with someone Preston was dating. But he's become a jerk. And for the first time in my life, I've found a girl who makes me feel alive.

Summer is not at the library. My gut contracts. She made up the whole let's meet story to escape from me at school. I'm about to leave when I find her in the reference stacks, looking at a thick book. She shoves it back onto the shelf, but not before I notice the title: *Guide to Unlocking Past Lives*. "Hey. Thanks for coming. I wasn't sure you would."

"Yeah, me neither."

"So you're into reincarnation?" I figure I'll start slow, work my way up to the real topic.

"Not exactly. It's garbage. People aren't born over and over again. It's way more complicated." She heads for the end of the row and sits at a study carrel in the back corner of the deserted library.

I pull a chair from a nearby carrel, squeeze in beside her, and open the math book.

"You're prepared. I'll give you that. Did you go to spy school or something?" The ghost of a smile teases her lips.

"Just motivated." I keep my voice low. Libraries and secrets go together.

We sit in silence for too long, beyond comfortable into uneasy. She doesn't look at her phone, no apparent interest in the time. Or tap her nails on the tabletop; no long nails on her slender fingers. "You bite your nails."

"You brought me here to talk about my lack of a manicure?"

"No. I brought you here to talk about..." Not sure where to go with this. I should have dropped it at school after blurting out "I'm adopted". How can I make her see we're meant to be together, and my birth status is proof of that fact?

"Look, Kota. We started off all wrong. People say you're a good guy. It's just me. I don't remember much, and it makes me cautious."

I see a small pulse on the side of her neck and imagine her heart beating in time with it. Something comes over me. I want to press my lips to that subtle movement and be one with her lifeblood. To sink into her, not a sex thing, but a consuming desire, a burning that sets my body on fire.

The library is gone. The carrel dissolves. There is only Summer and me. I grab her hands—warm, warm hands—and stare into her bottomless eyes. *"Goanio' dai io.* Beautiful." It's as if I'm seeing her for the first time, her pale skin nestled into my dark, a flicker of blue in her eyes, her hair unbound and free.

"Kota?" She jerks away. "What's the deal?"

The spell is broken, the library returns, my cheeks burn. "Sorry. I just, uh, zoned out." I don't understand either.

"Yeah, totally." Summer slides her chair a few inches away from me. "Why are we here?"

"I have to make you understand." Now that it's time to talk, the words stick in my throat. "I told you that I just found out I'm adopted. I don't know squat about my parents or background. I mean, it's obvious that I'm Seneca, but beyond that—zippo."

"Oh. That must have been a shock. You okay?" Summer's forehead is scrunched up. Compassion? Confusion? "Why, exactly, are you telling *me*?"

So it's confusion. She hasn't made the same leap I did. "We're alike. Unknowns. Meant to be together." The impassioned plea I imagined doesn't come out.

"In a way. But you're with the people who loved and raised you. Your past is yours, even if you don't know specifics about your birth background. There's nothing...um, nothing really, in my memory. I'm not sure how I can help."

I open my mouth to tell her that she's my soul mate, but even in my mind it sounds crazy. We've never been on a date, barely know one another, and most of our conversations have been arguments. "Not asking for help. Just thought if you knew about me, maybe it would help you. Not to feel so different."

"Ah, Kota." Her voice is soft. I can barely hear it. "There's nothing you can do to really help me. I'll either find what I need...or not. I think my birthday is in April."

"Oh, great." Not sure what that has to do with

anything. "You'll be seventeen?"

"Maybe. I guess."

"Me too. June fifth. That means next birthday we'll be adults. Big eighteen."

"Good for you." A huge sigh lifts and collapses Summer's chest. She stands, her hand on my shoulder.

The feel of her through my shirt makes my heart race, as if I've been jolted by a wire that's not grounded. I glance up and catch a fleeting glimpse of something new in her face. Soft. Vulnerable. Sad. I reach for her.

She pulls away before my skin meets hers and shoves her left hand into her pocket. "Thanks for sharing such an important thing with me." She stares into my eyes, as if she can see through me. Her irises flash yellow before settling into green. "Am I searching for *you*?"

It's clear that her question is of the utmost importance. But I don't know the answer and refuse to give a meaningless response. "I don't know what that means."

Summer's shoulders droop. "Then there's no use in us being together. Ever."

"Well, well, well, study time, you two?" Kayla, two large books balanced in her hands, skids to a stop beside us.

"Math." I close my unused book and turn to Summer. "I hope this helped."

"Thanks. See you, Kayla." Summer hurries away.

"Did I interrupt?" Kayla takes in Summer's retreating back. "Does Marlie know about this?"

"It's school stuff." I shrug it off and leave Kayla's snide grin behind.

The trip home is uphill. Like my life.

NINETEEN

Summer

In the week since I met Kota in the library, I've seen him many times at school. His look is hungry, as if he would suck me in if he knew how. I blew him off at the library and have done nothing to encourage him since. I asked him, point blank, if he's the one I'm searching for. He had no clue what I meant. So it's not him.

The help I gave to Marlie didn't get me reconciled, so it's not her. Which leaves only one option. Preston. I have to up my game with him. Maybe it's not about feelings at all, but some other thing with Preston that will release me from earth.

"Line up. Double file through the halls. Quietly, people. There are classes in session." Mrs. Mayhew herds us to the side door, where a bus awaits for our field trip to Hannastown.

By the time I head out of the room, the only partner left is Doug. Seriously?

"Like, cool, right? You and me, heading out to pow-wow land." Doug puckers up and makes a woo-woo-woo sound, muffled by his hand. "It's the way Indians talk."

"Funny. Kota is Native American, and I never heard him do that."

"Old school, baby." Doug tries to smack my butt.

I avoid his hand. "Sexual harassment, *loser*. I'm not your baby, and don't touch me or your ability to *ever* father babies will be gone. Understand?"

"I get it." Doug rolls his eyes. "That time of the month?"

"Yeah, so you better watch it." It's clear that debating anything with Doug—Douchebag Doug as Kota calls him—is useless. It's going to be a long afternoon.

The bus merges onto Route 22 and stays on the highway in traffic for about fifteen minutes. After a right on SR 1055 and a left on Front Street, we pull into a parking lot about twenty minutes later. There's a tall stockade fence on the right—likely the rebuilt fort—and three log cabins across the road on the left. The site is surrounded by snow-covered, rolling hills and barren trees. Not sure why I expected green grass, farmland, and leafy trees. It *is* winter, duh.

We head for the first cabin. Candlelight glows in the wavy glass windows. Inside, the chill has been banished by a roaring fire in a stone fireplace. A kettle hangs over the flames on an iron arm, a sweet cinnamon aroma filling the small room.

A costumed docent greets us, her long skirts sweeping the floor. "I am Mistress Barbara, proprietress of this establishment. Welcome to Hannastown, built on land purchased by Mr. Robert Hanna in 1769 following the Treaty of Fort Stanwix. This site housed the first English court west of the Allegheny Mountains."

"Please tell us about the important document that was signed here." Mrs. Mayhew prompts her.

"Of course." Mistress Barbara isn't pleased to be interrupted. "On May 16, 1775—a year before the Declaration of Independence—the Hanna's Town Resolves was signed on this site. The local people, most of whom had fled from the tyranny in England, agreed to take up arms and resist British authority. It was the first such declaration in any of the British colonies."

As she drones on, I glance around. There's a side room with a hemp rope bed and tick mattress, steps to a loft, and a separate saloon. Fine china, lanterns, ladles, pewter, and utilitarian redware pottery decorate the hutch in the main room.

A chill travels down my arms. Redware? Now how did I know that? Or any of it?

"Check it out." Doug nods toward the bed. "Bet that old thing saw some action back in the day. Wanna give it a try?" He rocks his pelvis forward and back.

"Not with you." I step away from his disgusting display. "It would have been too crowded for 'action'. Travelers slept five to a bed."

"Very good." Mistress Barbara smiles at me. "We have a historian in the group. Have you been here before?"

Marlie, leaning against the wall, rolls her eyes. Preston, texting, looks up. Kota, alone in the corner, raises one eyebrow.

"Um, no, don't think so." But what do I know? This place has been here for a very long time. Maybe I did materialize here. But if so, obviously it did nothing to help me.

"This was a welcomed rest stop along Forbes Road, which was a thoroughfare to the west. There was an ample supply of water from numerous springs nearby." The docent heads for the door. "Let's move on to the fort while we're warm, and then we'll visit the remaining two cabins."

I linger in the back of the room as the others shuffle out the door. The fire in the huge stone fireplace beckons me. I can't look away. Each flame leaps in the air, jagged in outline, consuming the wood below in a frenzy of destruction. The crackle becomes the sharp retort of rifles, the red and yellow a reflection of brown skin, the rising smoke the scent of burning buildings. I suck in a breath, longing to flee, unable to move.

"You coming?" Kota's voice breaks the reverie.

"What? Oh. Yes." I tear my eyes away from the burning.

"Your eyes..." Kota stares at me. "They look like flames."

"There you are." Preston strides across the room. He pushes Kota aside and takes my hand. "C'mon, babe. Everyone else is outside. You okay?"

I keep my eyes downcast. "Sure. Just storing up the heat." I leave the two guys and head for the door.

Behind me, I hear Preston. "There's more to this than you know. Stay away from her. I won't tell you again."

"I'm sick of you and your threats. Leave me alone." Kota sweeps past me without a glance.

I step onto the porch and descend the steps before Preston catches up. When he does, he again reaches for me. "Your hand is warm." He wraps his cold one around mine.

"What did you mean? When you told Kota there's 'more to this than you know?'"

"Oh, you heard." Preston keeps walking.

"Are you the one?" I pull him to a stop and face him, holding my breath. If Preston isn't the one meant to save me, I'm doomed.

His eyes are blank spheres, his face expressionless. His lips barely move, as he whispers, "Yes. I'm the one." He pulls me behind a fat pine and presses his cold lips to mine.

I break the contact. "How do you know what I mean?"

"Trust me."

The timbre in those two words settles it. I wrap my arms around him. My lips part. I accept his tongue in my mouth. I wait for it: the remembrance of my sin, a sense of release from guilt, the resulting joy, and final escape into eternal rest.

"Mr. Burke and Miss Sullivan." Mrs. Mayhew's tone is as icy as the air. "This is a *school* event. We are representing Fawn Valley. Get back to the group. Pronto."

"Sorry." I scurry away, face hot.

"No harm, no foul, right, Mrs. Mayhew?" Preston stays with her, says something else I don't hear, and she laughs.

I cross the road and join the rest of the group, already gathered inside the high stockade fence that represents the old fort. So I'm still here. In the real world. Preston, no matter what he said, didn't send me to my rest. Maybe the interruption is the reason. Maybe there's more to it, real love needs to bloom and displace the nagging guilt that continues to plague me. Maybe, maybe, maybe. All I know is that nothing has changed. I have no idea what sin I committed and have yet to discover what else is expected of me. At least I know that in some way, Preston is part of it. As long as I have that fact in place, I must be on track to be reconciled before my seventeenth birthday. But the vice around my heart doesn't loosen. And I wonder if Preston is just saying what he thinks I want to hear in order to get laid.

"The original fort was burned on July 13, 1782." Mistress Barbara frowns at my late arrival. "Court was in session that day, with people from the surrounding areas in town to have their cases heard."

"Someone set the thing on fire with a cigarette or something?" Doug looks around the group and grins. "Maybe they were smoking some weed. Fatal tokes, man."

The docent ignores him. "Based on what we have already learned, does anyone *else* have a theory about what happened?"

Everyone looks at the ground, no one answers.

"Very well." She sighs. "In league with the British, Seneca Indians raided Hannastown. The residents and visitors fled to the fort and were safe, although the rest of the site was burned."

"Did anyone get scalped? What do you think, Kota?"

Doug smirks. "Any tomahawk action?"

Kota's ruddy cheeks pale, but he merely shrugs.

Kota's discomfort is obvious. Part of me wants to defend him. It's been more than two hundred years since his ancestors destroyed this town. He shouldn't have to carry that kind of blame. But the other part of me—that which dominates my heart, mind, and soul—has the urge to pluck a knife off the wall back in the cabin and ram it through his gut. The sheer violence of this urge is alien to me. Yet I can't get rid of it. The vague fear Kota engendered in me from the start blossoms into a malignant spot on my heart.

"Douglas, racial slurs will not be tolerated." Mrs. Mayhew nods at the docent. "Continue."

"The raiding party used rifles, knives, tomahawks, bows and arrows." Mistress Barbara gestures to a plaque. "Although there were no initial fatalities, this monument honors Peggy Shaw. She was twelve years old and got shot while running from the fort to rescue a small child. She lingered for several days before succumbing to her wound. Let's return to the cabins, where we have refreshments waiting."

The wind picks up and swirls through the fort, whistling as it squeezes in and out of the slatted boards. It seems to blow through me, but instead of being icy, it feels warm and humid. I watch the others trudge through the dusting of snow. Preston waits for me, until Mrs. Mayhew points him to the cabin and waves me forward. I walk toward her and, apparently satisfied that I'm on the way and not necking with Preston again, she continues on.

Peggy Shaw. I can see her—imagine her? Short, with twin braids, one hanging down on each shoulder. Her dress a loose linen thing to the ankles, pulled in at the waist by a homespun apron. High boots meet the hem of her skirt. Bonnet strings are tied in front, the bonnet hanging down the back of her neck as she runs. She's pretty, and energetic, and full of life. I want to talk to her.

If I go ghostly, can I? Is she a ghost, too, or am I losing it? What is it about this place?

"Hey, you better hurry, or Mayhew will be on the warpath." Preston is at my side.

Peggy is gone.

"I'm coming. I was just…thinking. It's quiet out here." I let him put his arm around me as we walk toward the cabin. It's warm against his coat, with his hand on my shoulder and thumb rubbing up and down the back of my ear.

He pulls me behind the bus and his hand slides up to hold the back of my head in his grip. "You're mine, Dovie. From now until forever."

His kiss is hard and rough, his breath sour, his face radiating heat. This is what I've been waiting for, the perfect relationship, something that will lead to rest and peace. There must be something I'm doing for him, some need I'm fulfilling that will expiate my unknown sin. I'd thought that when I discovered the answer, I would also know the question, but perhaps not. I don't have to understand the process, only go through the motions and let it happen.

"We have to get back. I told Mayhew I dropped my wallet and had to find it. I really wanted to find you. And now I have." Preston pulls away. "You go first so we don't arrive together."

I walk across the road, join the group in the second cabin, and accept a paper cup of warm cider. Kota gives me a strange stare, even though he's pretending to listen to Marlie talk about how boring the field trip has been. When Preston enters a minute later and winks at me, Kota shakes his head and turns away.

It isn't until the docent resumes her lecture that it hits me. My breathing quickens and my left hand turns to mist; I shove it in my pocket. Preston called me Dovie.

TWENTY

Kota

Mistress Barbara is wrapping up her presentation. Finally.

I shift my numb butt on the crowded bench and Marlie giggles as if my ass is there for her benefit.

"Mrs. Mayhew?" Summer, several students away from me, whispers to the teacher standing guard behind our back row.

"What now?"

"I need to use the restroom."

"Can't you wait until the docent is finished?"

"No. Sorry."

She must accept Mayhew's sigh as permission. I watch Summer inch across several sets of feet to the end of the bench, getting a quick whiff of her scent as she passes by me. I know nothing about flowers, but she smells like one that might grow in Gram's garden.

I seem to be the only one who notices Summer edging out of the cabin toward the outhouse. Preston is texting and doesn't look up. Doug catches my eye, smirks and mouths, "On the rag." Marlie continues to file her nails.

After two minutes or so, I turn to Mayhew, point to myself, and to the exit. This time her answer is an eye roll, but I take what I get and follow Summer out the door.

The bathrooms are about fifty feet behind the cabins, along a gravel path dusted with snow. Summer must be inside. I walk toward the building. Although it's afternoon, the light is already fading, evening approaching early as it does this time of year. The sky is gray with heavy clouds rolling across the expanse. In the west, the sun is setting behind the restrooms. I stop and turn to the east, where the outline of a full moon is already visible.

I spot Summer next to the inn, partially concealed by evergreen shrubs. She's motionless and staring at the sky. I must make a sound because she turns startled eyes toward me. "What are *you* doing out here?"

"Bathroom."

Her pursed lips tell me she isn't buying it.

"No, that's not true." I go with the truth. "I followed you."

"The moon has a red tint." Her gaze leaves me and returns to the sky. "Harvest moon. Time for the final harvest before Yule."

"And you know this because...?" She looks at me but doesn't respond. "You don't come across like a farm girl. Or a city girl. You're different than anyone else." Putting feelings into words isn't my best gig. I take a step closer to her.

Summer shivers and shrinks against the log wall of the cabin. "I really don't want to hurt you. But I *will* protect myself."

I notice she's clutching her keys in her right hand, jagged edges peeking through her clenched fingers. In a quick motion she bends and picks up a rock with a sharp edge. And then, suddenly, it's as if the rock is floating in mid-air, levitating like a magician's trick. Her left hand is translucent mist.

"What the hell?" Curiosity nudges aside disbelief and

146

confusion. "Your hand. It's not a hand anymore."

The rock falls to the ground. Summer lowers her arm to her side and tucks her hand away. Neither of us moves or speaks. Seconds pass before her mist-hand comes out of her pocket. It's normal. I glance at her eyes, spheres of dark red that send me back a step.

"What just happened to you?"

"I don't know what you mean." Summer shrugs.

"Cut the crap." I hold up my hand. "A minute ago yours didn't exist."

She doesn't reply and heads for the restrooms, but pauses at the top of a small hillock. Without turning around she whispers, "Do you feel it?"

"Feel what?" I can't tell her that I feel like touching her pale skin, feel like burying my face in her flowing hair, feel like holding her so tight to me that our bodies become one. There is a rightness about me when I'm with her, a sense of belonging that I never have—or had—anywhere else. Of course it would be with a girl who doesn't want me.

"Ghosts live in this place." Breath leeches from her mouth in the frosty air, as if her words are ghosts.

"It's okay. Ghosts aren't real. But any historical site can be kind of spooky, I guess." I move close to reassure her and end up doing the one thing I didn't want to do. I grab her from behind, pull her close, brush aside her hair, and lower my lips to the nape of her neck. My eyes close.

Summer doesn't squirm, push, or raise her voice. But every fiber of her body stiffens, and then collapses, as if she has vacated her clothes.

My eyes snap open, and I'm standing in the dusky light with Summer's coat in my hands. No Summer. She must have slipped out of it and retreated to the bathroom or back to the cabin. Somehow. I can't wrap my head around any of it. She might not like me, but why would she be so afraid of me? It makes no sense. None. From the corner of my eye I catch a glimpse of mist moving through the gully at the bottom of the hill, but when I look closer it's gone.

"There you are, Mr. Landis." Mrs. Mayhew comes around the corner. "We're boarding the bus. Get in line, please."

"Where were you?" Marlie deftly moves to my side. "Are you sick? Isn't that Summer's coat?"

I don't answer. Summer is coming down the steps from the cabin at the end of the line. How'd she get inside? Must be a back door, because she didn't pass me. She doesn't look my way and even if she did, Preston is keeping her busy. I walk up, hand her the coat, and lag behind.

The bus ride back to school involves Marlie interrogating me about holding Summer's coat and whining about breaking a nail. Her never-ending monologue gives me time to think. Summer got spooked at Hannastown. I saw her go off on her own more than once, and each time she returned, a haunted look glazing her eyes. Preston is touching her more now than when we left, so something's up there, too. Don't suppose he'll share what's going on anytime soon, even though his usual is to give me a blow-by-blow—literally—description of his dates.

"So I'll see you tomorrow?" Marlie pecks my cheek before we exit the bus. "Or you can come over to the house later if you want. My parents are going to a meeting and it's Consuela's night off." She licks her lips.

"Not tonight." I don't buy into her little foot stomp and sigh. For some reason I'm exhausted and only want to get home for a nap.

"Hey, need a ride?" Preston, after kissing his fingers and pressing them to Summer's cheek, joins me on the sidewalk. "My car's in the lot."

"I don't get you. First you threaten me to stay away from Summer, then things are like they used to be between us." I keep walking. Tired or not, I'd rather walk than take his offered lift.

""Nothing personal, my man." Preston keeps pace with me. "As long as you know your place, it's all good."

"Yeah, whatever." I exit school property and hike for home. After the bus ride from Hannastown and all that happened there, I need fresh air. By the time I reach the house, a niggling that's been with me since Thanksgiving pushes aside thoughts of the day.

Silence greets me as I open the door with my key. "Anyone home?" Good. I plop my stuff on the chair in my room and go downstairs to the basement. Mom keeps her gardening supplies here, Dad his fishing gear, and there is a set of file drawers.

The gray metal filing cabinet is as tall as me. Cobwebs connect it to the wall. I open the top drawer and find old bank statements from before we went paperless, income tax records, and receipts. Next drawer, warranties and instruction manuals for appliances we no longer have. Third one down holds outdated travel info, as if we need *Fun Hikes for Tykes*. A month ago I would have griped about this crap. Now I'm glad they keep everything.

But after going through every file, I haven't found what I need. Namely, information about where I came from, newspaper clippings, anything to connect me to...me. There has to be some kind of record. I go back upstairs and do the one thing sure to get me in trouble, pick the lock on Dad's work files. Again, nothing interesting. I lock it up. Computer search time, even though I'd hoped for something concrete.

I open the computer and an ad appears on the sidebar for cornbread mix. Mom has a big, hulking box of cornbread mix—Southern Country Brand—that's been in the back of the kitchen cupboard forever...

"Mom, what's the deal with this stuff?" I reach for the box of cornbread. There's microwave popcorn behind it, and I'm hungry.

"Oh, I've had that for ages." Mom moves it and hands me the

popcorn bag.

"Gross. It might kill us. Food has expiration dates. I'll toss it."

"No. Don't bother. Actually, it's a funny story." Mom's hands flutter as she gets the stepstool and shoves the box in the far reaches of the top shelf, deep in the corner cupboard. "Your dad got it for me as a joke when we were dating because he loves cornbread. I tried to make it and burned the whole batch. I keep it for sentimental reasons."

"Cornbread is romantic?"

"Cornbread is cornbread." Mom ruffles my hair. "It's what's inside that counts."

"Time for some cornbread." I head upstairs to the kitchen. The top shelf is too high to reach. I grab the stepstool, climb up, and feel around in the depths. Sure enough, the dusty box is still there. It's heavy and dense, as I expected, and the top is glued shut. So maybe cornbread is just cornbread after all. I shake the box and hear the faint rustle of paper. Or maybe it *is* what's inside that counts.

I slip a knife along the box seam on top, revealing the little notch where it can be re-closed. Inside there's a bag of cornbread, sealed with Scotch tape and not as thick as it should be to fill the box. Lining one side is a clear plastic bag. I pull it out, push crumbs off the kitchen table, and spread out the documents I find inside.

The yellowed newspaper article on top includes a photo of a nun holding a small, square blanket with a plaid design. *"Infant Abandoned at Carmelite Monastery."* I mumble out loud to dispel the silence roaring in my ears. "Sisters at the Carmelite facility in Latrobe made an unusual discovery Thursday night. Sister Mary Frances opened the front door to investigate noises heard after Compline. 'We finished a hymn to Mary, mother of Jesus, and I thought I heard a baby crying. When I opened the door, I found a bundle wrapped in a colorful blanket.' The bundle turned out to be a healthy newborn boy, less than an hour old, according to doctors at Latrobe Hospital who examined him. Meanwhile, police on the scene found the body of a deceased Native American female one-quarter mile from the monastery. The Coroner estimates the woman to be in her early to mid-twenties. Autopsy revealed she had recently given birth. She is thought to be of Seneca descent, based on a traditional amulet found with the body. Police have no identification for mother or baby, and no missing persons' reports have been filed locally. Efforts to locate next of kin continue."

My hands are shaking as I lower the newsprint to the table. This is about my real mother. And me. I check the date at the top of the page. "June sixth, which means the incident was on June fifth. It's me. Can't be too many abandoned Indian kids born that day around here."

The thud of books hitting the floor alerts me right before Mom's whispered, "How did you find those?" Her face is white, and she reaches for me.

"I saw an ad for cornbread on the computer. Clever—hiding this stuff in plain sight."

"We can look at everything together when your dad gets home. I'll make some dinner and bake brownies—your favorite—and we can have a fire..." Mom's voice trails off as I gather the papers together.

"All these years you guys lied to me." I see her expression and change it to, "Withheld this from me. I appreciate the offer of food, but not very hungry right now. I'll be in my room." The look she gives me makes me feel guilty, but oh well. I've been feeling a vague sense of guilt my entire life. I spend the rest of the evening in my room, going word by word through adoption papers and other articles, including one in National Report.

"Kota, can I come in?" Mom knocks and waits.

I open the door.

She hands me a cloudy plastic bag. "This is yours." And she leaves.

I sit on my bed and open the brittle plastic, which is taped shut at the top. Inside is a small, square blanket, like the one in the newspaper picture. The colors are faded turquoise, red, yellow, and black, with a rust-colored stain. The fabric has a faint metallic odor combined with old wool and something flowery and sweet. I lie on my bed and inhale, my nose buried in the blanket. My mother wrapped me in this. I don't know how she came to be dead in the bushes, while I was a quarter of a mile away, and it doesn't matter. She gave me life and kept me safe. I let the scent of her lull me to sleep...

"No'yeg." I cling to Mother and nuzzle for her milk, but she doesn't move. My arms and legs flail, fast at first, then more slowly. I'm hungry. And cold. But not as cold as No'yeg.

I awaken with a start. My phone reads 2:43. The room is dark. I tuck the blanket back in the bag and shove both under my bed. Instead of counting sheep, I think about all the colors of Summer's eyes until I drift off once again.

TWENTY-ONE

Summer

"What do you mean, he called you Dovie?" Finn frowns, indignant at first, then slowly understanding. "I didn't tell anyone. Honest, Summer. See? I don't even think about you by that name."

"You didn't maybe mention it to your mom? She could have told someone, who told someone—you know. If you did, it's okay. No probs." I don't want to make him feel bad, but there has to be a reasonable explanation for Preston using the name from my past. My real name.

"Cross my heart." Finn, solemn face downcast, uses his pointer finger to draw an air X over his chest. "And hope to die."

"*No.* You must never say that." I ruffle his hair. "Doesn't matter what anyone calls me. Maybe it'll help me remember. Want to play Blind Man's Bluff?"

"Is that a computer game?"

"No, it's—never mind. Probably not your thing. Want to go to the mall? We can do some Christmas shopping for Jill and Daniel." I get my coat and the car keys, grateful Daniel took me for a drivers' license—and that I got the questions right and passed the road test. I must have driven before, don't know.

"Can we go to Sneaky Pete's at the food court for lunch?"

"Sure." I call to Daniel, who's in the attic getting out Christmas decorations, put Finn in the car, and make sure he's buckled. "Let's go."

We sing some Christmas carols. Finn knows rock and roll ones, I only know old hymns. There are flurries in the air, but the roads are clear, and traffic isn't bad. Until we get to the parking lot at Ross Park Mall. I find a spot at the end of a row, and we join the throng of shoppers.

"Dad likes L.L. Bean." Finn pulls me in the door of an outdoor sports shop. We find a Life is Good fishing hat for Daniel and some fishing flies.

"What about your mom?"

"She got a Pandora bracelet on her birthday. How about a charm?" Finn drags me to the store, which is so jammed we have to sign in and wait to be called.

We peruse the hundreds of charms. Finn wants to buy a pig—because he likes pigs—but when our turn comes we settle on a sterling silver heart with a crystal center. They put it in a little bag with silver tissue, and we're done.

"Let's look around." I hope to find something Finn wants, that Jill and Daniel won't buy. In the center of the mall, by the escalators, is a kiosk selling remote control helicopters.

"Hey kid, take one for a spin?" The salesman must see the same look of longing on Finn's face as I do.

Finn maneuvers the toy then lands it and hands the man the control.

"How about it?" The salesman adds, "Maybe Santa will bring you one."

"Hungry?" I pull Finn away, knowing I'll return to buy him the copter, grateful for the allowance Jill gives me.

At Sneaky Pete's we both get burgers, chocolate shakes, and fries. Finn finishes the last slurps of his ice cream as his friend Josh runs up.

"Finn, how are you?" Josh's mom smiles, including me in it. "We're going to Toy World. Would Finn like to join us? We'll bring him home."

"Is it okay?" Finn is already on his feet.

"Sure. See you later." I buy the helicopter before leaving the mall, get a huge gift bag for it, and stow everything in the trunk.

"Summer?" A familiar voice, faint under the noise of cars honking and jockeying for spaces, makes me turn. Preston jogs across the lot. "I thought that was you. Shopping?" He's casual, at ease, well dressed, handsome.

"Hi. I brought Finn, but he went toy shopping with a friend and ditched me." This is the person who knows my real name. He's my ticket to reconciliation. I mentally kick myself. Why not simply enjoy the attention? Why search for deep feelings that don't seem to exist? Azul never said it would be love that saves me. My fanciful notion could be way off. Or maybe it was Azul who put the name Dovie into Preston's mind as a clue for me. "How about you?"

"Stopped for gloves." Preston holds up his hands, encased in waterproof leather. "Are you busy? I was going to call and see if you wanted to do something this afternoon."

The immediate negative response that comes to my lips dies there. "Sure, great. Just let me call home and tell them when Finn will be back."

We leave my car at the mall, and I climb in his Mustang, the bright red color perfect for the Christmas season. "Nice. Where are we going?"

"It's a surprise. Glad you're wearing warm boots." Preston weaves through traffic and heads north, away from the city. "This is a classic 1968 Mustang. My dad restored it—he paid someone to do the actual work—and gave it to me when I turned sixteen."

Small talk peters out after a while. I'm not good at it. There are too many blanks in my memory to sustain meaningless drivel for very long. The dense traffic and multiple businesses thin out, and Preston turns off the highway. In fifteen minutes we're surrounded by snow-covered fields, complete with cows, a few horses, and barns set back off the road. The scenery is soothing for some reason. Maybe I *am* a country girl.

"We're here." Preston pulls down a rutted lane of frozen mud with dense pine trees on both sides. "Elfland Tree Farm, complete with Christmas barn. You're going to help me chop down a Christmas tree for my family."

"They sent you to get a tree?"

"Usually Dad pays someone to put up the decorations, but this year I wanted to do it with you. Look for the tallest one in the forest." Preston pulls on his gloves, gets a saw from the trunk, and opens my door.

There are other people hiking around and we join them, up and down rows and rows of pines. Most don't meet Preston's 'tallest one' criteria, so it takes a while. The lazy snowflakes continue, coating Preston's hair in white. His cheeks are pink from the cold. He manages to handle the saw and still hold my hand.

Soon we're alone, those with shorter trees in mind left behind. A doe is startled by our approach. She leaps over a stump and runs, white tale flashing. Little gusts of wind whip snow into eddies, as if there are fellow ghosts circling the tree lot with me. I can't put it off any longer.

"Preston." I stop, take a deep breath, and stare into his eyes. "You called me Dovie. Why?" My insides shake as if I've swallowed the cold.

"I did? That's weird." Preston shrugs. "Don't worry. I'm not calling you by another girl's name." He looks over my shoulder. "I think we found our tree."

"No, wait." The hair on the back of my neck stands up. Something isn't right. "Dovie is a very unusual name. It's not like you called me Sara, or Abby, or Chloe."

Preston leads me to a tree stump where someone already cut down a tree. "Sit." He kneels beside me, and in that instant Preston—who looks, smells, and sounds the same—changes in some infinitesimal way. "Dovie Critchlow. I know your name. But that's all I know."

I can barely breathe. "Are you a...spirit?"

"What?" Preston laughs. "No idea what you mean. You've been reading too many ghost stories late at night. My family is rich, and I have connections. I did some digging to find out something about you, to help you remember. Because..." His voice trails off and he, who is never at a loss for smooth, drops his head. When he looks up his eyes are wet. "This sounds crazy, but I think I'm in love with you. Don't say it, I know we're in high school and have our whole lives ahead of us. But I think you feel it, too."

What do I feel? The surge of excitement I expect from Preston's declaration doesn't happen. He says the right things. Does the right things. He's the right one. So why is the press of my vague guilt still overriding everything else? My time on earth is finished in a mere four months. The logical thing to do is go to with this chance to save myself. Feelings are overrated.

"Dovie?" Preston stands and pulls me to my feet.

I let him embrace me, pressing my face into the warmth of his jacket. His scent is sour, likely the effect of hiking through the woods.

His arms tighten, twin vices surrounding me. "You are mine. Are we clear about that? I love you, and you love me. I need you, and you need me. We will be together forever."

His voice is hypnotic, as it caresses me with the assurance of his devotion. Azul pops into my mind; I nudge him aside. Kota is with me too, the echo of his 'we're meant to be together' so much like Preston's. But Kota can't be the one. This is my time with Preston. Through him I will remember the mistake—my sin—that haunts me. "We belong together." I echo his murmured entreaty.

Preston lifts my chin and kisses me, hard and fast, as if sealing me with his mouth for eternity. He releases me as the sound of other hikers comes closer. He blinks, and in that moment he's back to what I think of as the guy I know.

"I think you should call me Summer."

"Sure, of course." He grins.

"Do you think you could help me find out more about where I came from? Since you have connections." I pause and go for it. "And since we're in love."

"I like the way that last part sounds." Preston kisses me again, this time soft and tender. "I'll see what I can find out, although if the police don't know anything, not sure I can help that much. Whoever you are? Doesn't really matter to me."

We find what Preston calls 'the perfect tree', chop it down, and haul it to the car. Once it's tied on the roof, we head into the Christmas barn. The smell of sauerkraut and hot chocolate, yards of shiny tinsel and tree ornaments, and the sound of carols lull me into a holiday mood.

I'm drawn to a small box of vintage jewelry labeled: Any piece $5.00. Clip earrings, brooches, a cameo, and a few chains are lumped together.

"Check this out." Preston produces a woven band with a gold-color head of a snake set with turquoise eyes. Don't know how I missed seeing it in the box. He unwinds the bracelet and clasps it around my left wrist.

It fits my thin wrist as if made just for me. "Ssss—it's going to get you." I wave the snake.

"I'll take my chances. Don't even bother to take it off. Early Merry Christmas. To remember the day we fell in love." Preston pays for it before we leave.

"I don't remember the last time anyone got me a gift. Thanks."

There's something about the snake that attracts and repels me at the same time. But I keep it on, even after I get home and settle into bed for the night. I have trouble falling asleep. What am I supposed to do now?

TWENTY-TWO

Kota

"Do me a favor, Kota." Mom hands me a foil-covered plate. "Run this over to the Sullivan house. Jill always tells me that Daniel is a cookie monster, and I have all these cookies left over from Christmas."

As much as I want to go, I don't want to go. "Aren't they stale by now?"

"You think I would send stale cookies to our friends?" Mom swats me with the dishtowel. "They were frozen, thank you very much. If I keep them here, I'll eat them and violate my New Year's resolution. And put on another ten pounds. Now scoot."

"Yeah, fine. Give me a minute." I go to my room, change from sweats into jeans and one of my new Abercrombie flannels, and braid my hair. After the bombshell of "you're adopted" at Thanksgiving, I decided to go with the whole Seneca thing. My face is there already—no escaping the gene pool, even if it's a secret one—so why not go all the way?

All the way. Right. The night after Christmas, Marlie under the tree, tiny white lights and the glow of a fire. And

161

Mom with Dad at Benedum Center for a concert...

"Want to see what I got for Christmas?" Marlie is snuggled up to me on the couch.

"Sure."

I couldn't care less, but after Summer basically told me we would never be together—ever—I figured what the hell. I guess she meant it, because she and Preston seem to be inseparable these days. I even heard he got her some crazy jewelry for Christmas. All of which leaves me with Marlie. Maybe it's not fair to her, but I have no energy for finding a girlfriend, Preston is MIA in my life, and everyone at school has someone.

Marlie stands, stretches, and says, "Close your eyes, and you'll get a surprise." She giggles. "That rhymes. I'm a poet."

I close my eyes as directed, wishing for a nap instead of a surprise.

"You can look now. This is what Santa brought me."

Marlie is backlit by the fire. She's wearing a big smile to go with her new red lace bra and thong. "All I want for Christmas is you, you, baby." She sings—off-key—the lyrics to a holiday pop song, while gyrating her hips and bending low to expose her jiggling cleavage.

"Nice." I know I'm expected to paw her, drool, and grovel at her bare feet. But I just sit. The flames are red like her underwear, with hints of yellow. Kind of like the colors in the blanket I was wrapped in as a baby. Did my mother act like Marlie? Is that how she ended up pregnant? What about my father? Did he enjoy the lingerie and then take off when responsibility caught up with him? Bastard. No, wait. I'm the bastard.

"Penny for your thoughts." Marlie's Christmas slut-wear has somehow hit the floor. She continues to dance, unencumbered by elastic, wire, or see-through lace.

I've never seen a girl totally naked before, if you don't count the time when I was five years old and the neighbors had frozen pipes. They used our bathroom, and I saw their teenage daughter step out of the shower when I went in to pee.

"Do you have new Christmas undies, too?" Marlie hooks her

thumb in the waistband of my jeans and tugs. "Or do you go commando?"

I reach for her and encircle her hips with my arms, which puts my face at her navel. She thrusts forward until her skin meets my lips. Automatically, I kiss at contact.

"Ooh, baby, you are sooo bad." Marlie unbuttons my shirt and pushes it off my shoulders. She unbuckles my belt and pulls it off, twirling it in the air like a cowgirl in an old movie.

Although the movies I've seen don't include nude. I stifle a laugh at the thought of Marlie in a cowboy hat.

She pulls me to my feet, unzips my jeans, and pushes them to the floor. "Too bad, so sad. One more layer to paradise."

This is the moment every guy waits for, like, from the time they reach puberty. I can surf on my hormones. It couldn't be more private, romantic, or anticipated. A thin layer of cotton, and my virginity will be no more. Is this Marlie's first time? Is she on the pill? Where's the condom Preston gave me in middle school?

Marlie turns from me and spreads a furry throw on the floor in front of the fire. I look down at my body. Sheen of sweat on my heaving chest. Toes curled against the rug, legs locked. And between them no response. None. I'm tempted to go to the what's-wrong-with-me place, but for some reason that doesn't happen. I'm just not interested. No big moral dilemma. Except for my utter commitment to not bring another bastard like me into the world by mistake. Which is redundant.

"What's your problem? Need a little help?" Marlie sashays toward me, her eyes on my underwear.

"No problem." I grab my jeans, step away, and pull them back on. "You should get dressed."

"Excuse me?" Hands on hips, Marlie faces me.

"It's nothing personal. I just don't think we should do this."

"It's very personal. You're the first guy who ever turned me down. What are you, some kind of religious freak?" A nasty gleam replaces the lust in her eyes. "Or just can't get it up?"

"Just can't get it up." I know my face isn't kind when I add, "For you."

"We're through, Kota. I tried to make this relationship work,

but you're a freaking bastard. Always were and always will be."

"True, that."

Marlie throws a pillow at me, dresses, and storms out of the house, swearing more fluently than the guys when we shoot hoops. I pick up the throw and replace it on the sofa, go to my room, and fall into bed, still in my jeans.

"Are you taking these cookies to the Sullivans, or waiting for Valentine's Day?" Mom greets me as I enter the kitchen.

"All right, all right." I put on my coat. "Later."

"Be careful. And thanks." Mom smiles. "No samples for you. I'm making beef stew for dinner."

I munch a few cookies on the way. They won't be missed. I hike down the Sullivans' snow-covered driveway. It's beautiful, a cheesy winter wonderland. We didn't have a white Christmas, but these first two weeks of the New Year have been nothing but white.

"Look out."

A snowball explodes against the back of my head before I can process the warning. Finn grins from behind a holly bush, but not at me. His attention is on Summer, who is standing on the other side of the drive, a bucket of snowballs in her mittened hand.

"Sorry. Wrong place, wrong time." She doesn't look glad to see me, per usual.

I should get used to the punched-in-the-gut kick I get each time she frowns in that particular way—at me. "No harm, no foul." I hold up the plate. "My mom sent these for your family."

Finn darts behind me and joins Summer. "Let's pulverize him."

"Hey, I'm not the enemy." The little dude has the same frown as Summer. I thought by now he'd figured out that Halloween was all a misunderstanding.

"I know." Finn stands on tiptoe and whispers in

Summer's ear. She shakes her head, and he whispers again.

"No, Finn, we aren't going to have a snowball fight with Kota." Summer jerks her head toward the enclosed sun porch. "Just put them on the table. Tell your mom thanks."

I do as told, close the door behind me, and start up the drive. Two mounds of snow fly at me, one hitting my back, the other my butt. "Hey, not fair." I dive for a tree, scoop up two handfuls of snow, and fire back.

Finn, grinning, ducks. "Ha ha, can't get me."

Summer hangs back, but there's telltale snow on her gloves. I get closer to her. The usual alabaster of her cheeks is dusted with pink from the cold. Several tendrils of pale hair have escaped from under her hat. Her eyes, which were dark when I arrived, have become a dusky violet. Although she's wearing a heavy coat, gloves, boots, and a knit cap—with almost no skin exposed—my body reacts to her in a way it didn't with nudie cutie Marlie.

"Look out." Summer's words coincide with a cold blast of snow to my face.

"You aren't supposed to warn him." Finn gets off a snowball to Summer's face, too. He runs, Summer chasing him.

I take off after them. Time for Finn to get nailed. He runs faster, but his legs are shorter, so we all arrive at the meadow together. The snow is undisturbed, except for deer tracks along the edge. Pine branches, heavy with snow, extend over the open space. Finn trips on a hidden root and goes down.

Summer dives after Finn, graceful, fluid. "I've got you now." Soon she's rubbing snow in his face.

"You can't get away." I land beside Finn and stuff snow down the neck of his jacket.

The three of us tussle for a minute or two, then roll on our backs. Finn gets up and wanders away to make snow angels. Which leaves me lying beside Summer, not touching, but close enough that I can feel her warm breath when she turns her head toward me.

"I don't know what to make of you." Summer's whisper could be to herself. "Am I screwing up again?"

I resist the urge for a quick answer. Don't really understand the question. Flakes drift from the tree above us, as if it's snowing again. I'm afraid to move and break the spell that has me close to the one person in the world I want to be near. "It's something I don't get. I've lived here all my life, had a great family, a few friends. But I feel more connected to you than anyone else. Ever. I'm in freaking high school. Not supposed to feel this way." Realizing I just spoke the words I meant to keep to myself, I hold my breath.

"Sometimes I'm drawn to you. Other times you frighten me." Summer sighs. "There's more at stake for me than a teen romance. I'm not free to follow my feelings. It's complicated."

"So explain it to me." I think about her chameleon eyes and misty hand and know that any explanation is going to be beyond anything I can imagine.

"I can't." Summer gets up, dusts the snow off her jeans, and holds out her left hand to me.

I take it and stand, reluctant to break the contact. Her glove compresses, as if her fingers disappear inside of it. The cuff of her jacket sinks in as well. "Summer?"

"I told you. There's no way you could ever understand." She drops my hand and runs to Finn.

And I'm left alone, in her absence aware of a sharp cold that pierces my very soul.

TWENTY-THREE

Summer

"I need help with this before Mom makes me go to bed." Finn hands me a shoebox and red construction paper. "I want it to look like a car."

"You're confusing me with someone artistic." But I take the supplies from him and sit down at the table. "We could do this over the weekend. Valentine's Day is Monday."

"Nah, I want it done now so I'm ready. Every year the twins in my class—Evan and Aiden—always have the best valentine boxes. Their dad is a wizard in cardboard. Last year he made them coffins."

My fingers stop their web search for: How to Make a School Valentine Box. "Coffins?"

"Yeah." Finn grins. "Because their dad says love is dead."

This sentiment lingers in my head while we follow the Pinterest instructions and craft something that might, possibly, be considered a valentine car.

"Perfect." Finn holds up our project. "I'm gonna pulverize Evan and Aiden with this."

"Great." I smile at his excitement. "Maybe I'm a 'wizard in cardboard', too."

Long after Finn runs to his room to write the valentines for his classmates, I sit at the table staring out the window. Winter is lingering. The snow is gray-slush ugly. I'm still here. Two months and four days until my seventeenth birthday and oblivion. My stomach turns over.

I get out the valentine I bought for Preston at Ferri's. Generic red and white, silhouette of a guy and girl with their heads together, sappy words that don't quite get to "I love you". Because love is not what I feel for Preston. At least not as I understand love to be. Sometimes he's funny, loving, warm. He can also be distant, puzzling, cold. But since love isn't my goal, it doesn't matter. I scrawl *Happy V Day, Summer*, on the card and seal the envelope before I'm tempted to lie about my feelings.

Daniel comes in from the store holding something behind his back. "Where's Jill?"

"Laundry." I nod toward the basement stairs.

Daniel grins and pulls out a potted miniature red rose plant. "Don't tell. I'll hide this on the porch. Monday, before work, I'll surprise her."

"You'll get the good husband award."

"That's the plan."

"Going to bed. See you in the morning." I wave to Daniel and head upstairs. The loft is cold, so I switch on the electric fireplace. Soon the room is toasty, even though the sheets are cool when I slide between them. I finger the bracelet Preston bought for me at the Christmas barn. It encircles my wrist, the snake now familiar. Preston expects to see it on me every day, so I'm in the habit of leaving it on all the time. I drift to sleep with my thumb fingering the beady eyes of the snake...

The smell of rotten eggs opens my eyes. I'm in that place between sleep and the state of unnatural wakefulness Azul brings to me. But there's no *Azul*. Instead of his shimmery blue and surrounding cool, misty clouds, I'm faced with a barren landscape devoid of soft edges. Everything is hard, in shades of brown and black. Here and there tiny bits of steam escape from holes in the terrain. The stench of rot and sulfur permeates the air.

"*Azul?*" I wait for what seems like forever.

"I told you, the dilemma is yours alone to solve." *Azul's* whisper comes to me, even though I can't see him.

"Is this a joke?" I gesture around me. "It's like a movie set for Hell."

"How astute." A new voice, filled with gravel and poison. A figure approaches me, easily leaps across a chasm, and stands before me. His body is like *Azul's* used to be—a distinct form that flickers like a candle—but instead of a pleasing blue, it's rag-filthy gray. An aura of cadmium yellow surrounds him, a strange marriage of darkness and light.

"Who are you?" I take two steps back, but he remains the same distance from me.

"I am Detritus. It's good to see you again."

"I've never seen you before." My insides shake as I struggle to recall. Something is familiar, but surely I would remember in clear detail having met this...being.

"No matter. Soon we'll be together forever." Detritus smiles, a skeletal rictus.

"Never." But my heart constricts and breathing becomes difficult.

"Never say never." Again, the awful smile. "We will meet again on your seventeenth birthday. And then we shall never part. You chose me, and here I am."

My thoughts beg my mind: remember, remember, make it right.

"You won't remember. Don't even bother to try. That fool *Azul* has given you too much time, too many chances."

"Who are you? Besides Detritus, whatever that means."

"I am the one even specters fear. The one you will serve for eternity, to pay for what you did." Detritus moves, and it's like dirty water flowing across a road into a new puddle. "Ah, yes, I remember it well, even if you don't. Robbing one of their lifeblood, the most serious offense of all."

I struggle to pull myself back in time. Flashes—impressions more than memories—bombard me, all at once. Cold. Wet. Slippery. Still. My arms shoot out, grabbing, pulling, touching. My chest burns, breath bottled up inside, unable to escape. When I finally do suck in air, it's tinged with smoke, and I cough until my lungs could spit out of my mouth.

"As always. You let it slip away," Detritus breaks in. "Soon you will remember. But it will be too late."

A tendril of slimy, dirty white caresses my cheek, bits of the substance separating like fingers. "April eighteenth. Until then."

I awaken, soaked in sweat. The loft is hot, the fake fire still blazing. I throw back the covers, turn off the heat, and collapse to the floor in front of the window. The full moon bathes the back yard in silver, the creek a ribbon, a raccoon's mask visible by the water. My left hand dissolves first, followed by the rest of my body, until I'm cool mist floating through the window and into the moonlight.

I hover over the raccoon. "Life is so easy for you. A few years of washing your food, and nothing. No forever-after to worry about."

My spirit refuses to alight anywhere, mimicking the restless specters that roam ceaselessly for eternity. The moan I hear is coming from me, a low, sorrowful rumble filled with pain. Not sure if the dream-state memory is the same as self-awareness, but what Detritus said had the solid weight of truth. In his words, I robbed someone of their lifeblood. A fancy way to say I committed murder.

Who? Why? How? When? Where? I don't deserve answers, do deserve the consequence, even though the thought of eternal anguish sends tsunami ripples through my essence. I should go to Preston, right now, and beg him to save me. Even though I don't know what he or I have to do to make that happen. Hard to believe that sex could take away my offense—or my guilt. It's not like I can create a new life to make up for the one I took.

I will my spirit toward Royalty Ridge and Preston's mansion. It's as if there is wind buffeting me, although the bare tree branches are motionless. I'm pushed north instead of south, until I encircle a less elaborate dwelling. Kota's house. Curiosity sends me from the sky, through the wood siding, and into the interior. I take a moment to shake off the splintering effects of traveling through the solid frame of the house.

Kota's parents are asleep in a queen-sized bed, lying close, his front to her back. It's a sweet, simple scene that makes me long for such normalcy. And for love.

I float down the hall and through a closed door marked Indian Territory. Kota is curled up on one side, soft snores ruffling the long hair that lies over the side of his face. In sleep, he looks innocent and childlike; I wouldn't be surprised to see him sucking his thumb. The usual furrows on his forehead are smoothed out, his lips relaxed, the hurt in his eyes when he looks at me hidden behind lowered lids.

Without thinking, I slide down beside him in the bed, a ghostly embrace. My mist clings to his back, as his father embraces his mother. A brief frission of unease assails me, but soon I settle in.

Kota is shirtless. His skin is warm. His hair smells of shampoo.

I let a wisp of hand run through his hair, pulling it back from his face. "Kota. You scare me. And entice me." Is he the embodiment of something good—or evil?

Kota stirs and turns over. His eyes open, close, and snap wide.

I see the beating of his heart in the pulse at his neck, hear it thumping in my mind, sense its strength in my fingertips.

"I'm dreaming. This is a nightmare. I'm gonna wake up now." Seconds pass while Kota mumbles.

I don't move, not sure if it will cause me to materialize. How would I explain that? The moaning voice that belongs to my spirit self whispers, "I need help. I don't want to perish."

"I'm dreaming. This is a nightmare. I'm gonna wake up now." Kota repeats the mantra he must believe will banish me.

Again, I run a misty caress across his hair, letting myself dissolve completely into feeling rather than thinking. I do too much thinking, try to work all the angles, succumb to the fear. I have the urge to melt into him, to make us one. Not sex. A union, a melding, a…I don't know what.

Kota stares at my ghostly essence, as if looking into my soul. "I know you." His eyes struggle for recognition.

I need to go. Get out of here. Find Preston.

"Holy crap." Kota jerks his legs away from me.

I feel his movement in real-time. His skin is against mine, as my feet materialize first. They are solid, and that compact, warm heaviness of flesh is traveling up my legs. I have to leave. Fast. But I can't control myself.

"Summer?" Kota jumps out of bed. He breathes through his mouth, as if he can't get enough oxygen any other way.

"You're dreaming. This is a nightmare. You can wake up now." I repeat his words back to him, hoping I can ease from his warm sheets and drift away while he closes his eyes.

"What's happening?" Kota utters this under his breath.

I don't know how to reassure him, what to say.

"I don't belong here. There's nothing that interests me anymore. I'm losing my mind." He grabs the blanket and wraps it around his shoulders with trembling hands. His soul-baring admission shouldn't fit the situation, yet in the strangeness of it all, somehow it does.

"You're going to be okay." I try to imitate my ghost-voice—even though I'm now fully flesh—ease out of bed, and head for the door. He doesn't try to touch me or stop me. Once I reach the hall, I'm able to dissolve once more and float out of the house. I look back over my shoulder, expecting to see emptiness brightened by a nightlight.

Instead, Kota is in the doorway of his room. The blanket has slipped to the floor. His hands hang limp at his sides, one clutching his phone.

I turn back and disappear into the night. This time nothing prohibits my flight. I go to Preston's house, enter his room, and stare at his sleeping form. I'm not tempted into his bed. I don't want to feel his skin next to me. My body doesn't solidify. Detritus comes to my mind, with his threats and knowledge of me that even I don't possess. But I can't make myself do anything with Preston. At least not now.

With a sigh, I leave him and head back home. As I swoop through the wall, Finn comes out of the bathroom, pulling up his pajama pants. He stops, nods, and returns to his room.

I wait until my flesh is fully restored, go to him, and tuck the blanket around his little body. "Don't be afraid."

"I'm not." Finn grabs his threadbare, stuffed giraffe and hugs it to his chest. "You'll always come back, right?"

"Go to sleep. Everything's okay." I kiss the damp hair on his forehead, and my heart fills with simple, uncomplicated love for this little guy.

I get a glass of water, take it to my room, and sit it on the floor beside the futon, more for something to do than from thirst. A chill comes over me. I've killed someone. And I now know that in addition to the benevolent Azul, there is his opposite: Detritus. One desires my reconciliation. The other wants me destroyed. And I'm in the middle. The power to change my destiny lies within me. If only I can find the key.

LAUREL HOUCK

TWENTY-FOUR

Kota

I stand for what seems like hours—according to my phone, it's been ten minutes—staring down the hall. Where I either saw a ghost disappear or had a nightmare. With Summer in it. Starring as the ghost. I pick up my blanket and go back to bed. My pillow carries a faint, pleasant scent that doesn't belong to Mom's detergent, or to me. What the hell happened here? A shiver convulses my entire body.

Nighttime dark leaches into gray dawn as I lie with my hands beneath my head, pondering. The more I think about it, the more convinced I am that the world I thought I understood is only part of my reality. Summer appeared eight months ago out of nowhere, the girl with no name or history. Her eyes change color. She asked "Are you the one?" as if I should know what that means. And tonight, well, she haunted me. I never believed in ghosts and all that crap. But the soft mist that invaded my bed connected to me as only Summer could. I close my eyes at last.

"Kota, hurry up." Dad pounds on my door. "We're going to be late."

I get up, scratch my balls, and open the door. "It's Saturday. No school."

"You forgot what you're doing this morning?"

It hits me. "My drivers' test. Oh, shit, I mean, yeah, okay. Be ready in five." I pull on jeans from the floor, a blue sweatshirt with Fawn Valley Bucks on the front, and yank on my black Chuck Taylors. A quick pee, teeth brushed, hair braided on the run, and I'm good to go. I race to the front door and meet Dad in the driveway.

"Got your permit?"

"Yeah. In my wallet." I pull it out and show him.

He hands me the keys and gets in the passenger seat. "You've practiced, parallel parked more than your mother ever did, and know the rules of the road. You'll do great."

I drive to the DMV, register, and wait for the trooper who will go out with me. It doesn't take long, since we have an appointment. He makes me operate the windshield wipers, lights, and other equipment, then directs me to parallel park. I ace it. Out on the road, I'm careful with stop signs, red lights, and the three-point turn. We're only gone for fifteen minutes.

"Good job, Mr. Landis." The trooper checks off the final box on his form. "You passed."

I have my picture taken, get my temporary license, and catch up with Dad in the waiting room. "I got it." I hold up the proof. A pic of me looking like hell.

"Drop me off, and then you can take the car if you want." Dad smiles.

"Want? Oh, yeah." I climb behind the wheel and head for home.

Once I get the Mom-hug for passing and the Dad-lecture for driving by myself, I'm finally alone in the car. It's a minivan, not cool, but I'm not really caring. I steer through the Starbucks drive-through, get a tall chai latte, and head for…where? Marlie and I are through, Preston is an asshole, and Summer is…what?

"Summer is a ghost." I say it out loud; ridiculous.

But I have nowhere else to go. How pathetic. I park in the Sullivans' driveway.

A horn beeps behind me. Preston pulls in, his Mustang engine revving, blocking me in. I watch in the rearview mirror as he gets out and heads my way. "Finally got your big-boy pants on? I thought you were still driving your GI Joe Jeep."

"Great to see you, too." I get out of the van. "Just got my license. I can drive the GI Joe Jeep *and* your sister's Barbie car." I smile at him, waiting for his sarcastic reply that tells me he's happy for me. The old Preston-Kota thing. I've missed it in recent months.

Preston's eyes bore into me. "Why, exactly, are you at my girlfriend's house?" He glances aside as Summer joins us, drapes a possessive arm around her shoulders, brushes a kiss on her neck.

There's no good answer. If I tell him how much I want to see her, especially after last night, or that I want to share my big moment with her, he'll freak. My mind is a blank.

Summer glances in the van. "Did you bring the Starbucks?"

"Um, yeah." I open the door, grab the cup, and hand it to her.

"I have to give this to Jill, then I'll be back. Thanks for doing this, Kota. Moms can be a pain, right?" She heads for the house with my chai.

"So my mother called Mrs. Sullivan and told her I got my license. She asked me to stop at Starbucks for her on the way home." This sounds lame even to me, but it's all I've got. That, and a spot of warm inside that Summer sized things up and had my back with Preston.

Preston seems to weigh my words. "Just so we're clear that Summer belongs to me."

"Clear as mud." I temper my words with a sixty-watt fake smile, focusing on his car instead of him. "Hey, did you know your right front tire is going flat?"

"Crap." Preston examines the damage. "Looks like I

ran over a nail, and I don't have a spare. Tell Summer I'll be back soon." Preston gets in his car. "Be gone by then." He roars out of the driveway.

"He can be a prick." Summer has returned. "Sorry about your drink. Didn't want a scene." She is neutral, her face a pleasant mask. "Why did you come over?"

"I got my license." I leave off the part where she's the only person in the world I wanted to share it with.

"Great. Congrats." She turns to go.

"Wait." My brain flashes a warning light that my tongue ignores. "You came to my room last night."

Summer raises one eyebrow. "Excuse me?" Her eyes roil and end up a smoky shade of purple.

"You heard me. What are you? What's going on?" I hold my breath, wanting and not wanting an explanation.

"I'm a chick with little to no memory. And you're a guy with a drivers' license and an active imagination. That about covers it."

My insides feel like they're dissolving. I don't want to continue, can't stop. "No, you're a girl with a secret that's haunting you." The statement dangles, suspended between us. "I don't give a rat's ass where you came from, what you did, or who you are. I know there's something about me that freaks you out. Which is pretty messed up, since you're the one—" I stop, afraid to go too far and chase her away forever.

Summer looks around as if searching for an answer, a comeback, a solution to something I can't even imagine. She walks to a bench overlooking the creek, and sits.

I join her. This close, I smell the subtle scent left on my pillow during the night. The water is rapid from recent rain and the slight thaw that has melted some snow. There's a small waterfall that likely drips when summer dries things up. Right now there's a decent cascade that's mesmerizing. I could be a drop of water in that stream, ready to fall off the cliff into the unknown. "I have no purpose, not one I can identify. But there's an unmistakable nudge inside me to do *something*. And it all leads to you."

"Kota, I'm not like you—or anyone you know." Summer heaves an enormous sigh. "It's true that I don't know much about myself. What I do know is beyond bizarre. You wouldn't get it."

"Try me."

She never takes her eyes off the water. "Some people live and die. That's their story. They do things right and wrong and at the end, their souls find rest. That's the world you think you know. There's another dimension that's not as easy to understand. That's where I'm from."

"You're real. You're here." I lay my hand on her arm and feel the solid substance of her. "Last night you were different. But I recognized you anyway."

Summer nods.

"*Ouch.*" A hard pinch to my fingers has me jerking my hand away. Summer's bracelet—a weird snake thing—looks like a woven band. No rough edges. And yet it's as if the snake bit me. Two tiny pinpoints of red on my fingertip glisten with drops of blood. I suck my finger. I should tell her to get the stupid thing fixed, but I say nothing.

Neither does she, like she didn't even notice what happened. A deep, uncomfortable silence builds. Summer seems on the verge of speaking several times, stops to sigh, says nothing.

"It's okay. Whatever you want to tell me is safe." I can't take the quiet.

Summer takes a shuddering breath. "Fine. You want it? Here it is: I'm dead. A ghost. I don't know how long it's been since I lived and died. Or why I'm not able to rest. I did something wrong—very, very wrong—a lifetime ago. If I don't figure things out by April eighteenth, I'm lost forever." She finally looks at me. Her eyes are lifeless black, lusterless pupils that telegraph despair.

If anyone else had said this to me, I would have laughed and accused them of being drunk or high. Anyone else. Not Summer. Her flat voice, her chameleon eyes, her misty presence in my bed last night all testify to truth. I should run away, screaming, from the horror movie this seems to be. I can't. I don't want to leave, and I'm not afraid. "What can I do?"

"Nothing." Summer's expression doesn't change. "In another life we might have fallen in love. Who knows? But I don't have the time or luxury of feeling. Preston is the one who can save me. He doesn't know anything about all of this. But I know he's the only person who can make a difference."

"What if you're wrong? Maybe it's me, and you misread all the signs."

"Either way, I'll be gone in two months and three days."

We sit in silence, staring straight ahead.

"*Boo.*" Preston appears at Summer's side, the noise of the waterfall masking his approach. "Isn't this cozy?"

"Just leaving." I get up.

"Thanks." Summer doesn't look at me. "I'll try the formula when I do my math homework and see if it helps."

I get in the van and drive away, passing Preston's Mustang that's parked on the street. Guess he wanted to sneak up and catch me moving in on his girl. Except she doesn't really want me. And as for him, she only wants what he can give her. Release from here, rest there. As if I have a clue what that means. And yet, somehow, I totally get it. There's a pervasive guilt inside me, too. I realize with surprise that I can't remember a time before it was there. Is it about my adoption? My Native American blood? The time I ate most of a pecan pie and lied to Mom about it?

Home brings no respite from the restlessness that's taken hold of me. I like to solve problems. I hate things with no apparent solution. I sense that there's more to Summer than she knows or is willing to share.

No matter what she thinks or says, it's clear to me that I have a role in her story. And she in mine.

LAUREL HOUCK

TWENTY-FIVE

Summer

The calendar laughs at me as I flip from February to March. Finn's Valentine's Day box, which pulverized Evan's and Aiden's, is now in the basement. The heart-shaped container of candy from Preston has been eaten, the two dozen red roses long since dead. Kota, who wanted to help me, has kept his distance since the day he found out that I'm a ghost. That could be due to Preston's increasing presence—and pressure—in my life. Or maybe Kota finally had enough drama. I try to be glad he's leaving me alone. Not quite succeeding. Classic ambivalence.

And of course there's the pressing need to find out who I killed, why, and what to do to erase it from my tormented soul. Even I'm bored with the ongoing, unsolved mystery.

"There's something wrong with that man." Jill's whisper spirals up the stairs from the small greenhouse attached to the back of the house.

"He's a jerk. Plenty of those around. Don't...worry about it." Daniel, almost stuttering.

Jill, with a snort of disbelief. "What if he tries to hurt

her? You heard what he said."

I grab a shirt from the laundry basket and go downstairs, as if to iron. "What are you guys talking about? Sounds wicked scary."

A glance passes between Daniel and Jill.

"It's nothing." Daniel smiles. "Neighbors. Can't live with them, can't live with them."

Jill frowns. "It's not funny. Summer should know." She turns to me. "Mike's always been miserable, but he yelled at Finn earlier. And made some…comments."

I remember Mike the Moron waving his rifle at me—before I ghosted him and took the damn thing away. "I met him once. He's an idiot. Is Finn okay?" A wave of heat rises in my chest. Threaten me, who cares? I can't get any deader. But he better leave Finn alone.

Daniel doesn't meet my eyes. Just as well. Anger has colors all its own. I don't want him to see them. "He's fine. Worried about what Mike said about you."

"Mike told Finn to stay off his property and to keep the 'crazy girl' away from him, or he would do something about it." Jill glances out the greenhouse window, to where Mike's house is just visible through the still-barren trees. "If you see him, stay out of his way. We told Finn the same thing."

"Sure. No problem." I shrug, go in the basement, and iron my shirt.

Jill and Daniel go outside to rake leaves. I head back upstairs, get an apple from the bowl on the counter, and eat most of it before Finn runs into the house.

He waves. There's a blast of pee hitting the toilet, a flush, and he returns. "Did you hear about Mike?" Finn doesn't look at all scared. His eyes are shining. And his face is painted green and black, camo-style.

"Yeah, and that we're both to stay away from him and his property." I gesture to the sink. "Wash your face and hands. I'll cut up an apple for you." I get another piece of fruit and slice it while he lathers up with soap.

"Evan dared me to go to Mike's." Finn dries off and munches. "Everyone knows he's a nutcase—Mike, not Evan. So I did. It was *way* cool, Summer. Aiden helped with the camo. He and Evan followed me. I crawled through the woods on my elbows, like a Navy SEAL, and made it to Mike's stupid garden. Once I got inside the fence, I took the straw hat off the scarecrow and replaced it—" He gulps and grits his teeth.

"Replaced it with what?"

"Um, the hat you wear in the snow because it's not snowing now and you don't need it anymore and I didn't think you'd miss it and I'm really sorry."

The momentary thought, *my hat*, is soon replaced with a vision of a scarecrow in a pink knit cap. "Good one. Then what happened?"

"Not so good. Mike came out and saw me. He said some *really* bad words—Mom would never let me say them in my whole life—and started yelling about me getting off his property and keeping you away, too. Or else." Finn makes a slashing gesture across his throat. He finishes his apple and licks the juice off his fingers. "Don't tell on me, but I gave Mike the finger before I ran. Evan said it was the best dare ever."

"Finn, Mike's dangerous. Promise me you'll never go there again. No matter what your friends tell you to do." I grab his arm.

"Yeah, sure." Finn rolls his eyes. "You're as bad as Mom and Dad. But I'll listen to *you*." He glances at my wrist. "You've had that snake on your arm, since, like, forever. It's creepy."

"Preston bought it for me, and he likes me to wear it."

I don't share with this ten year old what I'm beginning to realize: Preston is controlling, volatile, and possessive. Maybe helping him to become a better person is my road to redemption. For murder. I shudder and look down. My hands, hands that took someone's life. My left hand dissolves at this thought.

"Hey, cool." Finn gets closer. "And your eyes are red. Let's go see Mike now. He'd totally pee his pants."

"We're staying away from him, remember?" I take in a breath, curl my tongue, and uncurl it as I breathe out. My hand returns to flesh. "I have a date, so I'll see you later. Your mom and dad are out back. Behave, little brother from another mother."

Finn bumps my fist. "Yeah, sure, big sister…" His forehead wrinkles in thought. "Big sister who plays Twister." He shrugs. "Sister's harder to rhyme than brother."

I grab sunglasses—really handy if my eyes decide to go crazy on me—a long-sleeved hoodie—in case my hand disappears again— and my cell phone—even though there's no one to call. I'm supposed to meet Preston at the mall, but decide to swing past his house and pick him up. He always drives. My turn to take some control.

It's a short ride to Royalty Ridge. Preston's house sprawls on the right. His Mustang is still in the driveway. Behind it is a MINI Cooper that looks brand new. Maybe a gift to his mom from his dad. They're always spending big money. I park at the curb and start across the manicured lawn, threading my way between tall pines.

The front door opens to Preston and Marlie. In each other's arms. The way they're going at it makes me wonder if his tongue is tickling her tonsils. She grinds against him. He pushes one hand between them and fondles her breast. They finally pull apart.

"Oh, baby, I'm still hot for you." Marlie isn't at all quiet about her needs.

"Not now. Be a good girl and run along. I have some business at the mall." Preston smacks her butt as she sashays toward what must be her car. "Another few weeks, and it's just you and me, babe."

I'm not sure what to do. Really, if Preston and Marlie want to screw their brains out, go for it. I'm not attracted to him at all. But I *am* in need of whatever magic he has that will solve my eternal dilemma. Nothing can stand in the way of that.

"Hey, Marlie." I step out from behind the Cooper. "Aren't you a little too hot for those pretty leather seats?"

"Summer." She stops, pulls her hair away from her sweaty face, and looks at Preston.

"I thought we were meeting at the mall." No explanation from Preston. In fact, he's more annoyed than concerned.

I wonder why I ever thought he was handsome or desirable. His skin looks unhealthy, there are furrows between his eyebrows, and his former carefree attitude is gone. *What is he to me? How will he help banish my guilt? What am I supposed to do?* My brain screams. I don't.

"Right. The mall. But I'm here, and so is she." I move away from the MINI.

"Get going, Marlie. We'll talk." Preston opens the door of her car, leans in to give her a casual kiss, and waves as she pulls away. He turns his attention to me. "Are you driving, or should I?"

"That's it? We're supposed to be dating, but you're practically screwing Marlie in your doorway. No apology? No break-up? No freaking human decency?"

"Not really." Preston looks at the Rolex watch on his wrist. "If we're gonna make a movie, we should leave now."

"Forget you. You're *so* not worth it." I turn to go, heart pounding. Am I throwing away my last chance to reconcile my soul? Is there something here I'm missing? What now?

A rough hand stops me and pulls me into the shadow of a towering pine. "It's really not that easy." Preston laughs in my face. "Dovie."

"Right, you surf the net, come up with a tiny bit of info, and hold me hostage to it. I don't think so." I grab at the snake bracelet on my wrist, intending to throw it in his smirking face. It won't come off. There's no clasp. It's a simple wrap thing, yet it's as if it's welded to my flesh. I

187

turn away, take a breath, and let my hand dissolve. I must get this thing off me. As long as I'm not flesh and blood, it should fall away. It encircles the mist.

"I'm hurt. I bought that for you." Preston feigns tears.

"Yeah, for five bucks." I give up. Later, I'll go to a jeweler, and they can cut it off.

"Not really. The bin at the Christmas barn had cheap trinkets. I had this lovely old piece in my pocket, ready to put on you when the time was right." He leans closer, and I get a quick whiff of rotten eggs. "You're almost mine, Dovie Critchlow." His voice is gravel and poison. I know that sound.

"Detritus?" Suddenly, I can see the black of his spirit, hidden beneath the polished form that I thought was Preston Burke.

"Ah, you recognize me. Good. I'm tired of playing adolescent games in this vain host. Sucking the lips off the delicious Marlie, holding hands with you, keeping that Neanderthal Kota at a distance. Quite tiring."

"Where is Preston?" I realize with a start that over recent months, the player who first approached me at school has been increasingly absent.

"Oh, I've made myself at home in his body." Detritus shrugs. "You seem to be the only one who noticed. Everyone else, even my BFF Kota, chose instead to think the worst of poor, dear Preston. What do you say we cut the crap, and you just come with me now? It will save us all a lot of heartache and trouble. You did the crime, now do the time." He cackles.

"I have six weeks left. I'm not going anywhere with you. And you better not hurt Preston." This time I manage to free myself from his grip.

"How sweet, trying to save the poor little rich boy. Forget him. Your own situation is quite dreary. And hopeless. After all these years, you still hadn't figured out your wicked deed, or your name, or anything else about your deplorable past, until I told you." Detritus sighs.

"You're almost out of time. But I can wait. Patience is one of my virtues."

"Leave me alone. I *will* figure things out. If I don't, then whatever." I feign a callousness I don't feel. My insides are shaking like there's an earthquake in my molecules. Throwing up, passing out, and splitting into tiny pieces all seem within the realm of possibility. He may be right—so far I've done nothing to save myself—but I refuse to give up early or easy.

"As you wish. I assume we won't be going out much anymore, but you won't have time to miss me. That bracelet marks you as mine. You can't take it off. Ever." Like the snake bracelet, his eyes become beady. His mouth opens, and a forked snake tongue flickers in and out. "Until April eighteenth, Dovie."

I back away.

Stumbling, the figure in front of me blinks his eyes and regains his equilibrium. "Summer?" Preston looks around as if awaking from a deep sleep.

"Are you okay?" I keep my distance, not sure if this is Detritus pulling a trick, or if he's left Preston alone for now.

"Yeah, sure. Did we have plans?" Preston scratches his head.

"Um, no. I just saw you and stopped to say hi. So, hi." I run to my car and lay rubber down the street. I drive until I reach Montrose Nature Preserve behind Jill's house. The small parking lot is empty. I don't even turn off the engine, but open the window to the cool breeze and put my forehead on the steering wheel. A tornado whirls inside me, picking up debris from my unknown past, my awful present, and my questionable future. Which isn't too far away.

"What am I supposed to do? Azul, you have to help me. Please."

Nothing, except the honking of a formation of geese overhead and the roaring in my ears. This is war. Me against my past and the powers of evil that want me to wallow in my guilt. Azul said there's a way out. I must find it. Soon.

TWENTY-SIX

Kota

Summer is at her locker. She's not with Preston. In fact, although I hadn't thought about it before, she hasn't been with him at all for a couple of weeks. And I would know. I've turned into a stalker, hiding in the crowd, lurking in the shadows, trolling two car lengths behind. Ever since I learned the truth about her. A truth that should have sent me running the other way, yet has done just the opposite. I wonder if my Native American mother gave me some vision-quest DNA that wants to commune with freaking spirits.

"Kota, my man." Preston breaks free of the stream of students passing by in the hall.

I search for what has become his default mode: sarcastic bastard. He looks pale, thin, and haggard. Very un-Preston. Still, better to be careful than get burned by his crap yet again. "Dude. 'Sup?"

"I don't know." Preston looks around as if seeing the school for the first time. "You have time to hang?"

Again, I search for the underlying snotty meaning. Can't find one. He looks like Preston of old, except maybe sick, or depressed. "Yeah, okay. Now?"

"Good. Thanks, man." Preston heads for the door leading to student parking. He passes Summer without a glance in her direction.

Summer shrinks back against the locker when she catches sight of him. Her eyes—pale brown morphing to black—turn to me. She practically melts into the locker— which, as a ghost, she probably can do if she wants. And she grips her books until her fingers blanch—more than usual.

"Hey." It's the first syllable I've spoken to her in two weeks. Ever since. Try not to go to the place where ever-since-what careens into happily-never-after. I pause; her scent makes my jeans tight. I follow Preston out the door.

Instead of heading for Eat 'n Park or Panera, Preston hits the drive-through at Starbucks, orders a grande mocha Frappucino for himself and a tall chai latte for me, and drives to Colson Creek. He parks off the asphalt with the hood toward the water.

"We gonna have a make-out session?" I laugh. This place is classic.

Preston stares at the bubbling creek, his coffee untouched. "Kota, something's wrong with me."

I wait, but there's silence. "Grades? Girls? Gonorrhea?"

"No, seriously." He turns hurt eyes to me. "Like I'm…losing my mind or something. I'm scared."

The last time Preston said "I'm scared" was in second grade at a showing of Godzilla in the park. I drink some chai. He's been such a dick for so many months, that this sudden change is suspicious. "Uh, like, what's going on?"

Preston runs his hands through his usually-perfect hair. It's oily, sticks out at odd angles, and hasn't been trimmed for a while. "Man, I wake up and have missed shit. Days, sometimes. Or I know I'm walking and talking, but it's like I'm watching from outside my body."

"Did you tell your parents?" Classic dodge.

"They're in Europe. Maria is staying in until they get

back, and she becomes the day maid again." Preston takes a deep breath. "I think I've totally screwed things up with Summer. And you. I don't know why—or what to do." Another deep breath ends in a wet sob. He covers his face with both hands, his body shakes, mucus runs from his nose.

"Hey, dude, no worries. We're good." I dredge a crumpled tissue from the bottom of my pocket and hand it to him. "End-of-the-year stress, that's all. But you could see your PCP, talk to her. Or come over and talk to my dad. He's okay."

A few minutes pass while Preston's tears subside. He blows his nose and tosses the soiled tissue and his full coffee cup out the window.

"You're messing up the park."

"Now you're an environmentalist as well as a Native American?" Preston turns the key, and the Mustang revs to life. His douchebag persona has returned. "Just messing with you. And you bought it. What a hoot. Wait until I tell Marlie." He glances at me. "Oops, hope you don't mind me sleeping with your former main squeeze. She *is* delicious."

My head is spinning, but I do believe one thing. Preston is losing his mind. What do they call that? Bipolar, maybe? "You can have Marlie. Hey, gotta get home. I have a paper due."

"I can have Marlie, and you want Summer, right? The old girlfriend switcheroo." Preston's voice is lower, filled with gravel as if he took up smoking and already destroyed his lungs.

"Sounds like a plan."

"I have a better idea. I'll do whatever I want with Marlie for now. But by this time next month, Summer will belong to me. Then maybe I'll come back for you. How do you like *my* plan?"

I keep quiet. It's dangerous to punch the driver of a moving vehicle, although my fist longs to sink into his smirking face. And to think I felt sorry for him two minutes ago.

"Nice chat." Preston drops me at my house and roars away.

"Asshole." I mutter under my breath, go inside the house, and make it to my room. My anger fades, replaced by a shaky sense of something being very wrong. It's more than Preston being a jerk. More than some mental health crisis. Preston isn't…Preston. Which makes him who, exactly?

I power up my laptop and search: mood swings in teen boys. Lots of stuff about being moody, cranky, symptoms of depression. Nothing fits with what I've seen in Preston. I think back to when it all started. His weirdness began when Summer appeared. And it's only gotten worse. Until today at Colson Creek. His breakdown had the ring of truth. Then the new and *un*improved Preston re-surfaced, spouting crap about Summer belonging to him.

"No. Get a grip, you moron." My words are hollow, very unsatisfying, as a bizarre thought occurs to me. "Gotta do it. No big deal. A computer search. That's all." I type in the search box: signs of demon possession. Until Summer, ghosts were stupid, demons phony, possession total B.S. Knowing that I'm attracted to a ghost, however, means all my prior ideas have to be shoved aside.

An hour of various sites educates me to the levels and signs of possession, what to do, who to ask for help. Most of it is sensationalistic garbage. Until I hit a new site: The Native American Medicine Man and Mysticism. I read several pages of a PDF file before shutting things down. I'm too tired to think. Preston possessed? I must have lost *my* mind. Just because shaman believed it to be not only possible, but a reality, doesn't mean someone I know is affected. That's old school. Baloney. Ridiculous.

I lie down on my bed. A quick nap, dinner, then that paper to do for English lit…

"You are confused." A blobby blue figure floats in front of me.

"And who are you? Besides a fat nightmare." I look around at the strange, cloudy landscape, where I'm weightless, drifting, unanchored.

"I am Azul. I cannot help you. Or her, now. You must understand. She must remember." Azul's voice chills me. Each word oozes sorrow.

"Understand what?"

"Yourself. Because once you know, and she knows, reconciliation is possible."

"Look, I'm taking a nap. Then I'm going to eat Mom's meatloaf with gravy, which sucks even when I'm hungry. After that, homework." I blink and try to awaken.

"You suspect that your friend is no longer your friend. You know that Summer isn't Summer. The spirit world has been introduced. Shake its hand." Azul pulsates. "Keep your friends close and your enemies closer."

"Old quote, dude. Not Yoda-worthy stuff." If I accept that this dream is real, I'm ready to be locked up. Must stop dreaming.

"You will awaken soon. But I am real. The situation is dire. Summer needs you—but she has misinterpreted the signs. Go to her. Make her listen. Provide what she needs." Azul begins to fade.

"What does she need?" I reach for Azul, suddenly terrified to be left alone in this place.

"She needs you."

"Kota, dinner." Mom.

Thank goodness.

I struggle to sit up. Naptime is over. Meatloaf is on the way. "Coming." I use the bathroom, flush, and spend more time washing my hands than necessary. The aftermath of the dream won't leave me. I'm in my house, I just peed in my toilet, the face in the mirror is the same one I always see. But a sharp, painful awareness is lodged in my gut. It confirms what I've suspected all along.

Summer and I, for whatever reason, are meant to be together. I now have proof of that. If you count dreams as proof. My ancestors did. But I don't know them, so no help there.

Dinner doesn't take long. No second helping for Dad or me, and Mom has a meeting at the library. A five-minute cleanup in the kitchen gets me props from both parents, well worth it. Because I need time alone. Instead of sitting around moping about Summer and wondering what the hell is going on, Azul—dream guru—has spurred me to action.

I type "ghosts" in Search and am rewarded with 40,700,000 sites. Too general. I try "real ghosts" and it shoots up to 62,800,000 hits. *Crap. Okay, how about "helping a ghost to rest?"* This time it's a manageable 13,200,000 helpful websites. Right. I give up and start clicking through those that appear semi-legit. Two weeks ago, I wouldn't have thought anything to do with ghosts was real. Now I'm trying to save one. Go figure.

Nothing is useful. No mention of anyone named Azul, unless you count its meaning of blue in Spanish and hello in Tamazight, whatever that means. Since it's Wikipedia, it might not even be true. The other stuff is a mixture of voodoo, sorcery, and nonsense. I smack my desk. "Hasn't anyone ever dealt with a real ghost before, you stupid freaking machine?"

As if in answer to my insult, or maybe the jarring of the desk, the screen goes black. It blinks, flashes, and opens to a new site. There's no name at the top. The page is split down the center with a jagged line. One side is a pale blue background with words in Corsiva Handwriting font, the one I use to make cards for Mom to avoid paying at Hallmark. The other side is red, the words printed in a font as jagged as the virtual tear on the page.

I start with what looks like the good news side. "Hope never ends. As long as there is breath, and courage, and fortitude, fight on. The power of the shadows cannot prevail against the strength of the light until the final sand has run its course toward eternity. Look deep within, mine your soul, find the answers—and you will find peace for all."

The other side is bad news. "Death is final. Darkness swallows up light, extinguishes hope, shreds eternity. The doomed shall roam forever in the gloom of perpetual night. Eternal wandering is the final stop. Look no further, accept the consequences—and let go."

A strange sense of something very wrong takes hold of me. I re-read the good news. Is it saying that to save Summer I have to look within myself for answers? I get up and pace around my room. How can *I* answer *her* questions? And yet, the unease in my gut has less to do with Summer than with me. Is there something I need to do for myself? How does helping me help her? Or is this just another wacko website? I go back to the computer, but the site is gone. I can't even find it in my browser history.

I pull on a jacket and go out back to the old Adirondack chair that Dad never put away before winter hit. It's covered with bird crap, who cares? I sit and stare into the woods behind the house, as if answers will come from behind a tree and smack me in the head.

When nothing happens, I attempt to look "deep within". And realize there's not much there. Beyond faded newspaper clippings, my own background is one big question mark. Would my birth mother have had answers for me? *Why did she have to die?* As my brain hits the word, die, a chill racks my body and a sob burbles to the surface. My mother died. *No'yeg.*

That word. Again. I pull out my phone and search for Native American translations. *No'yeg,* as I suspected, means mother. How did I know this? Maybe if I think harder, I'll come up with the secrets in my soul. And the way to free Summer before it's too late. For her. Or is it for me?

TWENTY-SEVEN

Summer

"Can I come along?" Finn arranges his features in the most engaging way possible.

I don't want to take him, shouldn't have mentioned it. For some reason, I have to go back to Hannastown. There's something there. I felt it on the school trip, and ever since, the mere thought or mention of the site sends chills up and down my spine. *So* not taking Finn to a place where there could be trouble.

"You're coming with me." Daniel smiles over his son's head. "We have to get our fishing licenses today. Trout season starts on April twelfth."

"But it's only March twenty-first." Finn shows Daniel the date on his phone. "We have weeks and weeks to do that. I want to go with Summer."

"No, it's cool." I ruffle Finn's hair. A pang shoots through me. Only twenty-eight days until I have to leave him. For good. "We can get ice cream tonight. If you eat your salad, for a change."

"Milkshakes?" Finn, bought off by Dairy Queen. Cheap date.

"Sure. Whatever." I wave as he grabs his fishing hat. Guess buying a license requires the proper gear. What a cutie.

Daniel and Finn leave, I grab a lightweight hoodie, and steer the car east on Route 22. Hannastown doesn't open to the public until May, but by then I'll be...somewhere else. Today I won't be able to visit the cabin, use the restroom, or buy something at the gift shop. But I'll have the open-air part to myself, without docents to interfere. Not sure what I'll find. Maybe nothing. The absolute urgency in my gut propels me forward, foot heavy on the gas pedal, hoping the cops are all at Dunkin' Donuts.

A few turns off the highway, thread the car through rolling hills on two-lane asphalt, turn into the small, unpaved parking lot. The place is deserted. No cars, no bikes, no people. Perfect. I get out and pull on my hoodie as the sun hides behind a cloud and the air nips at me. I wander around, trying to imagine it as the docent described: three busy taverns, thirty permanent families on twelve acres, travelers coming to be heard in court. And the fort, then a looming symbol of safety for the colonial frontier. Can't believe I remember the docent's spiel so well. Too well?

The wind changes in an instant, cool to hot. My skin sprouts beads of sweat. I take off the jacket and roll up the legs of my jeans. Should have brought water. I glance at a trough the rain has filled. The surface is flat, reflecting high clouds overhead and the tips of trees that are in spring bloom. As I watch the reflection, the branches become summer-heavy with leaves—time-lapse photography in action.

I can't look away from the water. It beckons me. I drop to my knees in front of the trough and plunge my head beneath the surface. Although not cool, the wet is refreshing. It seems to hum through my ears, encircle my brain, caress my cheeks. The need for breath jerks my head out of the water. I stand, tripping on the hem of a long skirt. *Where are my jeans?* I'm totally dry. Even my hair.

"Good day." A man in a buckskin jacket, brimmed hat, and carrying a long rifle leads a horse to the trough.

I spin around. There are many people on the dusty road, the women in long skirts, the men in breeches and homespun. Cabins dot the landscape behind three taverns that appear to be doing a brisk business.

"Are you well, young miss?" The rifleman doffs his hat. "Best get out of the hot sun and find a draft of sweet cider." He appraises me when I don't respond. "Do you live here? Are your people nearby?"

"This is Hannastown." I manage to squeak this out.

"Indeed." He nods.

"And the year is…"

Although his eyes narrow, he nods again. "It is 1782, in the year of our Lord."

"Thank you." I curtsy—*curtsy?*—and walk away.

The scent of animal dung is strong as I make my way through town, dodging people and horses. Everyone is going somewhere, except for me. What just happened? I didn't materialize, so this isn't my usual mode of transport. I'm wide awake, so it's not a dream. And something else is wrong, but I'm not sure what it is. I stop under a leafy tree to escape the heat. It's 1782, and must be summer, judging by the temperature and humidity. A rumble of thunder rolls through the sunlight.

"Hello." A girl, maybe eleven or twelve years old, holds out a redware cup. "Would you like a drink of water?"

Not sure what to do. Thirst makes the decision. "Thanks." I take the proffered cup and empty it in one long gulp. Handing it back, I notice I am eye to eye with the girl. We aren't tall.

"I'm Peggy." She giggles and hides her smile behind her hand.

I look down at myself. The snake bracelet still encircles my wrist, but nothing else is the same. I'm wearing a long, linen dress covered with a homespun apron that reaches

201

the tops of tied leather boots. It's 1782. I'm shorter than when I drove up to Hannastown. And it all comes together. "My name is Dovie Critchlow." I study Peggy's twin braids, bonnet hanging down the back of her neck, and sweet smile. This is the girl I imagined...saw...on my field trip here. The one who will die during an upcoming Seneca raid. "Peggy Shaw, right?"

"You do not live here." Peggy is sure of this, guarded at my knowledge of her.

"No. I saw you before, and someone told me your name."

"It was likely Paul Hadley. He tells *everything*. And he pulls my braids." Peggy giggles yet again, her default mode. "But someday I'm going to marry him. Why are *you* here?"

There is no good answer to her question. Why, indeed?

"Dovie, there you are. Land sakes, child, you almost put me in my grave."

The voice brings instant tears to my eyes. I turn to the sound and wrap my arms around the tall, spare woman who spoke. "*Mama.*" She smells as I suddenly remember: faint sweat, lavender, and lye soap. I cling to her, unwilling to be separated ever again. "Mama. I've missed you so much."

She sets me away from her and laughs. It's like music. "I love you, too, Miss Priss, but it has only been a few minutes since I left you." She shakes one finger at me. "You were told to wait by the trough. I know you are twelve years old, but we are in the company of strangers."

"Sorry, Mama." But I'm not sorry about anything. This is my mother. After what seems to be over two hundred years, I can't get enough of her. I hold on to a fold of her dress. "I'll stay with you."

"See that you do." Mama fumbles in a fabric bag and pulls out a sheaf of papers. "I have to appear before the court this afternoon."

"Court?" Did she do something wrong? Is that the burden I've carried with me for so long?

"That is why we came, after all, to settle the deed to our land now that Papa has passed." Mama looks around. "Now where did that child get to? We have a few moments to sup before my appointed time. But only a few."

I notice that Peggy has long since wandered away. Is that who Mama is looking for? A niggling memory tickles my brain. Another child...how could I ever forget? "Where is he? Where's Trey?"

I turn to a tapping on my left shoulder. No one is there, so I spin the other way. Trey's grin puts the sun to shame. Freckles sprinkle his sunburned nose, fair hair hangs into his green eyes, a dimple puckers his cheek.

"Ha, ha, I got you." Trey runs around me in circles, raising little clouds of dust.

I grab him on his way past and smother his sweaty hair with kisses. He is redolent of salt, tobacco, and a hint of peppermint. "My baby brother. Oh, Trey, my sweet, sweet Trey." Tears mix with his sweat until I taste the salt.

"I am *not* a baby." Trey stomps his booted foot and squirms against me, his voice muffled in my apron. "I am ten years old and the man of the family since Papa died."

"Where have you been?" Mama pulls him away from me by his ear. She sniffs in his direction. "Up to no good, I am thinking."

Trey shrugs. "I went looking for the privy. The man behind the counter in the tavern gave me a peppermint to help him with the tobacco pouch."

I reach for my brother and mother and pull us together.

Mama gives me a brief hug before stepping back. "Dovie Critchlow, what is the matter with you today?"

"I love you both. So much." I know I'm blabbering, teary, clingy. My heart is bursting with love for my family. Even the words "my family" make me want to dance. We're together again. Nothing else matters.

I follow Mama—who keeps a firm grip on Trey—to

the tavern. We're seated by a window with wavy glass. Flies buzz around platters of food the server brings to the plank table. Pewter mugs are filled with cool water. I don't recall ever enjoying a meal so much. It's not the food. It's sharing the time with those I love best. "If Finn and Kota were here, this would be perfect."

"Who is Finn?" Trey talks around a mouthful.

Mama's fork stops halfway to her mouth. "Kota? Is that not a Seneca name?"

Too late I realize I spoke what I was thinking. And wonder why those thoughts of loved ones included Kota. "They're no one. Just a joke."

Mama's hand shoots to my forehead. "Are you ill? You are not yourself today, Dovie."

"No, I'm cool—fine." I may be twelve and in the era of my true birth, but my thoughts and words are twenty-first century.

No way to explain that, no need. I'm ready to remain my real age and grow up in this century. On our farm. With our horse, and the chickens, and Mama baking bread in the stone oven out back, and me playing hoops with Trey, and swinging on vines into the creek. Memories assail me, all good, save for the day Papa caught the fever and left us.

"A hot day, to be sure." The red-faced serving woman gathers our plates. "Knew this July would be bad, the way the flies swarmed early."

Something she says makes the food in my stomach turn to fire. "It's July?"

"All month long, Dearie."

"And what's the date?"

Mama gives me a strange look. "Are you certain you are not ill?" At my headshake she says, "It is July thirteenth, 1782." She opens her pouch to pay for our meal.

This is the day. Words shoot through my brain: Seneca raid, Hannastown burned, *danger*. According to history, only Peggy Shaw got killed, I remember that. But since we're passing through and no one knows us, we could die, burn up, and not be counted among the missing. I have to get my family—*Mama, Trey*—to safety before it's too late. Before…I lean over and vomit on the floor as the import of the date hits me.

This is the day. This is the day. This is the day I die.

TWENTY-EIGHT

Summer

"Get moving." Mama shooes us out of the tavern, after she makes certain I'm not truly sick and pays extra to clean the floor.

"We have to leave. Go home. Now." I repeat what I've been saying since throwing up my lunch. "Something bad is going to happen here. I can feel it. Please, you have to believe me."

"Heat has got a hold on you. No need to fret. Soon as I see the judge, we can be gone." Mama looks straight at me. Her eyes soften. "You are my good girl, little Dovie. I have loved you since your Papa cut the cord and handed you to me—all red and wrinkled and wailing louder than a newborn lamb. I have to make sure the farm goes to you and Trey, and now is my only chance to do that. So care for your brother while I take care of business."

I know that look. And maybe, no matter what I say, I can't prevent what's going to happen. "I promise to take care of Trey. I won't let anything happen to him." I cross my heart with my pointer finger. "So help me."

Mama laughs. "He listens to you better than to me. I

won't be long. Wait under the oak tree." She kisses me and swats Trey as he turns his cheek from her. "No sass, Trey, you hear? Mind your sister."

I watch her walk away, my heart as heavy as the weight of humanity is to my ghostly form. I turn to my brother and hold both of his hands. "Trey, you *must* listen to me. If I say run, you run. If I say hide, you hide. If I say—"

"If you say eat a peppermint, I'll eat a peppermint." Trey interrupts me with a grin.

"This is serious."

He opens his mouth, searches my eyes, and his jaws snap shut.

I hold his hand, and we walk to the shade of the big old oak. My heart pounds, waiting, waiting for...what? War whoops? Silent tomahawks? The zing of arrows? I survey the strange scene of living, breathing history, wondering where to hide. The town will be burned, so taking refuge inside the cabins won't help. The streets and fields are too exposed. The fort, *yes*, the fort. It's here to protect people. We'll wait for Mama there and hope she finds us before all hell breaks loose. Maybe this isn't the day I died after all.

I gesture ahead. "We're going to the fort."

"Mama said to wait here."

"And she also said to listen to me."

Before I can take a single step, a gunshot rings out, then several more.

Trey jumps.

I pull him behind me and shrink against the bark of the tree. People run toward the fort. We join the crowd. There's pushing and shoving as everyone seeks shelter. I keep a firm grip on Trey's hand and drag him along. I'm too short to see over the heads in front of me, not sure how close we are to safety. And then the small, sweaty hand in mine is gone.

"*Trey. Trey.*" My shouts are lost in the screams, gunfire, and pounding of feet on packed earth. I take a deep breath to stave off the panic that makes me stupid. He can't be that far. He was just here. But where? *"Trey."*

My peripheral vision catches sight of Kota. Thank goodness. Kota will help me. But when I turn to look, it's not Kota at all. It's an Indian holding a tomahawk in one hand and a rifle in the other. I stop. Without Trey, I might as well be dead.

The crowd has thinned as the fort absorbs those swarming into it. I glimpse Trey on the other side of the road, hiding behind the trough. I pivot and head for him, diving beside my brother as a bullet zings past my head.

Between the fort and us, the road fills with Indians. They have powerful, shirtless torsos, loincloths, leggings, and moccasins. Their heads are shaved with one scalp lock, faces painted white with black, perpendicular stripes. In their hands are a variety of weapons: rifles, bows, quivers of arrows, clubs, spears, and knives. The noise they make is thin and eerie in its ferocity.

"They are closing the gates." Trey whispers in my ear.

The doors to the foot are, indeed, closing. There's no way we can get inside now. The acrid scent of burning wood and the sucking rustle of flames starts behind us. Looking over my shoulder, I see the tavern ablaze and a cabin being lit with a torch. I can't think. Should we risk it and make a run for the fort? Head the other way? We can't stay here, barely hidden behind the trough.

"Papa, Papa." The cry of a small child pulls my attention back to the road. A little boy is running hard away from the fort. From the shadows, an Indian raises his rifle.

One gate slips open. Peggy Shaw rushes from the protection of the stockade fence. She gathers the child into her arms and races back toward the fort. She's almost there when a shot rings out, and she collapses. Arms pull her and the boy inside, but not before I see the blossom of red blood soaking her white apron. And know she won't survive.

We have to move. "Come on." I take Trey's hand and

ease out of our meager hiding place. Instead of running, we move from tree to bush, trying to blend in with the landscape. Down a low grade, I spot a stone facing. I remember this place from the school tour. It's a springhouse, where cool spring water was used to preserve food. I wait and watch for a moment when there are no dark eyes upon us, and drag Trey down the hill.

We enter the small, shadowed enclosure together. Damp and dank, it smells of mold and earth. The water is waist-high and cold, so cold. Perfect to keep milk and cheese fresh. Perfect to hide two children. I wade as far from the entrance as possible, hugging the slimy stone walls, Trey by my side. The water comes up to his chest. His quick, rapid breaths make tiny ripples. Very little sound penetrates, but the scent of burning wood gets worse.

Trey chokes. "The smoke." Tears run down his cheeks, maybe from smoke, maybe from terror. His eyes are wide, and his dimple is gone.

I hug him close, feeling the tremors that rack his thin body. Or maybe it's me that's shaking. My feet become numb from the cold. How long do we stay in here? When will it be safe to come out? How will I know? Did Mama make it to the fort in time? Will she search for us? Too many questions, but they keep the fear at bay.

Trey's head, leaning against me, comes up. He nods toward the square of light at the opening.

I hear guttural words spoken that I don't know, yet somehow understand: "*Wadigusa wea.*" It is finished. There is a whispered reply, then silence.

"Can we leave now?" Trey's teeth are chattering.

I shake my head and put one finger to my lips.

Moccasins and legging-clad legs appear, blocking some of the light. Their owner pauses.

I put my mouth against Trey's ear and whisper, "If I pull you underwater, hold your breath. Don't move or make a sound." I shouldn't take the time or make more words, but I have to add, "I love you."

Trey jerks his head away from me, grabs my shoulders and reaches up until he can whisper, "I love you, Dovie."

Brown hands, holding a long, jagged knife, signal that the time has come. Soon an inquisitive set of brutal eyes will search our hiding place. They simply *cannot* find us.

I nod to Trey and take a deep breath.

Trey closes his eyes, takes a breath, and pinches his nose closed. He surrenders to my encircling arms.

We sink below the water together. The cold closes in over our heads. And my heart.

Although I can feel Trey's fine tremors and his heart beating like a baby bird's, he doesn't move or make a sound.

With my eyes open under the water, I see feet. I feel the water displaced by the Indian's presence. He stands very still. Doesn't leave.

Go away. Please, go away. My lungs begin to burn, hot, suffocating, yearning for air. There's a pulsating in my head, a rhythmic mental heartbeat. *Thump, thump, thump.* I concentrate on this and try to ignore the need to breathe.

In my arms, Trey starts to struggle. Little movements, panic-borne disobedience that could get us killed. I tighten my grip on him and place my hand over his nose and mouth. It can't be much longer. There's no way the Seneca can see us or know we're here. Unless we make our presence known. No more than thirty or forty seconds have passed since we submerged, but it seems like a lifetime.

Spots appear before my eyes, and I feel my grip loosen on Trey. He behaves—no sass, as Mama said—and I manage to hold on another second or two before I *simply must breathe.* I rise to the surface, still holding on to Trey, and suck in deep mouthfuls of the smoke-tinged, fusty air. My lungs heave in and out, in and out as I search for any sign of our enemy. He is gone.

Careful, I whisper to Trey, "We did it. He's not here

anymore."

Trey doesn't reply. He's limp, neck flaccid, eyes open and rolled back in his head. His lips are blue. The little chest that seconds ago was heaving is now still.

"Trey?" I poke him. His head lolls in the water. Louder, "Trey, wake up. Please, *wake up*." I shake him. I'm alive. He is not.

Heedless of what lies outside the springhouse, I pull Trey's suddenly heavy body out onto the grass. We're exposed in the open air, vulnerable. One cabin nearby has escaped the flames. I move behind Trey's head, put my hands under his armpits, and drag him across the rocky ground to the log house.

"Trey, it's safe here." I gather my brother to me and rock back and forth, keening softly, not wanting to alert the Seneca raiders, but unable to hold in the grief any longer. "Trey, I'm sorry. I'm sorry I'm sorry I'm sorry." Under my sobbing words run the litany of my thoughts. *I killed you I killed you I killed you.*

A sound that is almost inaudible checks my tears. I look up into a face so like Kota's that fear and relief collide in my belly. The Indian holds a tomahawk in one hand, the gleaming blade slick with red. In the other hand he holds a flaming torch.

"Hanisse 'ono."

"No. I am not the devil." Nor do I speak his language, but the menace and meaning come through somehow. I look at Trey's body on the floor beside me and suddenly don't care what happens. And besides, I know the end of this story. I die. Right after I kill my brother. So I deserve whatever is coming. I deserve all the pain, fear, horror this man can heap on me. For what I've done. And for spending centuries not even remembering it. Not even remembering Trey.

I stand and hold out my arms.

The Indian rushes me, a loud cry splitting the air, his weapon slashing forward. It's a cliché of slow motion. As he gets close I smell coppery blood, smoke, sweat-stink. He ignites the homespun curtains on the windows, and with a sudden whoosh, an inferno from hell surrounds us.

My twelve years don't flash before me. I don't move. I don't close my eyes. Instead, I focus on Trey's face, sweet, still, forever ten. It's the last thing I see before the sharp bite of the blade takes my breath forever.

TWENTY-NINE

Summer

My eyes open. I am soaking wet. My head is pounding. "Trey? Mama?" I turn in a circle, heart pounding, waiting to be attacked again, maybe more brutal this time. Where is everyone? Things look different. The cabins are back, but fewer, and no sign of the raging fires. At my feet is the trough where Trey and I hid, but it's new and only half-full. The stockade fencing is new, also, and there's no real fort, only an empty enclosure.

I look down at jeans clinging to my legs and the cotton of an Old Navy T-shirt plastered to my body. Confusion flickers in my brain, and with it, my left hand disappears. I died. A long time ago. Trey died. I don't know what happened to Mama. It all comes roaring back, accompanied by so much pain that I double over, right hand clenched across my stomach.

Azul now has his wish: I remember what I did, my grievous sin that has left me unreconciled for over two hundred years. I killed my brother. If I hadn't held my hand over his nose and mouth, he might have surfaced, caught a quick breath, and stayed under longer. It's my fault. Total. Complete. Irrevocable. I don't deserve eternal rest.

"Hey." A deep, inflectionless voice.

I swing around. One of them is still here. His Seneca features are a blank canvas, punctuated by dark, slightly oblique eyes, the irises surrounded by a narrow ring. High cheekbones and ruddy skin are the same as the Indian with the knife who took my life. And would have taken Trey's, had I not done so first. The only difference is the hair. Instead of a scalp lock, this one has a dark braid. It reminds me of Peggy Shaw's braided hair, she who was shot and killed. By the Seneca.

My mind can't cope with the sight of this monster. "*Murderer.*" I leap at the Seneca Indian standing less than two feet away. My left hand returns to aid the right as I pummel his face, kick him in the balls, scratch at his eyes. I hear horrible, awful words spewing from my mouth in rhythm with my attack.

He falters, grabs his crotch, and retches, but doesn't go down or pull out a weapon. He fends off my blows but doesn't fight back. His scent is citrus-sweet, no hint of blood, smoke, or sweat. "Summer, *stop*. You're safe."

Weakness assails me as the sobs come and tears cloud my vision.

Instead of taking advantage of this, the Seneca catches me as I fall. He carries me to a grassy hillock and places me on the ground. His hands smooth the hair away from my face. He murmurs, "Summer, it's okay. I won't hurt you. It's okay. Summer, I'm here."

Then I know him. "Kota." I brush off his hands and sit up. A quick glance at the bottom of the hill almost sends me spinning off again. It's the springhouse. Where Trey died. I hold it together with great effort. I try to stand, but notice the lower half of my body has vaporized; my head and torso are hovering a foot above the grass.

"Right. Kota." He gives me space, looks toward the field behind us.

"I'm sorry. I…thought you were one of them."

"You mean part of a Seneca raiding party?" He says this with heavy sarcasm.

"Yes."

Silence reigns between us. I've offended him, I guess, but tough shit. Who is he to have such a thin skin about present-day, when his ancestors butchered my family? A whisper echoes inside of me: *You killed Trey, not them.*

"What happened?" Kota turns to me.

"Why are you here?" His presence has turned the chill into a cold sweat.

"I asked you first." He moves away from me a bit, seeming to sense my discomfort.

"I came to look around."

"And then?" Kota stares at me. All sarcasm is gone.

I suspect, from the flicker in his eyes, that mine must be roiling with color. My eyeballs feel pulled outward as if they could bore into the kindness and concern I see in him. He already knows I'm a ghost. Why not spill the rest?

"You can tell me anything. Maybe I can't help, but I can listen." Kota watches me.

I shake my head to clear it. The need to share what happened is too strong to ignore. "I came here to look around. Somehow…" In the normal-looking daylight, what I have to say is too fantastic to believe. If Kota doesn't understand, so what? "I went back to the day Hannastown was attacked. I saw my mother. I killed my brother…kept him from crying out and smothered him. A Seneca killed me."

Kota nods. "So that's what you did that's haunted you. Your brother's death."

My silence is assent. I can't speak over the stricture in my throat.

"Were you a kid?"

"Twelve years old." I choke out the awful details of what happened.

"Seems to me you were trying to save his life. Neither

of you were getting away. At least he died in your arms, which had to be a comfort to him." He pauses, reaches for my hand, then pulls back. "Now I understand why you've always been afraid of me. But Summer, it *wasn't* me. Maybe an ancestor, but who knows? After so long, I can't be responsible for what happened. And I would never, ever hurt you."

Kota's logic is annoying. "My head understands that. My heart...I'll work on it."

"Since you know what's causing your guilt—misplaced, if you ask me—are you going to *Preston* to make it better?"

With the word Preston, the snake on my wrist seems to constrict. Detritus has taken over everything about poor Preston. What does that mean to me? Now that I've remembered my offense, does my salvation lie in freeing Preston from Detritus? Knowing the cause of my dilemma isn't the same as knowing the solution. How much do I tell Kota?

"It's complicated. But I have to believe there's something connected to Preston that I must do to be reconciled."

"You don't have much time." Kota clears his throat. "I don't mean to tell you how to manage eternity, but just consider this. What if it's me that can save you?"

"You're the enemy." I see the quick hurt. "Were."

"Exactly. It's perfect. My ancestors caused you pain. And through me that pain will be taken away." Kota, again with the logic.

"That's too easy. Unless you know something I don't. But thanks for trying." Talking has taken the edge off my terror and grief. My lower body materializes. I stand. "I'm going to walk around for a few, then go home. You never answered my question. Why are you here?"

Kota gets up. "I'm not sure. I was just hanging out and the thought popped into my head: go to Hannastown. And I saw my mother opening the shed to get out the porch furniture, a job I wanted to avoid." He laughs, then sobers.

"I had to be here. After what you told me, I think some force of nature sent me to you."

Azul. Not a force of nature, but still trying to help me, even at this late date. That has to be the real explanation, but not one I can tell Kota. That he accepts me as a ghost is more than I could have hoped for. As far as I know—which isn't all that much—I've never admitted that to another living soul. But to drag him into the whole spirit world thing, no way he'd handle that. And in spite of my misgivings about him, Kota is a decent kid who should have a decent life after I'm gone. In three weeks.

"Do you want to be alone? 'Cause I can take off." Kota takes his car keys out of his pocket.

"Your choice."

Kota doesn't answer, but he doesn't leave. The keys are tucked away.

I descend the hillock and peer into the springhouse. It has been repaired, and there is still water in it, but it's shallow now. I close my eyes and remember Trey's small voice. *I love you, Dovie.* Can't linger here. We walk past the cabins, the trough, and cross the road. There's a stone plaque inside the stockade fence with Peggy Shaw's story on it. It doesn't begin to tell about the sweet little girl with the shy smile who got shot for helping another kid.

Kota by my side here is fine. He isn't the enemy. But as I look at the snake on my wrist, I'm still convinced it's Preston who holds the key to my eternal rest. It's only fair to tell Kota.

"You must be exhausted." Kota's hand grazes my face.

I notice he has a few scratches on his cheeks and a bruise at his temple. "Sorry for losing it. You should put ice on that bump and some antibiotic ointment on the scratches."

"Yeah, whatever. No big deal." He keeps touching me.

The mesmerizing feel of his fingertips on my skin could put me to sleep standing up. I move closer to him and close my eyes. Without meaning to, my lips part and seek his. Our mouths connect, not in a flurry of tongues and spit, but soft and gentle, almost weightless. I don't know how long we stand together. Could be seconds, maybe minutes. What I do know is that my heartbeat is normal, the fire in my gut has been extinguished, the throbbing of my head has ceased.

"Summer." Kota breathes my name, like a prayer.

My hands slip around him and catch his braid. I finger the coarse hair; it tickles. His heart thumps against the right side of my chest, while mine beats inside the left. We're so close together that it's as if I now have two hearts instead of one. I pull away, fighting the impulse to separate from him, even as I recognize the necessity of doing so..

"Kota, if I had more time, or if I was truly alive…" I shrug. "But that's not the way it is. My destiny lies with Preston, for whatever cosmic reason. I don't get it any more than you do, but I know it's true. There's no time for what I want in earthly terms, because soon this option will be over for me. Thank you for being my friend."

"I get it. But I still think you're wrong. If things don't work out, I'll be here for you." He gives me a small, sad smile and strides toward the parking lot.

I hear his engine turn over, gravel spits from under his tires, and silence descends on Hannastown once again. It's time to leave. The only ghost left here is me.

THIRTY

Kota

I should have told Summer about my dream—Azul—and my suspicion—Preston possessed. What if she gets into trouble because I was afraid to talk about stuff that's too bizarre to believe? She told me about being a ghost and traveling back in time, and I can't mention a freaking dream? Guess I know who has the balls around here.

Which makes me think of that day when she kicked me in mine. Although it's been two weeks since then, my stomach turns over, and I imagine an ache between my legs. That girl carries a punch. Hannastown two weeks ago...that means two more and she's lost. Since I see her every day at school, and she's still around, chances are real good she hasn't yet discovered how to make things right. My opinion—which she rejects—is that her brother's death was a terrible accident, unavoidable the way things went down. She has done nothing wrong.

"Hey, Kota." The ghost girl of my dreams smiles at me from her seat in the cafeteria. "Want to sit with me?"

"Sure." I plop down across from her, remembering the first time we sat together and her eyes did their voodoo thing. "How's it going?"

"As you can see, still here." Summer's eyes blanch to yellow. She drops them and stares at her salad.

"You talked to Preston, right?" He might be a jerk, but if he can save her, whatever. "Want me to say something for you?"

"*No.*" Summer looks up. "Don't go near him, at least not until after I'm gone. He'll be okay then. Give him time. He's going to need a good friend when it's all over."

"What does that mean? Why will *you* leaving make *him* better?" She speaks in riddles sometimes.

"He's not himself right now..." Her voice trails off.

"Well, well, look at this. My two besties sitting with their heads together." Preston sits close to Summer. His fingers run over the snake bracelet she never takes off. "What have you two kids been up to lately?"

I study my former best friend and consider what Summer just said. Does she know he's under the influence of something dark and evil? *If* that's what's going on. Is that why she told me to stay away until she leaves? Like a light bulb in a cartoon, I get it. Summer knows something is wrong with Preston, plans to do a good deed and save him, thus saving herself. Maybe I don't fit in to the scenario after all. My head agrees; my heart doesn't.

"We're just talking." Summer's arms are covered with gooseflesh.

"About you, as a matter of fact." I feel the belligerence rising inside.

"Oh, yeah?" Preston takes the bait.

"Step outside with me, and I'll tell you all about it." I stand.

"Sure." Preston drops a kiss on Summer's head. "Go wherever you want. You know I'll find you."

I head for the enclosed courtyard where we're allowed to go during lunch. Very few do, but there are two girls sitting on a bench eating bag lunches. They look at my face, gather their debris, and leave us alone.

"Something on your feeble mind?" Preston lounges on a bench, straightening a perfectly straight shirt cuff.

"Who are you? What have you done with him?" I tower over this Preston impersonator.

"I like it. Right to business." His voice gets deeper, like he's swallowed a handful of stones. "Preston is a tedious, shallow young man, ripe to be picked. You'll get him back soon enough. If he's up to all the changes. If not?" He shrugs. "One less whiny, self-important youth in the world."

"You got a name? Besides asshole?" Knowing the profanity won't help, I can't think of enough insults to heap on this dirtbag.

"My name is Detritus." He cackles. "You can call me Detritus."

"You can't have Summer." I flex my not-insignificant muscles.

"Really." Detritus flicks his fingers in my direction.

I fall back on my butt, hop up, dust myself off. Inside, I'm shaking. This is the stuff of nightmares and horror movies. The little boy in me screams. The sixteen-year-old smirks. I play a hunch. "Really. We both know *she* thinks Preston is her ticket to eternity. Even though she knows you aren't Preston anymore. You and I understand that *I'm* the only one who can save her." I quote the words from the weird website I found. "'The power of the shadows cannot prevail against the strength of the light.' You're a shadow. I'm light. Give up now. Before I bring in Azul." I throw words around, pretending they're daggers, when in reality I don't have a clue.

A stream of smoke comes from Detritus' ears, and a low, serpent hiss issues from his mouth. His fingernails elongate into talons. He comes toward me.

I concentrate on finding my center, recalling the directions online: look deep within, mine my soul, find the answers—and you will find peace for all. A great lightness comes over me, as if my muscles are made of feathers and my body is a piece of lint. I am unbound, invincible, ready to do battle for Summer's soul. I almost feel like I'm flying.

In an instant, Detritus looks normal—like Preston. "You are one surprise after another." He leaves the courtyard.

I sit on the bench he vacated. Heaviness returns to me, as if my momentary preparation for battle changed as fast as Detritus did. What did he see in me that ended things? Will he leave us alone now? Not a chance. But maybe, if I continue to search my soul, I'll find whatever strength I need in coming days. I now know the enemy. But does Summer? She has some idea that Preston has a problem, that much seems clear, but she can't know Detritus up close and personal. I have to tell her, or risk putting her in his hands for eternity.

It seems like the day will never end. Pop quiz in math, C on a history paper, a chapter to read before tomorrow. Even my last period study hall is a waste. Marlie and Kayla are behind me, whispering, giggling, annoying the hell out of me. On purpose.

"Psst. Kota." Kayla kicks my desk.

I turn my head. "What?"

"I borrowed Marlie's red undies. Want to see *me* in them? Since *she* didn't turn you on?" She murmurs under her breath, "Ooo, baby."

And they say boys kiss and tell. But I don't give a crap what anyone says or what my reputation might become.

"Can't talk?" Marlie weighs in. "Maybe your tongue got tired working out on Summer. Wait until Preston hears about it."

It goes on and on. Mrs. Bechtel doesn't seem to care what we do, as long as we're in our seats and she can get her lesson plan finished. I try to concentrate on American History, but all I can think about is Hannastown. Which *is* history, but not what I'll be tested on.

The ringing of the bell is like releasing a racehorse at

the starting gate. I bolt from the room and shove my way through the throng of other kids wanting to escape. It takes forever, since I bump into a girl, she drops her books, and I have to help gather them. By the time I reach Summer's locker, she's not there.

I stop Doug, who has the next locker. "Hey, have you seen Summer?"

"Oh, yeah." Doug licks his lips. "Wish I could see more, if you get my drift."

I hold back from slugging him. "Did she leave already?"

"Gonzo, man." He leans in closer and lowers his voice. "Wanna get high? Got some good dope. Cheap."

"Not my thing." I race to my own locker, grab what I need, slam the door, and head for the bus. I text Summer as the bus stops and starts a bazillion times.

Meet me
Busy
Have 2. When?
IDK
PLZ
2nite @ 8, FVH track
K

Which leaves me hours to kill before meeting her at the school track. Not sure why there, don't care. I finish off homework, eat the chicken noodle casserole Mom left in the oven, and attempt to watch *Breaking Bad* reruns on Netflix. It all passes in a blur as I try to decide how to present the whole Preston-is-Detritus thing to Summer.

I leave the house early to avoid seeing my parents when they get in from long days at work. My note on the counter, *Went running at the track, back by 9*, is honest. Sort of. I drive to the school and park in the empty lot, making sure my car is in a slot farthest from the road in case a certain Mustang happens to drive past. I jog around the track once, to avoid as much lying as possible, and stop under the goalpost. My phone says it's 8:13. Where is she?

"Over here." Summer beckons from the bleachers.

I join her on the first row of metal seats. "Thanks for meeting me." Now that we're here, and several hours have passed, Detritus seems more like a product of bad cafeteria food than some creepy demon dude.

Summer waits for me. Her eyes are hazel with brown flecks. It strikes me that they are never blue. She looks so pretty and normal—like any girl in school only better— that again I wonder if all the ghost stuff has been brought on by breathing Doug's second-hand smoke.

"I thought we could be alone here—and see anyone who might decide to crash the party." Summer turns on the bench to look in my face. "Is this about Preston?"

"He's not Preston anymore." I take a breath, preparing a gentle way to tell her. Instead I blurt out, "His body is being possessed by a character named Detritus. He wants to hurt you."

"Not sure how you know, but I've met Detritus already." Summer's eyes darken.

I tell her the whole dream Azul thing, Detritus' morphing to demon state, I-must-be-crazy scenario. "But if all this is true, you're in danger. And Detritus didn't argue when I told him I'm the only one who can save you."

Summer snorts. "Which means it's not true, and he's leading you down a dead end." She smiles. "No pun intended."

"How can you make jokes? In fourteen days you'll be gone, incinerated, whatever." I stand, my sneakers clanging against the metal of the bleacher. "I'm right. You're wrong. From the very beginning, I've known we have a connection. I thought it was lust, but it's not." I thump my chest. "I know you're a ghost, and I'm not. But I feel it inside—if I don't save you, I'm somehow going to be lost, too." I deflate, a balloon that has the air sucked out of it.

"I'm over two hundred years old. I just look like a kid. You're sixteen—almost seventeen—and have the real feelings to go with it. I killed someone. You wouldn't swat a fly. I'm going to permanent death soon. You have decades ahead." Summer stands and wraps her arms around my chest. Her head rests against my chin.

I feel her warm tears, her fluttering heartbeat, the ragged breaths that are holding back sobs. Urgency for her plight morphs to panic about my own. "It's like I was dead before you came. Just being near you makes me alive. When you go, whether to roam or rest, I won't survive."

We stand together for a long time. I don't cry. Not because I don't want to, but because I can't. Tears won't come.

Summer pulls away first. "I have to get home. I promised Finn we'd read together before he goes to sleep." She gives me a hug and whispers in my ear. "You're the best friend I've ever had. You'll be fine without me." And then she's gone.

I sit in the bleachers as darkness falls. *Best friend.* Not what I feel for her. Not even close. She thinks she has the whole Preston/Detritus thing figured out. Wrong. Something is moving and shaking inside of me. A freight train ready to leave the station. A space shuttle prepared for lift-off. A missile ready to launch.

The short drive home does nothing to help me decompress.

Lock and load, baby. It's on.

THIRTY-ONE

Kota

"Kota, seriously?" Mom stands, hands on hips, beside the full garbage can that's parked in its usual place near the garage.

"What?"

"You were supposed to put this out last night. I've always been able to count on you." Her face softens. "Is something wrong? You haven't been yourself since...I don't know, at least a few days. Are you still upset about the," her voice drops, "adoption thing? We should have told you sooner. You know we're willing to help you search for your extended biological family."

"No, it's fine. I just have a lot of tests coming up. Wiped out, I guess." I manage to smile. "Sorry about the trash. I'll do it next week."

"Okay." Mom pats my arm on her way past. "Dinner's not for an hour. Maybe take a little nap."

I want to grab her and bury my face in her shoulder. I may or may not have tests coming up. Not much has made sense for the past five days. Since my encounter with Preston/Detritus, and Summer's revelations, I've been in a fog. Able to put one foot in front of the other, and not much more. I head for the house and the solitude of my room.

My bed feels good, even though I'm not into naps. Maybe Mom's right. I'm just tired, restless, uneasy. The guilt I feel for forgetting the garbage can is excessive. It's trash. One more week, and it's gone. One more week—nine days—and *Summer* will be gone. My eyelids are heavy, as if someone drugged me. Sick of the storm of feelings inside, I surrender to it...

My eyes pop open, or maybe they never closed. I'm floating as if in buoyant water, yet there's air under me. I spread my arms wide, a hawk in flight, aiming my hands up and down like ailerons.

"You must focus." Azul creates a wall of blue that halts my forward motion.

I glide to a stop in front of him. "What's happening to me?"

"You have a role to play, yet you gave up. Letting go is not an option. You must break through to the other side." Azul's form begins to spin, a tornado of swirling objects: a beaded pouch, a colorful blanket, eagle feathers.

"Yeah, so? I'm Seneca. Tell me something I don't know."

"Kota. Hear me." A woman—maybe twenty years old—dances toward me through twinkling stars. The scent of dogwood—like the tree in our front yard—clings to her. She wears a wraparound skirt, embroidered blouse, and moccasins. "Once, long before your birth, we knew how to listen to the stars. Over millennia, we turned from Truth. Now you must find the key that will open the lock you placed on your own heart. Listen, again, to the music of your soul."

"Mother?" I can't breathe and need no answer. This is my No'yeg. But instead of running to her, I hide my burning face.

"Listen and learn, my son." Mother's voice trails off.

I peek through my fingers and see her spinning away, a shooting star that dies.

As the vision fades, I sit up in my bed. My clothes are drenched with sweat, the sheets twisted, pillow on the floor. I get up and open my bottom drawer, pulling out the baby blanket. Hard to believe the cops found me wrapped in it shortly after my birth. It's exactly like the one I saw with Azul. I sniff it. Under the coppery scent of old blood is the faint aroma of dogwood. What was my mother trying to tell me? How did I lock my own heart? What will unlock it? I don't understand the spirit world. But Summer does. At the thought of her, panic rises in my gut. I've wasted five days. Days when I should have been helping her. Instead, I let myself wallow in shit I don't even understand.

I get up and grab my phone off the nightstand, punching *phone, favorites, Summer.*

"Hello?" Summer's voice is low, guarded.

"It's me. Kota. Are you alone?"

"For now."

"I don't know what's happening to me. I think Detritus put a spell on me or something. I haven't been there for you, or fought him, or…" I stop, uncertain.

"You can't fight a spirit battle with earthly weapons." Her voice is kind, as if explaining basics to a toddler. "I know you want to, think you're supposed to. But this fight is mine. Now that I know what went wrong in my life, Azul has to help me. Azul. Not you."

"So why does it feel so wrong to stay out of it?" I need answers. About me. And yet, without her, it doesn't feel like there *is* a me.

"I don't know." Summer is silent for a beat. "Just leave me alone. Please."

Dead air replaces her breathy voice.

I throw the phone across the room, and rest my head in my hands. She doesn't want my help? Fine. Screw her. I ask a simple question, and she tells me to get lost. Let her roam forever. Except my ranting is all lies. Which means I have to keep my mind sharp and get to work. Summer may not know she's depending on me, but she is. So are Azul and my birth mother. Beyond bizarre that these unknown, mystical beings seem more real to me now than the life I've lived for sixteen years.

I find Mom in the kitchen. "Hey, going out for a while."

"What about dinner?" Mom holds up a box of spaghetti. "Meatballs and garlic bread, too."

"Sounds great, but I have to see Preston. School, you know." I heft my backpack full of books. "We'll grab a pizza while we work." I realize I'm not hungry anyway.

"I'm so proud of your commitment to your studies." Mom gives me the good-boy look. "I'll put the leftovers in the refrigerator if you need a snack later. Love you."

"Thanks." I blow her a kiss, grab the car keys, and go to the garage. From Dad's hunting supplies, I get a knife with a serrated blade. I tuck it into the back of my jeans and pull my shirt over it. I feel better with some kind of protection. A roll of duct tape goes into my backpack. As a final gesture to my heritage, I use Dad's soft drafting pencil to draw black stripes on my face. I'm ready for war.

The drive to Preston's is so uneventful that I begin to doubt my whole supernatural theory of what's been happening. The trees are getting greener with the April rains, still budding, but the pale green contrasts against the cerulean sky. The air is cool and fresh, and the sun is heading for the horizon in the west. Maybe I'm having an adolescent crisis, need a few days off at the looney bin, and it will all make sense.

I park in Preston's driveway and march to the front door, lifting my hand to knock.

After several minutes, Preston opens the door. "Kota. Dude."

"You look like hell."

His eyes are bleary, underscored with dark circles. He's lost weight; his jeans droop off his hips as if he lives in a city 'hood. When he walks, it's a shuffling gait, back stooped, hands loose at his sides. His clothes are rumpled and need to be washed. So does he. I keep my hand poised to pull out the knife, in case this is a Detritus trick.

"I feel like hell. Flu or a virus. Don't know." Preston leans toward me. "Do I have a fever?"

What if Detritus pops out and bites me with fangs? I ignore this thought and feel Preston's forehead. "You're kinda hot. Did you see a doctor?"

"Nah, my folks are still away. Maria stayed for a couple nights, but I told her to go home. I'm old enough to take care of myself." He trips, hops on one foot, and rights himself. "Some strange shit going on up here." He taps his head and turns away from me.

"Like what?"

He doesn't answer.

"You aren't crazy. Detritus is real." I think. Maybe.

"Detritus?" Preston pulls at his greasy hair. "Never heard of him. But I feel like I'm being torn apart—on one of those medieval torture racks we saw in *Doomed Dungeon*, you know? I can't focus, sometimes days go by, and I don't even know what I've been doing."

My heart slows. I've lost days recently. Has Detritus taken over my body, too? How can I know? What can I do about it? "Preston, listen to me." I push him down on the bottom step of the curving oak staircase that leads to the second floor. "There's some weird crap going down. It's about Summer. A good-versus-evil scenario. The bad dude has been using you to get at her. Maybe even using me. And he has to be stopped."

"You been hanging with Doug, getting high?" Preston's voice has no inflection, but also no menace. Right now, he's Preston. "But dude...I think you're right. It's hopeless."

I put my arm around his shoulder. "We can fight this guy. But you have to help me. When you feel like you're splitting apart, do everything you can to hold it together. I'll stay with you. We'll do it together, just like always. You and me. Then we'll go to Summer and save her."

"You and me. Sure. Save Summer." Preston hoists himself up, leaning on the bannister. His face registers surprise as he doubles over, grabbing his stomach. "Dude, help me."

"Don't let him in. Be strong. I'm here." I pull out the knife, but short of stabbing Preston, don't know what to do with it. "You can't have him." I shout this in Preston's ear. "We are light, and we will destroy the dark." The words I'm spouting sound like bad movie dialogue.

"Can't. Hold. On." Preston falls to his knees, panting, thrashing, biting his lips until blood runs down his chin. "Kota, *help me*."

I grab the tape from my pack, dive onto Preston, and secure his wrists with it. I hold him close, like he's a baby. "Resist him. You can do it. If you don't give in, he'll go away."

Preston goes limp in my arms, shudders, and slides out of my grasp. "Having fun yet?" Preston's body rises, but it's Detritus in his stead. He easily removes the tape and salutes. "Bravo. As entertaining as a Shakespearean play. And as useless."

"Preston is weak. I'm not. I won't let you in." I'm afraid to have thoughts, in case he can read my mind.

"If I chose you, you would most certainly become my vessel." Detritus straightens Preston's shirt and jeans, and smooths back his matted hair. "But I have no need of two. This one has been perfect."

"The darkness cannot overcome the light."

"Are you still spouting that nonsense? It's dreary and trite, inadequate for centuries. I have always been a dark creature—able to masquerade as light." His snake-tongue licks the blood off the lips of his host. He holds up his wrist to show me Preston's Rolex. "Tick tock. Nine more days—eight, really, since the sun will soon set. Love the little bonding moment with your old pal Pres, but as you can see, totally hopeless."

Detritus takes his eyes off me long enough to tie his shoe.

I pull out the knife. My hand sweats and my stomach rebels. Kill Preston? *I can't. I can't.* But he's not Preston. He's Detritus. Evil. Dark. *I must end this now. For Summer.* I raise the knife and plunge it toward Detritus' back, wanting to send him straight to hell. My hand freezes in mid-air. My heart pounds as my head realizes I'm trying to battle the supernatural with everyday weapons.

"*Delightful.*" Detritus stands, and with a flick of his wrist the knife is across the room. "Did you actually think you could kill *me*? I'm the one who brings death, when and to whom I please." He makes a sound of disgust.

A chill invades me, a Titanic-sized iceberg ramming into my soul. A thought flashes across my mind: *Like an ice floe, is there more underneath the surface that I don't even see yet?* "I'll find a way to destroy you, even though killing is your thing, not mine."

"Such bravado." Detritus pushes past me. "It's obvious that killing comes easily to you. We both know that. Sadly for you, this time you tried it on someone who is immune to your violence. Be forewarned. I've tolerated your puppy-love tricks. But no more. The next time you want to take me on, you will die to this world...and live to mine. Now get out."

I race to the car. My thoughts roll and tumble all the way home. He can't touch Summer until her birthday. There's something I'm missing. I *will* figure it out...or die trying.

LAUREL HOUCK

THIRTY-TWO

Summer

"It's going to be okay." I pour a glass of milk and set it on the breakfast bar. "Your parents will be back from their business trip in two days. It's great that they let us stay here by ourselves. We'll get to do some cool things while they're gone." I hold up two containers. "Syrup or powdered sugar on your pancakes, or both?"

Finn doesn't touch the milk or the pancakes on his plate. "I don't care about any of that. For a ghost, you're not too smart." He gets off the stool and opens the pantry door, where Jill keeps a calendar. His stubby finger jabs at the date. "It's April sixteenth."

"So it is. Spring break. What should we do?" I know where he's going with this, don't want to linger at the obvious.

"You're headed for an epic fail, and you want to talk about Mom and Dad's business trip, if I want syrup or powdered sugar on my pancakes, and how to have fun?" Finn slams the pantry closed. He sits down and shovels his pancakes—sans syrup or sugar—into his mouth and chews hard. When the milk glass is empty, he thumps it on the counter.

"You want to talk about it? Fine." I pour coffee for both of us, a perk of being home alone, and sit with him.

Finn pours six teaspoons of sugar into his cup, adds milk, and stirs. "Your birthday is in two days. Did you think I'd forget that turning seventeen means you're gonna be a spectator?"

"Specter." I almost don't want to correct him. It's cute. And it's true. I'll be a spectator of other souls as they rest in peace, and I roam forever. "You worrying won't help anything. And either way, I'll be gone, so just pretend I'm at rest."

"Look, I'm ten, not stupid. This isn't about my imagination." Finn takes his time before replying. His eyes fill with tears. "Dovie, I love you."

These simple words, an echo of my real brother's, rip open the scab I've cultivated since my visit to Hannastown. I wrap him up close to me and rest my chin on his head as my own tears flow. "Oh, Finn, I love you, too. It's hard to say goodbye." We sit until his hair is wet.

"Isn't there something you can do?" Finn gets up and walks around the kitchen on the balls of his feet, bouncing like Tigger.

"Yes, of course." I look at him and realize he'll see right through a lie. "I have to do something with Preston."

"You mean sex?"

"*Finn.* No." I used to think that romance was the key. But with Detritus in control, there's no such thing as romance.

"Then what? Can I help?"

I take in his earnest little-boy face and innocence. And know he can't be part of anything to do with evil. "Preston is having some…problems…and I'm going to talk to him. Help me set things up here. Then go to Josh's house for a while. When I come for you, everything will be done."

"What kind of problems?" Finn won't let it go.

Can't scare him with the whole Detritus thing. "He's

confused about his identity."

"He's gay? Or thinks he's a girl in a boy's body?"

"No, nothing like that."

Finn ponders. "Like possessed? By a demon?"

I sigh. The kid already knows I'm a ghost. Maybe better for him to understand evil and know to avoid it, than pretend it doesn't exist. "Yes."

"Then I can't go to Josh's. You need me." Finn runs to his room and returns with a familiar book. "I'll hypnotize him and get rid of the demon."

It goes back and forth, but it seems clear Finn isn't going anywhere. I won't let him be part of the final battle, but will make him believe he's important to the process. We do some online research and prepare by getting out a Bible, the little bottle of holy water Jill brought back from a trip to Lourdes, a roll of duct tape, and the set of handcuffs Finn got from his Uncle Mal, the cop. I skim his hypnosis book and let him teach me what to do, under the guise of him practicing to do it.

"We're ready." Finn looks over everything. "Call Preston. This guy is going *down*."

"Okay. But you have to go to Josh's for a while. If you're in the house, he won't come. I'll let you know when I need you. So don't go outside or anywhere else. Stay close." This should keep him safe. After what I did to Trey, can't risk Finn's life.

"Synchronize our phones." Finn, movie addict, makes sure our numbers are on speed dial.

I walk him to Josh's house. Before he goes inside, I hug him. "Stay here. Promise me. I'll call when it's time."

"You got it." Finn is solemn. "Be careful." He rings the bell and joins Josh inside.

I wait until I'm back home to call Preston. My finger shakes as I tap his name. It rings five times.

"Summer?" It's Preston. Thank goodness.

"Hey, can you come over? We need to talk."

"Not feeling good," Preston mumbles.

"I'll make you some tea. But I have to see you. It's important."

"Yeah, 'kay." He hangs up.

I pace while I wait, uncertain if Preston or Detritus will show up. I need Preston. With the tea made, the Bible in place, and Finn safe, I'm free to worry. My left hand goes in and out of flesh, the reflection of my eyes in the hall mirror is a kaleidoscope, and the ache in my heart intensifies. If I can find rest, I'll be reunited with Mama and Trey. It means leaving Finn, but either way I have to say goodbye to him. At the sound of the Mustang, I curl my tongue in my mouth, suck in a breath, then exhale as my tongue unfurls; my hand regains flesh. Showtime.

"Preston, hey. Thanks for coming." I open the door and usher him inside. "You look like hell."

"That's what Kota said." Preston looks around with bleary eyes, as if he's never seen this house before. "Can we make it quick?"

I set a cup of steaming wintergreen tea on the table, said to protect against evil. I wait for him to take a sip and get settled before pulling out a chair so I'm seated directly in front of him. "I know what's wrong with you."

"What, you've remembered you're a doctor?" He manages a smile.

"It's not physical. This is going to sound really, really bizarre." I search his face. Still Preston. "There's an evil spirit possessing you."

Preston stares at me. He doesn't laugh, as I half expected. "You and Kota both get it." He runs a shaking hand across his unshaven face. His voice is a tortured whisper. "It's like I'm me, but a puppet-me, you know? I hear and see the things that are happening, but I can't control them. Sometimes I forget stuff. Once...I even had...talons. I thought it had to be one of two things: insanity or possession. But there are times I'm totally with it—like now—so it can't be pure crazy."

"You believe me."

"Sure. Kota said it's some dude called Detritus. He tried to help me escape from the bad shit, but the evil guy took over." Tears form in Preston's eyes. "There's nothing anyone can do to help me."

"I can fight with you." My heart swells. Kota tried to go up against Detritus. For me. Even knowing what he was up against.

"Do it. Quick, before Detritus comes back."

"You have to trust me."

"I'm in hell, Summer. Please. Help me."

I don't waste any more time. I use Uncle Mal's handcuffs to secure Preston's hands to the arms of the dining room chair, then the duct tape to immobilize his ankles to the chair legs. I sprinkle holy water over his head. "This is good versus evil. Whether you're religious or not doesn't matter. Just close your eyes and listen hard."

Preston nods. His lids snap shut.

I open the Bible and begin to read. "'Your adversary, the devil, prowls around like a hungry lion, seeking whom to devour. Resist him, standing firm, and he will flee from you.' We are here to destroy the works of Satan, with the power and authority to cast out the demon who has invaded your soul." I read the other passages I marked earlier, until Preston is breathing evenly.

"You are comfortable. You trust me. Everything that happens, you will remember. You are feeling heavy, sinking into the chair, relaxed, at peace. Do you understand?"

"Yes." Preston's face is slack. A line of drool inches from the corner of his mouth.

"You have the power to block Detritus from you. Tell him. Send him away. *Do it now.*"

"I have the power." Preston mumbles, then throws his head back. "Leave me. Go back to hell. You cannot possess me any longer."

"Hear this, Detritus." My voice takes on strength as I speak. "Your host is no longer yours. The body you tore

241

apart is healing, knitting together, stronger, able to resist your advance. I cast you out in the name of all that is holy and right. *Be gone*." I sprinkle Preston with holy water again and wait for a full minute. "Preston, you may awaken, healed and cleansed, when I reach the number one. Five-four-three-two-one."

Preston's body arches, his limbs contort, and a long, low scream erupts that seems to come from deep in his belly. He coughs violently, and his wrists fight the handcuffs. He falls forward, a rag doll without bone or joint. His head shakes. He lifts it, blinks, and looks around. "Summer? Is it over?"

I search for any sign of Detritus in Preston. Nothing. "Do you feel different?"

"I heard everything you said. It felt like my body was being ripped into two pieces. But I concentrated on your words and imagined everything inside me knitting back together."

Preston looks like Preston. I remove the handcuffs and tape and help him to stand.

"I've been a jerk." He takes my hand. "But you saved my life. Can we start over? Get to know each other without evil dude in the way?"

I squeeze his hand. "I'm leaving soon, thanks to you. You saved my death." I reach up and smooth out the frown that appears on his forehead. "Don't even try to figure it out. By helping you, I set some old wrongs right. I'll be forever grateful."

Preston gives me a quick hug and steps back. "Oh, just so you know. Kota did buy the flowers for homecoming. I stole them—Detritus did—and the tickets from his locker. You should be nice to him before you leave. And don't worry, I'll apologize to him. We'll be friends again."

I wave as he leaves. The Bible goes on the shelf, and I clean up the house. I leave the handcuffs for Finn to put away. Each moment I expect Azul to come and whisk me to eternity now that I saved Preston. Inside, excitement and sadness war as I contemplate leaving Finn—and never getting to say goodbye to him or to Kota. Kota who did love me and protect me, but whom I feared. Misplaced feelings, it turns out, his Seneca heritage not the threat I perceived it to be.

"Summer?" Finn dashes in the front door. "Are you okay? You didn't call me."

I want to be mad that he's here without me bringing him back, but it's safe, and I'm glad for a chance to get one last sticky-fingered hug. "Everything worked, thanks to you. I made up for what I did wrong by releasing Preston."

Finn clings to me. "I'm glad you can rest. But I don't want you to leave. Can you come back sometimes to see me?"

"I don't know. But if I go soon, you run next door and tell Josh's mother that I'm gone. She'll take care of you and call your parents."

"What should I tell Mom and Dad? They'll think you ran away." Finn sniffles and wipes his nose on my sleeve.

"Tell them you don't know where I am. That's the truth." I pull out a tissue and hand it to him. "Remember, this was the best place I ever landed, because it ended my nightmare. I'll remember you, my sweet brother-from-another-mother, for eternity."

We both start as the doorbell rings.

Finn reaches in his pocket and looks up at me. "I left my phone at Josh's. It's probably him."

I release him. "No problem. But don't have him stay to play in case I disappear."

Finn grins and mimes zipping his lips. "You got it. Our secret."

I look out the kitchen window as I get a glass of water. Storm clouds roll in, blocking the sun. A noise makes me turn. For the first time in an eternity, I can't move.

"Hello, Dovie." Mike the moron, our neighbor, is standing just inside the room. Detritus gleams from his eyes. His arm is around Finn's neck, holding him close.

Finn's eyes are huge, and his little chest heaves. He does not cry.

"So, you thought bypassing Preston would save you." Detritus chuckles. "I was done with him. Your little exorcism was nothing more than theater. I did quite a good job with the whole release-the-host thing, don't you agree? Mike here is an even better host, since he's stronger and has a much less well-developed sense of morality. He'll do things that Preston never could, even with me as his guide."

"I'll go with you. Right now. Just leave Finn alone."

"So sad. Now you'll have the death of two little boys on your soul: sweet Trey and dear Finn. And not enough time to reconcile for either one." Detritus tightens his grip on Finn, whose lips are turning blue. "But there *is* a way out for you. If you give me this innocent soul, I'll release you. Be with your real brother and mother. Rest forever."

"Never. You can't have Finn."

"Summer, s'okay." Finn's words are choked out.

"You see? The child *wants* to be with me." Detritus' free hand caresses Finn's hair.

My mind races. I drop the glass in my hand. It tumbles to the floor and shatters. Water explodes into the air, setting off reverberations in the liquid. Shock waves from my past spread out, snatch me up, and pull me in. Two hundred years flash before me, manifestations throughout the ages as I struggled to reconcile my soul. Wave after wave of memories washes over me. And then it hits me. I glare at Detritus.

"You can't take him unless I give my permission for him as my surrogate. Because his soul is pure. And I'll *never* give him up." I pick up a piece of jagged glass and throw it at Detritus.

He easily dodges. "You are tiresome. But sadly correct. That means the three of us will have a little party here. And the day after tomorrow, Dovie Critchlow, you will finally be mine." He snatches the handcuffs from the table, attaches Finn to his wrist, and smirks.

I keep my distance and affect disinterest. But now Detritus knows Finn. Could he return for him at any time, just to torture me further? My heart sinks, and my mind tries to find a solution before I must surrender. And leave Finn unprotected for eternity.

LAUREL HOUCK

THIRTY-THREE

Kota

The words "look deep within, mine your soul, find the answers—and you will find peace for all", keep echoing through me. I failed Preston. I've done nothing to help Summer. Time is running out. And the turmoil in my soul is threatening to overwhelm me. Summer isn't answering her phone or her door; I can only hope she hasn't been swept away early. Her birthday is tomorrow. I have less than twenty-four hours to figure out what to do. I push down the gas pedal, and the van speeds up.

The GPS takes me past Hannastown. Summer learned her story, but I found nothing there. She went back to her roots. I'll go to mine. I keep driving for six more miles to Latrobe and park near the Carmelite Monastery, grabbing my pack from the seat as I get out.

There are small frame buildings, painted gray, one with a white cross on the side. Living quarters for the nuns? Nearby is a chapel, a simple redbrick one-story with white trim. A white statue is in front with pink flowering trees around it. I sniff the scent of dogwood.

I walk to the door, also painted white, and stop on the

concrete. My heart accelerates. Is this where the nuns found me? Did my mother lay me on this cold slab with only a threadbare blanket to protect me? Why didn't she knock and ask for help instead of abandoning me and walking a quarter of a mile away to die? I wait for the ghosts of the past to speak to me.

"Can I help you?" A soft, gentle voice from the shadows breaks the stillness.

I spin around. Not a ghost. A nun. "Um, just looking around."

The nun's eyes open wide and she takes in a quick breath. "If you are interested in the religious life, the nearby monks at the Benedictine Archabbey of St. Vincent would welcome your questions. We are an order of sisters here."

"No, not here to join up. I do have questions, though."

She smiles and opens the chapel door. "I'm Sister Louise. Let's go inside."

We enter a plain church with paneled walls and a wooden altar at the front covered with an unadorned white cloth. I sit in a back pew and wonder how to begin.

"Take your time, son." Sister Louise perches beside me, her calf-length black dress rustling softly. She smells of soap and onions.

"Were you here sixteen years ago?"

Sister Louise's hand goes to the crucifix hanging around her neck. "You grew up."

It's as if she knows me. "I'm in high school."

There is a beat where emotions race across her plain face. "It *is* you. Our baby."

I nod, unable to trust my voice.

"I'm so glad to see that the Lord has blessed you, and that you stopped to visit us." Her smile fades when I don't respond. "Why are you really here?"

I keep it short and sweet: found the old newspaper article, came to see for myself, interested in any details. "And I wondered…where they found my mother's body."

"None of us were there. We took care of you—a blessed event for all of us that evening, I must say." Sister Louise pats my arm, proprietary, like a grandma. "Come outside." We stand by a brick archway and she points through tall pine trees. "After the police arrived, they found the remains down that way, a quarter of a mile, we heard. I'm so sorry for what happened, but pleased to see your adoptive family has raised you well."

"Do you mind if I take a look at where she died?"

Sister Louise frowns. "You'll have to go alone. I'm due in the kitchen."

"That's fine. Please. It means a lot to me." I hold my breath, not sure of their rules.

Sister Louise lowers her head, a moment passes, and she looks up. "I suppose it's all right. But not for too long. The chapel closes at 4:30 P.M. After that we don't expect any visitors to be here. What is your name, son?"

"Kota Landis."

"Kota. That's Seneca, I believe. We did quite a bit of research here after the event, when we learned the poor young woman was of Seneca descent. If memory serves, the word *kota* means ally."

This is news to me. I wonder if it's coincidence, or if my being an *ally* to Summer was destined from the start. I'll never know. "Thank you." I head for the pines, and she goes the other way.

I take my time, looking at the surroundings, trying to imagine what it was like almost seventeen years ago. The trees would have been smaller, although some look old enough to have been mature at the time. I stop every few feet, waiting for something—anything—that will help me to "look deep within". The sun goes behind dark clouds, the breeze picks up, and it feels like rain. That's nothing new for spring in western Pennsylvania.

In less than ten minutes, I've walked a quarter mile, according to the app on my phone. The manicured grass has given way to needle-strewn ground as the trees collide into forest. I search, but don't know for what. After so many years, I'm not going to find evidence of my birth mother or what happened that night. I set my backpack on the ground, open the zipper, and pull out the blanket I was wrapped in after my birth. I put my nose to the wool and inhale. The stench of blood is stronger than I remembered, almost hiding the sweet aroma of dogwood.

When I take the blanket away from my face, I am surrounded by profound darkness. The air is warm, humid, more like June than April. Dizziness overcomes me, and I go down on one knee, then face-first into the pine debris. The needles are sharp, the scent of Christmas strong.

I curl up in a ball, my vision blurred, breathing difficult, as if I'm underwater. Rhythmic pressure surrounds me, buffeting, squeezing, kneading me like bread dough. My heart beats fast. A slower thumping sounds in my ears. I sense panic and hear awful moans; neither are mine. The pressure builds around me as the moans turn to screams. A gush of warm fluid—both salty and metallic—carries me from heat to sudden cold. My cries mingle with another's as I gasp.

"I have a little man, a small *hokwe*."

I know this voice from my dream. I try to say, *No'yeg*, but am unable to form words. My arms and legs flail in frustration.

Mother picks me up, wraps me in soft wool, and holds me close, singing. "*Hey, hey watenay. Hey, hey, watenay. Kay-oh-kay-nah. Kay-oh-kay-nah.*" Her voice gets weaker and weaker, until I can barely hear her. "I'm sorry to leave you, my baby. Remember that I loved you from the first moment. If your Papa hadn't died, we would have been a fami…" Her words trail off.

Mother, no. I reach for her. The sound of her breathing has stopped, her heartbeat is silent. *I killed her. I killed my mother.* My shame runs deep within me. It's my fault she died. I give up trying to move, speak, or even cry. I deserve to die for what I did.

Soft light illuminates the thicket. "Small one, your moment has come."

A blue form pries me from Mother's still arms. All breath leaves me, and I become as light and cool as air. My soul rises from my body and begins to sink toward the ground until corralled by the strange creature holding me.

"I am Azul." His voice is the coo of a dove. "Infants who die are meant to go straight to eternal rest. But you carry guilt on your tender soul that threatens to condemn you. I am able to give you one chance, as if you still live. Perhaps you will forget your shame. And then, at the end of a natural lifespan, you will rest. But if by the age of seventeen your guilt continues and you have failed to reconcile your soul, you will never find peace."

Azul's warmth encircles me. He transports me a short distance, places me on a cold, hard surface, and breathes into my nostrils. My body transforms from light and cool to heavy and hot. "May you never need to remember Azul."

I cough and cough and begin to cry. I killed my mother. Warm arms, smelling of soap and onions, soon pick me up. Bright lights flash, and loud voices hurt my ears. I'm given milk, warm, clean clothes, a soft bed. Memories of *No'yeg* begin to fade. I want to remember her always, and that she's dead because of me. But I'm lulled by the comfort. My mind shunts vague, pervasive guilt into my infant heart where it begins to fester.

I come to with a moan, my grown body still lying in pine needles, the Indian blanket clutched in my hands. The tumblers in my locked brain click into place. I killed my mother. I'll be seventeen on June fifth. My soul has never been reconciled. I'm a ghost...*a ghost*. And if I don't discover what to do about it soon, I'll be lost forever.

A great lethargy comes over me. I roll onto my back and stare at the sky, which is again light. According to my phone, I've only been here for a few minutes. But long enough to find out that I've been dead for almost seventeen years—and that what I did has been gnawing at me for just as long. It hasn't been the adoption, or my heritage, or my appearance after all. No, it has been the awful, unforgiveable sin of killing my own mother.

A squirrel runs down a tree and pauses beside me, standing on back legs.

"I'm a ghost. Aren't you afraid of me?" The squirrel scampers away as a great roar fills my ears. My muscles become like feathers. I am light and airy. When I look down, my body has morphed from heavy flesh to cool mist. I float through the trees and come back to the Indian blanket. My flesh returns, along with nausea and dizziness.

"When I tried to fight Detritus at school he must have realized that I'm dead." I address the squirrel, now perched out of reach on a tree limb. "That's why he backed off that day. He's waiting for his chance to block Summer *and* me from eternal rest. What am I supposed to do?"

I wait for some epiphany. Nothing happens. "Azul?" I close my eyes and try to dream him. Nothing. "You said you couldn't help me, but I didn't remember or understand. Help me now." Silence.

Chattering, the squirrel runs up the tree, leaving me totally alone. Azul told me I have it within me to reconcile my soul. I've been drawn to Summer since she arrived, ghost to ghost, although neither of us understood. The Seneca thing was a stumbling block for her. Now that's gone. I am Summer's reconciliation, and she is mine.

I have to find her before it's too late. For both of us.

THIRTY-FOUR

Kota

I pause by my van in the monastery parking lot. Is it better to go ghost or drive to Summer's house? Since I've done no more than a quick float through the trees, I stick to what I know. I back up, throwing gravel, and almost miss the figure gesturing to me. No time for cheery conversations. I wave and prepare to pull out.

"Wait. *Kota.*" Sister Louise hurries toward me, holding up her black skirt as she runs.

I stop and roll down the window. "Thanks for your help, Sister. I have to get home."

She stops, out of breath, and grabs onto the window frame. "I'm so glad we met. I want to give you something." In her hand is a white cloth, wrapped around something. She hands it to me. "I spoke with the other sisters, and we all agreed this should be yours."

"What is it?"

"Open it and see."

I unwrap the fabric. Inside is a small beaded thing—no more than maybe five inches by three. The shape is a snapping turtle. It's backed with soft leather. The beads are

253

circular in stripes of green, orange, white, blue, and pink. "Where did you get this?"

"When your mother's case was closed, the police officer from the scene got permission to give this to us for safekeeping. It's an umbilical cord amulet."

"Gross." I try to hand it back to her.

Sister Louise won't take it. "These are hand-stitched seed beads on buckskin. Pieces of the parents' or grandparents' hair might be worked into the design. The internet said this is a Seneca tradition. Once the umbilical cord falls off the baby, it's placed in one of these. The person carries it with them always for luck. The turtle is a symbol of long life. Your mother had it on her person that night. For you."

My life wasn't very long. Or lucky. I don't say it out loud. Sister Louise doesn't know I died that night, and that she's talking to a ghost. "Thanks." I sniff the leather. The faint scent of dogwood clings to it. *No'yeg.* My heart constricts. How I wish I hadn't killed her. "I'll take good care of it."

Sister Louise leans in the window and places a soft kiss on my cheek. "I see strength in your eyes. God bless you." She steps aside. "Come back to visit real soon."

I tuck the amulet in my pocket, wave, and take off. Delayed grief over my mother's death won't help me now. Although *my* seventeenth birthday isn't until June, I'm afraid that once Summer leaves—to rest or to roam—I'll be doomed. I put the pedal to the metal and speed down Route 22. What are the cops going to do, take away my drivers' license?

Summer's house is dark inside as I walk down the unpaved driveway. Although dusk hasn't fallen, the place is surrounded by trees, and there's usually a light burning. If she's not here, I don't know where to go. She hasn't made friends, doesn't have a job, isn't with Preston.

I lift my hand to push the doorbell then pull it back. A faint sound reaches my ears. Not a scream or a moan, more like a muted squeal. Enough to send goose bumps up my arms. I duck below the windows and slink to the back of the house. There are several doors, to the small greenhouse, the basement, storage areas. Everything is locked. A new, heightened sense of awareness ratchets up my unease. Something is very wrong.

I'm a ghost. Summer got into my bedroom, through locked doors and windows. So I should be able to get inside here. But how? What's the deal? No time to read the manual or practice. I've probably vaporized twice, once in the face of great stress with Detritus and earlier today after finally figuring out my status.

I close my eyes and imagine my muscles turning into feathers, my flesh into mist that rises on a humid summer night over the creek. When my eyes open, I'm hovering two feet above the flagstone patio, transformed into wisps of white. I circle the house, avoiding the windows. I saw Summer's ghostly vapor when she came to my room. I don't want to give myself away. Because the only thing that could cause the panic throbbing in my gut is Detritus. If he's inside with Summer, there's trouble ahead.

At the back of the house again, I approach the flimsy wooden door of the basement, hold my breath, and ram into it. Instead of the hard smack I expect as a human, I pass through. Ripples disturb my essence, like a stone skipping across a pond. I shake it off and let my mist leech up the spiral stairs, pausing at the top.

"Don't hit him again." Summer is up in the face of a man I've seen once, a neighbor named Mike. Her right hand is clenched into a fist. The left is white mist.

Finn sports a bright red spot on his cheek and a look of defiance on his face. He's handcuffed to Mike. Casually, he turns his head and spits in the man's face.

"How childish." Detritus' voice comes from Mike's mouth. He wipes off Finn's spittle. "You should thank me for taking the time and effort to be tied to this little brat. I could easily kill him now and wait for another," he glances at a watch on his wrist, "seven hours to take you away.

Out of the generosity of my heart, I'm letting you spend this time together. A little birthday gift, if you will."

What the hell am I going to do? Detritus knows I'm a ghost, so the element of surprise is gone. Do I have more power as a ghost or a guy? Is vapor stronger than flesh? Frustration hums through me. Summer could change if she wanted, and she's in human form, so maybe that's the best way to go. I hold my breath, imagine my real body, and wait.

The airy cool transforms into hot substance as I materialize on the stairs. With it comes nausea and dizziness. I look down, glad to see that clothes accompanied the change. I slide my hand inside my pocket and touch the amulet—it's supposed to be good luck after all. There are matches in there as well, and the knife is tucked in the back of my waistband. I know it's lame, hoping for physical protection against a supernatural demon. What else do I have?

Once the dizziness subsides, I ascend the rest of the way, not bothering to hide my footsteps on the metal stairs. "Hello, everyone. Someone forgot my party invitation."

"Ah, how sweet. The damaged knight, come to rescue his murdering damsel in distress. The stuff of fairy tales." Detritus bats his eyelashes and affects a feminine pose.

"Not too manly there, demon-dude." I catch Summer's eyes—bright red and shiny—but focus on baiting Detritus. If I look at her too much I'll collapse. Better to concentrate on taking him down. Somehow.

"Gender is not an issue for me." Detritus shrugs. "Mortals make too much of such things, male, female, who sleeps with whom, all that rot. I am ageless, timeless, sexless. But not powerless." He holds up one hand, the fingernails elongate into talons, and he opens a long, bloody scratch on Finn's other cheek.

"Aren't you the big bad creep?" Finn displays his handcuffed wrist. "Beating up on a kid who's chained to you and can't fight back. I've seen worse on video games, *loser*." He has the nerve to wink at Summer and me.

The kid is tough, for sure. I wonder if Detritus can see that Finn's little body is shaking.

"You are all pathetic, thinking you can anger me." But Detritus' face reddens, and the veins in his neck pulsate. He unlocks the handcuff from his own wrist, drags Finn across the room to the iron bannister of the spiral stairs, and locks him to the railing.

Score one for Finn. At least he's not up close and personal anymore. I position myself in front of the kid. Summer joins me. Three against one. Maybe we have a chance.

"Kota." Summer whispers my name, but her focus is on Detritus. "This isn't your fight. Leave while you still can."

In the maneuvering, I've taken my eyes off Detritus. I look at him now.

Detritus is shedding Mike, like a snake sheds its skin. The top of Mike's head peels away and sloughs off in long pieces. Underneath is a face that looks like raw meat, muscle without skin. The eyes are beady black dots, the nose two flat openings, the mouth sports dripping fangs. His body is androgynous, draped in a black garment embroidered with an upside-down cross, a bastardized nun's habit that would make Sister Louise faint. The talons on his hands are filthy, one dripping with Finn's blood.

"Umm." Detritus sucks the blood from his finger. "Innocent blood is the sweetest."

"Enjoy it now. When you take me, Finn will be out of your reach." Summer puts a protective arm around Finn's shoulders.

"For now." Detritus nods. "But who among mortals is without shame in a lifetime? There are many who will meet me one day. Perhaps he won't be as delicious by then, but I'll cope. I've waited all these years for you, thanks to that blasted Azul and his manipulation of time. You should have been mine long before this."

"It's easy to take a girl and threaten a kid." I manufacture a laugh. "I notice you have no threats for me. I'm a Seneca *warrior*. More than you can handle. Why not take me tonight and leave Summer? She's not nearly as important a catch as I am. I died as an infant, and this is my first time to materialize. That doesn't happen every day. An innocent baby with only one sin on his soul—the murder of his mother. Think how sweet I would be…for eternity."

Part of me can't believe I'm even in this situation, much less offering myself in place of Summer. But I don't care what happens to me anymore. It seems unlikely there's a way out for either of us, but I'll try almost anything to save her. I never knew my real family. She can be reunited with hers. And I love her. Pure and simple, I love her. I don't want to get fondled, laid, or married. I just want to love her. If that means as a sacrifice, so be it. I'm not brave—foolish more likely—but I have to follow my heart.

"What are you talking about?" Summer stares at me. Her voice is barely audible. "You…died?"

"Long story. Who knew we were both ghosts?" I throw her a shrug and a grin. "Told you we were always meant to be together."

The mantel clock chimes. I count with the bongs: one, two, three, four, five, six, seven, eight, nine. How can hours have passed? Without any progress or hope. I see Detritus nodding his head to the chimes, a knowing smile on his thin lips. He leaves—still keeping us within his sight—and goes onto the sun porch, his face turned toward the full moon.

"I don't believe you." Summer whispers into my ear, keeping her eyes fixed on Detritus. "You're making it up in some lame attempt to save me."

I don't bother to answer. Instead I let my body vaporize, circle the room, and return to flesh at her side.

"Oh, man, this is too cool." Finn whistles. In spite of his injuries, he's into the ghost thing. "I can't wait to tell Josh." The joy leaches from his face. "If I'm still alive."

"Let's figure out what to do instead of playing games." I keep my voice low. "You've been at this longer than me. Any ideas?"

Summer holds up her wrist, the snake bracelet snug on her skin. "This has something to do with it all. Preston—Detritus—made me put it on, and I still can't get it off. I think it has power, or he wouldn't have been so adamant I wear it."

"Great. The asshole has power, and we don't. What if we both dematerialize? Not sure how that would help, but flesh and blood can't fight him."

"Do it." Finn weighs in. "Fly out of here. You already said he can't take me, so he'll leave when you guys do."

"The kid has a point. We can draw Detritus away." I give Finn a thumbs up. "You're a brave kid."

"Brave or not, no way." Summer shakes her head. "I won't leave. Maybe Detritus can't take Finn's innocent soul, but he can hurt him, maybe even kill his mortal body. I won't let another little brother die because of me."

"Trey is not your fault. Why can't you understand?" How can I make her see this?

"And as a newborn baby you killed your mother on purpose?" Summer rolls her eyes. "That doesn't even make sense."

We both stand there, lost in our thoughts. I don't even register the passage of time, the ticking of the clock. Maybe she's right about me. I didn't ask to be conceived or born. Or for my mother to die. A spark of hope pushes aside the pain and swallows the guilt.

"Is it possible Trey's death *isn't* my burden to carry?" Summer's eyes cling to me. "Neither of us were destined to live that day. I did my best, didn't I?"

"You were trying to save him. It's time to let go." I pause and know it's true when I add, "And my mother's death is a tragedy—but not my doing." For the first moment in my life—or death—I'm free. I grab her hand.

Both of our hands dissolve. Her mist mixes with mine, until it's impossible to tell which belongs to whom. An electric jolt travels into my shoulder, down my chest, into my lower body.

Summer shivers and closes her eyes.

"*Look out!*" Finn screams.

The warning dispels my mist and brings solid flesh back to Summer.

A fierce blow knocks me off my feet. My head explodes with stars, and I collapse. The umbilical talisman falls out of my pocket and skitters across the wood floor, out of reach.

"*Get off him.*" Summer's bravado turns to whimpers as Detritus pokes at her eyes with his talons.

The chimes on the clock signal it's half past the hour. I crane my neck to look at the mantle. Eleven-thirty. The momentary peace of passing guilt morphs to numbing panic. Soon it will be midnight. April eighteenth. And Summer will be lost.

THIRTY-FIVE

Summer

I blink several times to see around the instant tears that Detritus' sharp talons produced. Rage bubbles inside me, tinged with regret. If I'd only believed Kota from the start, maybe we could have both reconciled our souls in time. That's surely why we were meant to be together. But I was naïve, eager to believe the lies placed in my heart by evil, quick to turn away from the light.

"Go back to hell." Kota springs up off the floor, producing a knife from the waistband of his jeans. He runs at Detritus, blade extended. "You can take me, but I'll *never* let you have Summer or Finn. Even if I have to roam forever."

Independent of my own brain, muscles, or will, my left hand shoots out to deflect the blow away from Detritus. I try to pull it back, but my arm is rigid, as if an iron rod has been placed in it. The knife glances off the snake bracelet on my wrist and flies out of Kota's hand.

"Drama. What a droll way to end it all." Detritus pulls me close to him, caressing the woven snake. "I remember the day I gave this to you. Little did you know it would be with you for eternity, marking you as mine."

In my peripheral vision, I see Kota looking at the kitchen windowsill, where Jill has pots of herbs growing. He inclines his head in that direction and sidles toward the plants.

Finn's eyes glance at Kota and quickly away. "Eternity. Is that a long time?"

"What do they teach children these days?" Detritus releases me and chucks Finn under the chin. "Eternity is forever. Never-ending. Without beginning or end. Timeless."

"So Summer will *always* be with you?"

"She will be my slave from now on. I may enlist her aid to gather other filthy souls." Detritus produces the rictus of a grin. "Maybe even send her to damn this pathetic, doomed Native American on his seventeenth birthday."

"The guilt on my soul is gone." I feel the absolute rightness of this statement, as if light has flooded into the darkness of my being. "Trey died. But I didn't kill him."

Detritus takes a step back. "You don't believe that. Your dear brother Trey's tortured body has been crying out for justice these many years. Admit it. You know it's true." His voice is wheedling and insistent, a teacher speaking to a wayward student.

"No. You're wrong." I notice that as I grow more confident, he seems to shrink. "And since I have no sin on my soul, there's nothing to reconcile. You *must* release me. Those are the rules of the universe." And even if he's somehow able to break those rules, I'll choose being doomed forever before I let him take Finn.

Kota sniffs two of Jill's plants before grabbing the large container of sage. He pulls something out of his pocket, there's the rasping strike of a match, and a whiff of sulfur. The plant smolders, sending fumes into the air.

Detritus stumbles, catches himself, and backs away until he's almost out the door. His eyes roll back in his head and he moans, pulling at his hair and gnashing his teeth. He falls to the floor writhing as if in great pain.

"Finn, where's the key for those cuffs?" Kota keeps his eyes on Detritus.

"Lost." Finn twists his hand, trying to slide it loose from the metal.

Kota runs to the kitchen desk and grabs a paperclip. He pulls it apart and jiggles the handcuff lock.

I retrieve Kota's knife and try to saw through the metal, being careful not to graze Finn's tender skin. Sweat breaks out on my forehead. The shackle remains intact. I throw down the knife. "How can Detritus take me? I *know* I didn't kill Trey."

Kota speaks through gritted teeth as he resumes working the lock with the paperclip. "There were two parts, right? Remember your guilt, and perform some act to atone. Maybe you still need to go through with the atonement, even though you did nothing wrong."

"But what is it? I thought it was falling in love with Preston. Then saving him from Detritus. Neither worked."

"It's *always* been about you and me." Kota snaps the paperclip in two without releasing Finn. He stoops to pick up a colorful object from the floor.

Kota and me. Me and Kota. I close my eyes and try to summon Azul. "We saved each other from our guilt. Why aren't we free? Help us, please."

No sound, except the blasted clock, chiming fifteen minutes to midnight.

"Burning sage. A cheap hoax, old school. Useless." Detritus, sooty and blackened, returns. His eyes blaze, and his chest heaves. "Sadly for you, not good enough to banish me. Nothing can do that. Give up now, and accept your eternal damnation."

"You miserable snake." I stride toward him, fists clenched, ready to pummel him. "You can take me, but I'll *never* serve you. I'll fight you for eternity. Kota will find a way to protect Finn and to escape you." I heap invectives on Detritus, knowing it won't change anything, unable to stop. Better to use up my time distracting him from the other two than risk him hurting them.

"Leave him. Come to me." Kota gives me a quick flash of what's in his hand. It's a small, beaded thing, colorful, old, in the shape of a snapping turtle.

I turn my back on Detritus and go to Kota immediately. I have to trust him. We stand together, shielding Finn behind us. I feel powerful with Kota.

"I'll kill the child." Detritus cackles. "There's nothing you can do to protect his mortal body from my wrath."

"Your bracelet. Against the handcuff." Kota pins my wrist against Finn's. "It has power."

The bracelet tingles on my wrist and comes to life, the snake's fangs slashing. But instead of the handcuff breaking open, it's Finn's flesh that's left in bleeding ribbons.

"*No.* It hurts." Finn flails at me.

"Let him go." I struggle against Kota, trying to pull the snake away from Finn's wrist. Is Detritus now controlling *Kota?*

Kota stares at me. His eyes are roiling with stripes of color that match the turtle: rings of green, orange, white, blue, and pink. "Trust my love."

It's almost impossible to see through my tears, breathe through the suffocating pressure, keep my heart from leaping out of my chest. But I have no other ally. "Finn, please. Believe in us." I immobilize his small body and again place the snake against the cuff on his wrist. It *has* to free him so that he can run far away from this madness.

Finn shudders and goes limp in my arms. Just as Trey did when I held him underwater.

Detritus grabs for me as the clock begins to chime the hour.

Kota yells, "*By the power of my ancestors.*" His muscles strain as he presses his turtle amulet against the handcuff.

Beads pop and fly through the air as the amulet morphs into a turtle with powerful jaws. It clamps down on the metal cuff, which snaps apart. The turtle strains toward the snake, but it slithers up my arm, out of reach.

Finn is free. His eyes pop open, he stiffens, and he cowers behind Kota.

The snake attacks me. Holding my breath, I vaporize, but can't shake it. I drift toward the ceiling where the face of Detritus waits to swallow me. Visions of death invade my mind. Dark, dreadful things pull at my soul and rip at my heart. My essence turns a putrid green and emits a foul stench.

"No, we have to stay together." Kota surrounds me with his own vapor and draws me back to the floor. He thrusts the snapping turtle against the snake once more as the clock strikes twelve.

The turtle bites off the snake's head. The serpent dissolves with a hiss and a whiff of decay.

Detritus stumbles back, clutching his throat. "You will pay for this insult in the worst possible way. You have escaped me, but not my wrath." His words gurgle as blood the color of burnt toast oozes from his nose and mouth. He elongates his arm and reaches between Kota and me. His clawed fingers sink into Finn's neck and pull him away from us, to the far side of the room.

"Summer, help me. Kota!" Finn gets out four words before his lips turn blue, and he ekes out a choking cough.

I float toward him.

Detritis opens his mouth. He emits a high-pitched noise that creates a ring of impenetrable sound waves around the two of them.

My essence is ineffective to pass through it. My curses bounce back to me. My corporeal body materializes but cannot breach the barrier.

Finn's eyes beg me to help him.

"I love you." Kota settles to the floor, takes on flesh, and grabs me by the shoulders. He turns me away from Finn. "Do you love me?"

I wrench away from him.

"Summer. Dovie. Look into your heart. Answer me. Now." Kota's touch, for the first time ever, is rough.

"Finn—"

"Answer me." Kota's eyes burn with a feverish light.

A great languor comes over me. The scene I'm in recedes, as if I'm seeing it from afar. Instead, my attention is captured by Kota's heart. It's as if I can see it beating, a drum declaring his love for me. I touch his chest and feel his heartbeat. "Yes. I love you. For now and for all eternity." I take Kota's hand and place it over my heart.

The wall in front of Finn shatters, the crystal breaking with great, unearthly sound and vibration.

Finn stumbles from Detritus and closes the space between us, grabbing onto my waist. His body shakes, a tiny, frightened bird in the eye of a predator.

"You can banish me but not destroy me." Detritus begins to smolder, giving off a stench of death and decay. "Evil will exist forever."

"You will never hurt us again." Kota's voice rings out, assertive and confident.

With a hissing sound, Detritus disappears in a puff of black smoke.

I hold Finn close, his presence likely more comforting to me than I am to him. "Are you okay?" I examine him. His flesh is intact, healed, clean.

"I was so scared." Finn clings to me. "You saved me. Kota saved me."

Kota looks at me. "It was never about us saving ourselves. We had to save someone else. Someone with a pure heart."

"He is correct." A blue glow fills the room. Azul, in distinct form once again, nods. "You had to remember your guilt, realize it to be misplaced, and be willing to sacrifice your eternal rest for another's life. That is the power of perfect love over evil—the key for each of you to reconcile your souls."

"Is the bad dude gone?" Finn peers at Azul. "For

good?"

"You understand the supremacy of the light. Darkness will never come for you." Azul's voice is soft and soothing. "Summer and Kota will be permitted to enter their eternal rest."

"I don't want them to go." Finn's chin trembles. He didn't cry under the onslaught of evil, but now the tears flow at goodbye.

"It is the way of things." Azul nods.

"But what about my parents?" Kota frowns. "They'll search for me."

"Once you leave this earth, it will be as if you never existed. None will remember either of you. Your time here was nothing more than fleeting shadows, never meant to be permanent."

"Will I forget them, too?" Finn hugs me tighter.

"You were brave and strong, a light in the face of darkness." Azul smiles. "Your reward will be the memory of those who were willing to give up their lives for yours. You will always remember what happened here today, but without fear. It is time to go to your friend's house until your family returns."

"I love you, Summer." Finn stands on tiptoes to kiss my cheek.

"I love you, brother-from-another-mother." I kiss the top of his head and hold back my tears.

"Take care, little dude." Kota hugs Finn.

I watch Finn go out the door. I will miss him. But my heart is suddenly protected from the pain that knowledge should bring. I turn to Kota. "What happened with the snake and the turtle?"

"Allow me." Azul sweeps his hand across the floor; the amulet is restored. He lays it in Kota's hand. "The turtle symbolizes life and strength, a heritage of Kota's ancestors. The snake stands for death and evil, a tool of darkness to enslave those within its coils. In the final battle, the power of death could not overcome that of life."

"So why were Summer and I brought together?" Kota scratches his head. "I was sure something important—lasting—would be between us."

Azul fades from sight. Only his voice whispers, "Rest in peace."

THIRTY-SIX

Summer

Clouds surround me. I find myself in a place of solitude and harmony. It's warm, and light, and airy. There's no weight to my body or soul as I float unencumbered by any longing, despair, pain, or sorrow. I'm no longer a ghost of white mist, no longer a girl with no past. My form is fluid, rolling waves of crystalline purity.

I don't know how long I've been here. It doesn't matter. There is no day or night, no tired, hungry, or thirsty. I sense I'm waiting for something, but there is no urgency or worry. I don't miss Finn, not in a hurting way. I'll see him again one day. And I've been reunited with Mama, Papa, and Trey. My soul has been reconciled at long last.

I am content, yet not, and this one thing confuses me. Azul promised *total* peace.

"Summer." Kota glides next to me. It's the closest we've been since we left earth. "Your eyes are cerulean. They're peaceful, calm—like the sky on a cloudless day. You aren't a chameleon anymore."

"Are you satisfied here?" I wonder: does he feel as I

do? Is there something missing in his eternal destiny, too?

"Sure." But he looks away from me. "We're at perfect rest, right?"

"But don't you sense it? There's something…missing." I can't put into words what I'm feeling. Don't want to be ungrateful. I could have ended up with Detritus. Kota could have, too, or roamed for centuries like I did.

Kota doesn't answer. His sparkle dims as he moves away from me.

"*Wait.* Don't go." I remember the absolute conviction he's had since the first time he saw me. Long before I ever felt it. "You said 'we're meant to be together.'"

"And here we are. For eternity." Kota pauses. His essence is gray-tinged.

"I can't believe we're just supposed to reside in the same infinite space." A great wave of emotion, alien in this place, rises up in me. I have the overpowering desire to touch him, embrace him, caress him.

My substance moves forward until I'm directly in front of Kota, eye to eye, face to face, form to form. I reach out. My hands melt into his and we hover, joined in this way, for many minutes.

"Your eyes." He stares at me. "I've never seen so many shades of blue."

I feel myself taking on nuances of color I never knew existed, not just in my eyes, but throughout my form. I sense the change in me—from a chameleon of penitence to one of passion.

"Summer." He whispers my name in a puff of fragrant breath and puts his lips to mine.

I kissed a few boys in my earthly days. This is not a kiss. I don't know what to call it, but heat rises inside me. As I glance down, my color morphs to a simmering red.

Kota presses his glowing form against mine. I lean in to him.

Our fluid bodies blend, creating a hue I've never seen before. Merged together, the feelings of his entire life flow through me, and mine into him. A shudder of pure pleasure creates undulations that rock me to my core. My essence hums to a tune that his emits. We stay this way, locked together, as the waves of emotion slowly subside.

"I. Oh. My." The upheaval inside me fades at last. I'm transformed from a storm-tossed wave to a glassy sea.

Kota grins. "I was never *with* anyone on earth. But I can't imagine it would have felt this good."

To have gone beyond physical fulfillment to a higher plane is something I don't try to understand. I accept it. "You're my first. There will never be any other. In you, I have a future and a reason for my past." Confusion nibbles at me, a puzzle piece out of place. "We were never meant to reconcile one another's soul?"

"I think we each had to understand our past and solve our own problem." Kota ponders this. "But what about us? *Why* are we meant to be together?"

"I don't know." I struggle to put the rightness of what we have into words.

"Ah, my children. So many questions." Azul's whisper is gentle as it echoes through time and space. "You both have solved many mysteries. Surely this one more thing you can fathom."

My mind swirls with images of my long wanderings. Scenes from the ages—people I've known, places I've been, things I've learned. And Kota—initial fear, grudging acceptance, and finally, joy. I look into his face and see that joy reflected back at me. "I understand."

"Tell me." Kota's eyes search mine.

"You were never meant to be my reconciliation." I take his hand. "You're my *reward*."

Kota's essence surrounds me. "And you are mine."

We are elemental. We are fused. We are one. And we are home.

ACKNOWLEDGEMENTS

To God Be The Glory.

I am grateful for my family and friends, who always knew this day would come.

Thanks to Heather, Erik, Evan, Aiden, Max, KC, and Alaina for making me strive to be a better person.

Special Thanks to Mischa, of the chameleon eyes.

To my SCBWI Writers Group: Marcy, Linda, Cheryle, Tom, Helen, and Susan. You Rock!

Grateful thanks to Sky Williams, photographer extraordinaire.

And finally, I want to thank the incredible Inkspell team for making this journey possible.

ABOUT THE AUTHOR

Laurel has been writing since the age of six, when Crawls the Caterpillar inched across her lined notebook paper propelled by a fat yellow pencil. She has published magazine and newspaper articles as well as blog posts with All The Way YA, SEAPC Magazine, and on her website. Her portfolio includes multiple children's stories in a variety of genres. She has two Young Adult novels—both paranormal romances—with Inkspell Publishing.

In addition to writing, her passion is for travel to exotic locations around the globe. The people she meets, the places she visits, and the quirky way she looks at life all inspire her work. She loves complex characters and intricate plots that mesh into multifaceted books, melding romance, mystery, adventure, and history.

Laurel was a chosen participant at Better Books, a craft-based workshop near San Francisco. She is active in the Society of Children's Book Writers and Illustrators, and has been a presenter at their Fall SCBWI Conference in Pittsburgh.

When she's not deep into a writing project, Laurel is a medical missions' nurse, traveling for Southeast Asia Prayer Center, Hope in Haiti, Caring Hearts, and Convoy of Hope. She lives in Oakmont, Pennsylvania, with her husband and their fur baby, Mabel. All of that, plus she's the world's biggest fan of chocolate milkshakes and hugs.

Website: www.laurelhouckpages.com
Facebook: Laurel Houck
Twitter: @LaurelHouck
Instagram: laurelscottage

www.ingramcontent.com/pod-product-compliance
Lightning Source LLC
Chambersburg PA
CBHW030157200626
46812CB00017B/2267